SEAL TEAM SIX: HUNT THE LEOPARD

BOOKS BY DON MANN AND RALPH PEZZULLO

The SEAL Team Six Series

Hunt the Viper

Hunt the Dragon

Hunt the Fox

Hunt the Jackal

Hunt the Falcon

Hunt the Scorpion

Hunt the Wolf

Inside SEAL Team Six:

My Life and Missions with America's Elite Warriors

SEAL TEAM SIX:
HUNT THE LEOPARD

DON MANN
AND
RALPH PEZZULLO

MULHOLLAND BOOKS

Little, Brown and Company
New York Boston London

Copyright © 2019 by Don Mann and Ralph Pezzullo

Hachette Book Group supports the right to free expression and the value of copyright. The purpose of copyright is to encourage writers and artists to produce the creative works that enrich our culture.

The scanning, uploading, and distribution of this book without permission is a theft of the author's intellectual property. If you would like permission to use material from the book (other than for review purposes), please contact permissions@hbgusa.com. Thank you for your support of the author's rights.

Mulholland Books / Little, Brown and Company
Hachette Book Group
1290 Avenue of the Americas, New York, NY 10104
littlebrown.com

Mulholland Books is an imprint of Little, Brown and Company, a division of Hachette Book Group, Inc. The Mulholland Books name and logo are trademarks of Hachette Book Group, Inc.

The publisher is not responsible for websites (or their content) that are not owned by the publisher.

Printed in the United States of America

Originally published in hardcover by Mulholland Books, August 2019
First Mulholland Books mass market edition, August 2020

10 9 8 7 6 5 4 3 2 1

> *"If you are filled with pride, then you will have no room for wisdom."*
>
> —African proverb

> *We dedicate this book to those who oppose oppression in all its forms.*

SEAL TEAM SIX: HUNT THE LEOPARD

CHAPTER ONE

*"In a moment of crisis, the wise build bridges
and the foolish build dams."*
—Nigerian proverb

MONKEYS CALLED to one another from the trees
past the high aluminum fence, crickets chirped, and
other insects buzzed to the beat of "Smile for Me" by
Simi from a distant radio. At 2208 the temp and humidity had dropped to a bearable ninety-two degrees
Fahrenheit and eighty percent humidity as Crocker
jogged around the AFSF (Armed Forces Special
Forces) base in subtropical eastern Nigeria for the
third time.

He recalled some of the facts he'd gleaned from
a briefing three weeks earlier at SEAL Team Six
(DEVBRU) headquarters in Dam Creek. Nigeria was
the most populous country on the continent of Africa
with an estimated 180 million people. It was also
mind-blowingly diverse—five hundred different ethnic groups, three hundred languages, and more than
ten thousand spoken dialects, according to the Ministry of Arts and Culture, and divided equally between
Christian and Muslim. Christians dominated the
south; Muslims in the north. Alive in practitioners of

both faiths was an underlying loyalty to ancient tribal beliefs.

The area southwest of where he was now was home to the Yoruba ethnic group and the location of the ancient city of Ife, where, according to Yoruba mythology, the first human being, Oduduwa, climbed down from the heavens, threw a handful of dirt on the primordial ocean, and created life on Earth.

Everything seemed to hum around him—the earth under his feet, the air, the dark Prussian-blue sky.

Why is it that the world feels more vibrant and alive at night?

It's why he'd always liked it best, all the way back to his shit-kicking, wild-riding teenage years in western Massachusetts—gangs, fights, running from the cops, chasing girls. The freedom and danger.

He loved them both. That effervescence. That sense that everything was alive and changing constantly. And your actions, your thoughts, your mere presence played a small part in creating the future whether you were aware of it or not.

Faster!

As Crocker picked up speed, his left knee started to burn.

Arthritis caused by a buildup of uric acid, the team orthopedist had told him. "Time to slow down and settle into an office job."

To which Crocker had responded, "Not happening, Doc."

He ignored the pain—or weakness leaving his body, as he called it—and kept running. He didn't want to think about time and possible ravages to his mind and body, or how he felt about his career after the nastiness that had gone down in Syria four months ago, or where he stood with his new friend Gayle, the widow of a SEAL friend, or Cyndi, who had called him unexpectedly hoping to rekindle their romance.

He wanted to keep pushing forward into new challenges, through additional barriers, always focused on his personal mission of fostering and preserving freedom and protecting the good and innocent. Tonight he couldn't resist thinking about one of them. The Frenchwoman, Séverine, who he'd met in Kurdistan and had died in Raqqa, and the affection he still felt for her. A special woman, she possessed the best qualities—kindness, intelligence, inner beauty, courage, and a commitment to helping others.

Séverine, I miss you…

He had failed to protect her. In fact, she'd died thirty meters from where he was fighting, crushed under falling debris from a US drone attack.

Nor did he go back to try to rescue her. The circumstances in Raqqa had made that impossible—he was injured himself, ISIS terrorists were on their tail in overwhelming numbers, he was carrying a young hostage he and his men had rescued. But the circumstances didn't serve to assuage his guilt, which twisted in his head.

"Sweet Séverine…I'm sorry."

He said it out loud as he ran, sweat running down his face to his chest, and tried to imagine what she would think of this part of Africa. Then he sensed an almost imperceptible pause in the insect cacophony from the trees beyond the fence.

He almost expected to hear Séverine speak to him. Tonight, in this exotic, life-affirming place, everything seemed possible, even communication from beyond the grave.

Instead the silence ended with the distinctive *rat-ta-tat* of an AK-47.

Crocker automatically stopped in his tracks and crouched low to the dirt. *What the fuck was that?*

Was the gunfire directed at me?

His focus sharpened and he scanned three-sixty. Trees, a fence, a flagpole with its green-and-white-striped flag, a cluster of barracks, a brick HQ building and canteen, several guard towers. The guards manning the tower ahead waited a half minute before they swung a beam across the tree line, but didn't return fire. Nor did the three boys kneeling outside the fence look up from the lizard they were playing with.

Their nonchalance didn't surprise him. Crocker understood that he was in a different country with people who played by a different set of rules. A strange corner of the planet, where it was hard to distinguish the terrorists from the local militiamen, tribal vigilantes, and armed farmers who patrolled the bush. The shots could have come from any of them.

After two weeks he'd seen how locals seemed to take most things in stride—even the savage Islamic radical insurgency, Boko Haram, that operated with impunity throughout northern and eastern Nigeria, where he was now.

When no more gunshots came, Crocker swatted away the flying insects, wiped the sweat from his brow, tightened the laces on his Saucony Liberty ISOs, and continued running.

Welcome to the jungle, we've got fun and games…

Axl Rose could have been singing about Nigeria.

Welcome to the jungle, watch it bring you to your knees…

As the local military official who'd greeted him two

weeks ago at the Lagos Airport had put it, "Nigeria is an inward-looking country waiting for God to rescue it from itself." The gulf between rich and poor was staggering, as was the contrast between old traditions in rural parts of the country and modernity in the major cities. Nothing seemed to work, but somehow it did—starting with baggage claim at the airport, where Crocker and his teammates had waited two hours for their luggage, and were told that was normal.

Chaos was the norm, too. Nobody seemed to follow rules. Like one of the soldiers the SEALs had come to train, who showed up an hour late wearing flip-flops instead of the combat boots he'd been issued. Crocker had asked, "Where are your boots?"

"I lent them to my brother."

"Why?"

"Because he needed them for work."

Crocker and his men were on a six-week assignment to teach CQD (close quarter defense), intel gathering, and counterterrorist tactics to elite AFSF operators. They'd been trained to adjust to circumstances and make the best of all sorts of conditions. Their goal: To coordinate smoothly with members of the 133-man brigade they'd come to train, even though it often moved like a car stuck in rush-hour traffic.

Not that the Nigerians weren't polite, respectful, intelligent, and extremely good-natured—always up for a joke, a prank, a good meal, or sharing a story about some beautiful woman they had met at a club. They were. They spent their downtime reading, watching movies, and playing soccer and *abula*—a local game similar to volleyball, except played with bats.

The operators of AFSF 72 he'd gotten to know didn't expect their government to work. They accepted that it was corrupt and controlled by the elites who ran the country. Since gaining independence from Great Britain in 1960, Nigeria had endured six coups, a civil war, seven military dictatorships, and four constitutions.

Yet the people he'd met in nearby farms and villages seemed content and optimistic, even in a hard place like Yola—a sprawl of corrugated tin-roofed houses and diesel-choked streets, fiercely hot in summer and a sea of mud during the rainy season. As poor as most of them were, they were exuberant in spirit and expressed themselves in music, dance, jokes, stories, and the colorful clothing they wore.

On the radio in the distance, "Smile for Me" ended and "Fallen in Love" by a different Nigerian woman singer began. Another contagiously happy tune that invited him to laugh, dance, make love, and enjoy life.

Why not? After the grim destruction Crocker had witnessed in Syria, he was up for a party. He promised to spend the next four weeks familiarizing himself with the local culture, and hopefully getting to know the friendly British-born teacher, Ndidi Collins, from the nearby American University campus he'd met one morning during a drive into town in a three-wheeled taxi, called a *tuk-tuk*. She'd recommended his first meal in Nigeria, *jollof,* the one-pot West African rice dish made with tomatoes, onions, nutmeg, ginger, cumin, chili peppers, and grilled chicken or fish. She described it as "unicorn dust and love mixed together."

Passing the three boys playing with the lizard again reminded him of his brother Michael—once a coke addict and dealer, now a successful car dealer with kids, houses, and business investments—and their childhood hijinks with rodents, lightning bugs, and other insects in rural Massachusetts. Back before Crocker had become a gangbanger, and before he'd tasted *jollof*.

Another peal of gunfire echoed from the trees, followed by what sounded like a cry of anguish behind him. Realizing that it was a young person calling out in Igbo, the local language, Crocker stopped and turned. One of the boys now stood grasping the fence, his face in distress.

Things could change on a dime. Crocker accepted that. He welcomed it. And now his hands were covered with blood. As he felt for the boy's pulse, his mind was focused on two immediate goals: keeping the boy alive and saving his leg. Boys like the one he was attending to now needed to run and play. It was important.

He was a skinny kid with a big head, maybe seven years old. The playmate who stayed by his side and wept whispered his name, "Azi." The other boy had fled, as boys in all parts of the world did when they were scared.

"Azi?" Crocker asked. "That's his name?"

"*Ee…*" It meant "yes."

Not that it mattered now. The AK-47 round had entered from the rear at an angle about four inches above the knee, and had exited out the back outer side of the thigh, probably after glancing off the femur and maybe shattering it. The wound wasn't superficial, as evidenced by the boy's elevated and weak pulse.

First thing to do, and quickly, was stem the bleeding.

Crocker turned to his teammate Akil, who had just

arrived and was carrying an MP5. "I'm going to need my medical kit and some QuikClot." QuikClot Combat Gauze contained a hemostatic agent impregnated with the inorganic mineral kaolin, which promoted clotting in a matter of minutes.

"What the fuck just happened?" Egyptian-American Akil asked. "We heard the shots."

"Get the QuikClot."

"Where'd the bullets come from?"

"The QuikClot and my med kit."

"Boss, you're exposed here. We'd better move him first."

"No time!"

"Boss…"

"Go! And alert the major."

Seconds later, an emergency siren wailed from the front gate. The boy shifted and moaned as though he were trying to escape his body. In his periphery Crocker saw armed AFSF commandos leave from the gate and enter the woods. Others fanned out around the base perimeter.

Crocker wasn't thinking about his own safety. Maybe he should have been. Instead he was laser-focused on saving the boy and his leg. He pulled off his sweaty shirt and ripped it in half. Wrapped one piece above the exit wound to serve as a tourniquet. The other half he carefully placed under Azi's head. Then he grabbed the boy's feet and lifted them over his head, elevating the wound above his heart.

Azi's friend watched through the opening between his fingers.

"*Onwu?*" he asked.

"What's that mean?"

No time to bridge the communication gap as precious

seconds ticked by. Crocker wore no surgical gloves, his hands and wrists were sticky with the boy's blood. Flying insects circled. It was a hard to make out detail in the minimal light from the posts above the fence.

Reaching with his free hand, he felt the blood continue to ooze from the wound.

Not good…

If the bleeding didn't stop soon, the kid would slip into a coma, suffer brain damage, and die. More shots rang out from the line of trees. A grunt of alarm came from the friend's mouth.

"Ndi nwuru?"

"Don't worry…Follow me…"

Crocker took him by the shoulders, held a finger up to his lips, and pushed him to his knees. The boy's natural impulse was to resist.

"Stay," Crocker whispered. "Listen…" knowing there was a very slight chance the kid understood English.

"Kedu?"

"Stay…Watch…"

He lifted Azi's feet and placed them on the kneeling boy's shoulders as more gunfire sounded. He couldn't tell if it was coming from the soldiers or someone else.

The younger boy's flight impulse activated again, and Crocker held him in place.

"Ihe mere?"

"Stay still. You'll be okay."

The kid didn't seem to agree. Crocker used one hand to hold him in place, and the other to feel for Azi's brachial artery by reaching under his arm just below the armpit. Soon as he found it, he pressed down firmly with his ring and middle fingers.

The bleeding slowed, but not enough. So he moved his fingers closer to the boy's heart and applied pressure there.

Better…

That's when he heard footsteps to his right and the little friend's sharp intake of breath. Crocker didn't bother to look up.

Heard: "Boss! Boss! What the fuck…"

Familiar voices. Akil, Tiny Chavez, and CT arriving armed and carrying the medical kit.

"You bring the QuikClot?"

"Possible Boko Haram probe, southwest."

"Tell me you brought the QuikClot!"

"Got it."

"Boss, we got to get you outta here."

"Rip one open and hand it to me. Now!"

CHAPTER TWO

*"If thy enemy wrong thee, buy each of his
children a drum."*

—African proverb

AN HOUR later Crocker reentered the AFSF base
camp in a fugue of exhaustion. Guards at the gate
waved, raised their thumbs, and shouted, *"Ezi oru!"*
and "Good job! Good man!"

He tried to smile. After surgery to stop internal
bleeding at a bare-bones local hospital, the boy's life
and his leg had been spared, at least for the time being.
The next few hours would be critical.

Azi's condition was weak. Even the smallest in-
fection could cause him to slip into a coma or die.
Crocker would check on him first thing in the morning. Now he needed rest.

He needed to be briefed, too. He wanted to know
who had fired the shots, why security at this critical
base continued to be so lax, and why the locals had
been so slow to respond.

His legs carried him across the dusty PT grinder to
the old concrete structure where his DEVGRU Black
Cell team had set up: Akil (navigator), Mancini (second in command and weapons), Rufus "Tiny" Chavez

(explosives), CT (comms), and newcomer Gator (sniper) who was temporarily taking Rip's place while he recovered from injuries sustained during their last deployment. Crocker was the team leader and primary corpsman or medic.

Soon as he walked in the door, and the breeze from the overhead fan hit his skin, he saw that all of the men were awake even though it was an hour past midnight. This surprised him, because they had to be up at 0500 for an hour of PT before sunrise, then chow, showers, and the start of training at 0730. And Tiny, who hadn't been feeling well, liked to sleep.

"What's going on?" Crocker asked.

He blinked, and Tiny Chavez was in his face. He'd abandoned his game of *Overlook,* a multiplayer game that one could play as a detective robot trying to find and destroy normal robots, or an overseer seeking and eliminating defective robots.

Their teammates called him Tiny because of his massive arms and shoulders, the right one displaying a colorful tat of Jesus. He wore baggy shorts and a Gold's Gym T-shirt and vibrated with nervous energy. His dark hair was clipped close to his skull.

"How's the boy?" Tiny asked in his incongruous high-pitched voice.

"Lost a lot of blood, but I think he'll live. They locate the shooter?"

"No, but they just handed us a can of snakes."

Tiny's nostrils flared and his mouth twisted right, typically a sign he was upset. He was a skilled, soft-spoken operator with a little crazy in his eyes.

"What's that mean?"

A quick glance around the rectangular room showed CT on a bunk peering into his laptop and Akil listening to music. Both had buds in their ears. Gator and Mancini were missing.

"Where are Gator and Manny?" asked Crocker, blinking, then staring at his bunk as though it was some kind of siren calling him to sleep.

"That's what I was about to tell you about," Tiny answered.

"Tell me. What happened?"

Tiny's head was still halfway in the gothic landscape of Overlook tower, where the action had taken place tonight.

"What happened is…this—"

Akil cut him off. The big Egyptian-American former Marine saw Crocker standing on the tile floor near the doorway and removed the buds from his ears.

"Yo, boss, something big is going down. Major Wally's looking for you."

Tiny protested, "That's rude, dude. I was talking."

"I'm talking now, bro."

Major Walfor "Wally" Martins was their primary liaison with the Nigerian 72 Special Forces battalion they'd come to help train.

"What's Major Martins want?" asked Crocker, crossing to his bunk, sitting, and unlacing his Saucony running shoes. They were spotted with blood.

"Yo, boss…Didn't say. But Paige Spiranac, the golf goddess I told you about? The one I'm gonna marry. She's got a rad spread in the latest *Sports Illustrated* swimsuit edition."

Crocker turned to Chavez, who stood fuming. "Tiny…You were saying?"

Tiny, visibly pissed, turned to Akil and growled, "No way Paige Spir-ass, or whatever the hell her name is, is gonna want any part of your hairy Egyptian ass."

That got a chuckle from CT. "You got that right!"

Tiny hitched up his shorts and addressed Crocker. "You know that Nigerian J-2 guy Gator's been working with?" J-2 was intel.

"Uh…Lieutenant Peppie, yeah…"

"You know how they've been developing, organizing, and assessing intel from various local sources?"

Crocker's head hurt. "Yeah, yeah. So?"

"Well, tonight they were going over some scenarios together and this local farmer comes in with intel about some Boko Haram troop movement near the Cameroon border."

"Wait a minute…This happened while I was gone?"

"While you were at the hospital, right. And when he hears the intel, Gator's antenna goes straight up, like never happens with Akil's dick."

"The fuck it doesn't!"

"Stop horsing around."

Tiny continued. "Boss, Lieutenant Peppie was real reluctant to take it to 72 HQ because of what he says are politics. Everything with the brigade is politics, politics…Besides, it's Saturday night, and a bunch of the command guys are in town attending someone's bachelor party. And he's like, afraid to interrupt."

Typical Tiny, Crocker thought, *takes half an hour to get to the point.* "So?"

"So, Gator…You know Gator when he locks his teeth on something…He practically drags Lieutenant Peppie over to the 72 HQ. And when they present the intel to the duty officer, a Captain Mobido, or Mopito, or whatever, he like waves them away like he can't be bothered. And you don't do that with Gator."

"Don't tell me."

"Because now that whacked-out Cajun gets up in

the captain's face, and tells him he's a disgrace to his uniform and like a thousand other insults."

Crocker groans. "No…"

"Reads him the riot act, and calls him a coo-yawn."

"What's a coo-yawn?" Crocker asked.

"It's Cajun," Akil cut in. "Roughly translated means something like 'dumb fucking asshole.'"

"Great."

"The captain took it as a racial slur."

"Shit."

"Got hysterical and shoved Gator. Gator smacked the captain a couple times, then backed off."

"Fuck…"

"Of course the Nigerian captain runs straight to Major Wally. And now the whole Nigerian command is up in arms."

"Just what we need…" Crocker rubbed his face to get the blood moving. Last thing he wanted was to deal with shit like this now. But he had no choice.

"Where's Gator?" Crocker asked.

"Manny took him out to blow off steam."

"Where?"

Tiny turned to Akil, who turned to CT, who shrugged. "Beats me…"

"Get 'em both back here! Now."

Crocker started relacing his running shoes. Considered changing out of his soiled shorts and the medical tunic he'd borrowed, but decided not to bother.

"I'm going to talk to Major Martin. The rest of you coo-yawns go find Gator."

"Okay, boss."

As he walked beside Akil to 72 AFSF HQ, Crocker noticed a wind had started up, indicating that the weather was changing. The air revived him. He tried to remember what he had learned about Boko Haram from the CIA official who had briefed them before they left ST-6 headquarters in Virginia.

Boko Haram was a radical Islamist terrorist group that had wreaked havoc through northern and eastern Nigeria, seizing big parcels of territory, massacring entire villages, killing more than twenty thousand civilians, and creating millions more refugees.

Their name, literally translated, meant "western education is forbidden," which is why they aimed their savage brand of religious fundamentalism on teachers, schools, and schoolchildren—brutally slaughtering the boys and their teachers, and kidnapping the girls to turn them into concubines and slaves.

Much akin to ISIS in the Middle East, Boko Haram's goal was to install an Islamic state in western Africa based on Sharia law. The analyst who had briefed Crocker also said that despite their religious beliefs they earned money from drug and human trafficking.

Nice guys…

Akil stopped when they got within a hundred feet of the concrete building. "Boss, there's another part of this that bothers me."

Crocker was so tired he wasn't sure his brain could absorb new information. "What?"

"Our mission is to train, advise, and support, right? But we've spent the last two weeks running exercises, and haven't done shit to take the fight to the Boko bad guys."

"You saying the Nigerian military isn't doing its job?"

Akil grinned. "Now Gator gets a report of some

Boko Haram movement near the border, and the AFSF guys are too busy being insulted to see the bigger picture. That seem upside down to you?"

Crocker was trying to remember the rules of engagement (ROEs) of their JCET (Joint Combined Exchange Training). If he recalled correctly, the SEALs were allowed to accompany the Nigerians on live missions in an advisory capacity, and shoot back at the enemy if they took fire.

"The thing is, boss, we need to tread carefully."

It was strange to hear a warning of restraint from the usually uber-aggressive Akil.

"Why's that?"

"Lieutenant Peppie told me something the other day that might be pertinent."

"Pertinent? I'm impressed."

"The current president of Nigeria, Muhammadu Buhari, is a former military strongman who describes himself as a converted democrat, and previously supported the implementation of Muslim Sharia law throughout the country. Pertinent, right?"

"Interesting."

"Now he denies he ever had a Muslim radical agenda, but some local dudes, including Lieutenant Peppie, still question his sympathy for Boko Haram."

Major Martins sat at the wooden conference table, cleaning the meat off chicken bones in the remains of a cassava leaf stew at 0026 hours. 72 AFSF had received intel from a local source about a column of Boko Haram cars and trucks moving toward the border. Rumor was they were about to engage in some kind of exchange of weapons. The sources were "moderately reliable" according to the major. But given sensitive relations between Nigeria and Cameroon to the east, he informed Crocker that military and civilian leaders in the Nigerian capital of Abuja weren't inclined to act.

"I don't understand. Why's that?" Crocker asked. Bureaucratic bullshit irritated him wherever it reared its ugly head—as in the States, so as in Nigeria. He wasn't oriented toward concerns about image, or professional standing, or stepping on people's toes. You saw a problem, you found the best way to solve it, and you acted to the best of your abilities.

"Political difficulties," the major answered. The problem now: in order to prevent any possible incident between the two countries, the Nigerian government had closed the border two weeks ago, stranding hundreds of traders and travelers, including a group of tourists from Argentina, of all places.

Crocker wanted to ask what the hell South American tourists were doing in a war zone. But he nixed that. He was more curious to learn about the political beef between Cameroon and Nigeria.

He said instead: "Major, I realize our job here is to advise, train, and lend tactical support. But this intel, if it's reliable, I think it begs us to bend the rules a little, and at least find out what Boko is up to."

"You're a bender of rules, sir?" Major Martins was a thick-chested man with a round, friendly face, whose dark skin had been scarred by childhood smallpox. As an officer, he outranked Crocker, who was a chief warrant officer. He had no business calling Crocker "sir."

Crocker couldn't help being put off by the major's flippant attitude about what he perceived as a highly actionable situation. But he also understood that the cultural and historical gap between them was immense, that his knowledge of local politics was limited, and that he and his men hadn't come to Nigeria to stir up trouble, but to help and win hearts and minds.

"The way I look at it, Major," Crocker started, "rules are meant to be adaptable to circumstances." He was being about as diplomatic as he could manage given his state of exhaustion. "What we're talking about here are extraordinary circumstances that could yield very negative results."

Martins was a good smiler. He smiled again. "I'm a sensible man, Mr. Crocker. I like my position. My family enjoys the comforts it brings them. We have a saying in my country: A man who sells eggs should not start a fight in a market."

Major Martin, like many Nigerians, had a habit of communicating with proverbs.

Crocker answered politely, saying, "We're not selling eggs, sir. We're trying to eradicate Boko Haram."

Other officers in 72 AFSF sat at the long table listening, drinking tea and sodas, and reading comics and newspapers with no sense of urgency as Crocker spoke from his feet.

"It seems to me that if you really want to drive the enemy out of eastern and northern Nigeria, the last thing you want to see happen is for them to acquire more arms."

Martins looked up from the stew and waved. "Sit down, Mr. Crocker. Have a cup of tea, or a soda. What you say is, of course, correct. When a ripe fruit sees an honest man, it drops."

As Crocker looked for a place at the table, the lights went out, which happened often in this part of

Nigeria. Nobody made a sound. Instead, one of the junior officers switched on a battery-operated lamp, and two other men went outside to start a gasoline generator. The screen door banged behind them.

Crocker's eyes adjusted to the shadows, and Akil whispered in his ear, "Did he just call you a ripe fruit?"

"I hope not."

An aide said something to Major Wally Martins. Then the officer looked up at Crocker and nodded. "Our politicians go to London, for their education, to Paris for their holidays, to Dubai for shopping. The only time they come to Nigeria is to be buried. Does that make this a cemetery?"

Other officers at the table laughed.

What the fuck does that mean?

Crocker was tired. It was their country and their fight. But he hated seeing the bad guys advance or gain advantage, and reminded himself that it usually didn't turn out well. In the late '90s the US let Al-Qaeda bomb two of its embassies in Africa and didn't respond. Then they let them get away with bombing the USS *Cole* in Yemen and killing seventeen sailors. Didn't do shit, and how did that turn out?

He was working up a head of steam…He didn't want to see more children buried after a terrorist bombing, or hear about more girls being raped and kidnapped. Not while he was here and could do something to prevent it from happening.

He chose his words carefully so as not to insult their hosts. "Major, do you remember telling me that money and weapons help the rebels attract recruits, or would you rather I keep my opinions to myself?"

Major Martins smiled again, showing off a row of

brilliant white teeth. "Yes, I said that, and yes, it is a wise observation."

"Thank you."

"Mr. Crocker, you're an experienced soldier who has fought all over the world, and I respect that. But we're dealing with a case of what we call *aproko*."

"What's *aproko*?"

"Rumors, sir. Gossip."

"The intel comes from your source. People you pay for information."

"Lieutenant Peppie is an ambitious man."

Crocker wasn't sure what that had to do with anything. He asked, "What would you say, Major, are the odds these rumors are true?"

"Fifty-fifty," Major Wally Martins answered.

"So what do we risk, Major, by checking them out? By trying to reach the column and seeing what Boko Haram is up to, and possibly intercepting them if they are picking up a shipment of weapons and ammo?"

Major Martins pushed his chair away from the table and rubbed his belly. "You make a very reasonable argument, Mr. Crocker. The roaring lion kills no prey. I can't argue with that."

CHAPTER THREE

*"The skin of a leopard is beautiful, but not
its heart."*

—Nigerian proverb

YESTERDAY HAD been Chichima Okore's eighteenth
birthday, but she had kept that information to herself.
Today she couldn't shake the heavy sadness that
wanted to pull her into the ground—a state she tried
to hide from the seven other girls of her approximate
age with whom she shared a rusting shipping container hidden somewhere in the Sambisa Forest.

Chichima had vowed from the start of this ordeal
to be the strong one, the one who would record everything and never lose faith.

But now, after almost two years in captivity, she
couldn't hold back her frustration. She couldn't ignore
the stench and degradation that wore down her spirit.
Sitting on the edge of the moldy mattress, she lowered
her face into her hands and wept.

Through her tears, she said, "So much time has
passed…My friends and family have forgotten
me…I'm afraid I'm becoming a stranger to myself…"

The other girls were too numb to notice her distress. The lone exception was her gaunt friend

Navina, who sat beside her, took her hand, and implored softly, "Really, deep down, nothing has changed, Chichima…The ones you love are still the ones you love. The fox still drinks from the river…"

"I'm eighteen," Chichima replied. "I'm already an old woman inside…"

"Don't think like that."

"Where are our countrymen, our friends, our parents? Where are they, Navina?"

Chichima's name meant "sweet and precious" in Igbo. Today, her dreams, her childhood in the small farming hamlet of Malabu, even her identity felt like a distant memory. That carefree life amid the bush and surrounding rivers—monkeys chattering, hornbills cawing, the incessant buzzing of cicadas and crickets, playing with her brother, younger sisters, and cousins, helping her mother, and dreaming of one day moving to the city of Lagos and leading a modern life, had dissolved into the air.

Before she had turned six and started attending school, her father, a mechanic, was the only person in the family who could read or write. When her mother or one of her aunts wanted to communicate with family members up north, they would dictate to him what they wanted to say and he would write it down. He was also the only family member who spoke English, learned while he worked for a trucking company in the city of Jalingo. The rest of them communicated in Igbo, the language of their ancestors, which seemed to spring directly from the earth. Today Chichima wished she'd never learned English, or watched the Nollywood movies that depicted life in the cities of Lagos and Abuja, where her favorite actresses Damilola Adegbite and Venita Akpofure were glamorous women driving their own cars and living in houses with tile floors, air-conditioning, and sleek leather-covered furniture.

She wondered if the imam who lectured them daily for the past two years was right. Maybe there was an element of evil inherent in modern ways. Maybe Western ideas of personal freedom and self-fulfillment offended the Igbo river goddess Mami Wata, or the God of the Quran.

Maybe she was wrong to ever think she could be anything other than a country girl, living in a little house in the woods with a rusting corrugated metal roof and no running water, no electricity, no gas, and no telephone. She was part of a family that owned no chrome, glass, or even upholstered furniture, only tables, bed frames, and benches made by her father, brother, and uncles out of wood collected from the local forest. Even their kitchen sat outdoors, under an awning.

It had been Chichima's ambition to seek a better, more modern life that had led her to the Government Girls' School in Yola. Even though she started at fourteen, which was later than most girls, she had risen to the top of her class. Her curiosity had been like an unquenchable thirst. Her favorite subjects: history and English.

She learned that her people, the Igbo, lived in south-central and southeastern Nigeria on both sides of the Niger River. Starting at the end of the seventeenth century, an Igbo subgroup called the Aro people had formed a confederacy that spread its influence throughout eastern Nigeria and all the way south to the Atlantic Coast. To grow their economic power, Aro business families began exporting palm oil and slaves seized from poorer Igbo tribes. They sold the slaves to traders from Europe, who then exported them to colonies in the Western Hemisphere where the demand for manual labor was high.

This brutal history made a strong impression on Chichima's young mind. She tried to see past the horror of slavery to the tremendous impact Igbo culture had made on the United States in jazz, ragtime, various forms of dance, art, and the cultivation of yams and okra—both Igbo staple crops.

"We are one love, one voice, one heart beating," went the lyrics to the song by one of her favorite singers, Oona McOuat, who she had originally discovered on YouTube.

Chichima's ambition had been to go to the US to study at a university after she earned her high school diploma. Then she would return to her native country and become a teacher, to educate rural girls like herself so they could better understand the world and reach their full potential.

She had thought of it as a form of cultural-historical retribution. She would be returning significant things that had been taken from her ancestors—dignity, knowledge, and education. She would make her Igbo students strong enough to stand up for themselves and spread a positive influence throughout Nigeria, Africa, and the rest of the world.

It was a dream that seemed unattainable in her current circumstances, locked inside a shipping container at the base of the Mandara Mountains.

Just then, the lock rattled and the metal door creaked open.

Chichima was so weakened in body and spirit that she didn't respond to the armed men who ordered the girls to line up outside. It was only when Navina pointed to the short man with the crazy eyes and whispered, "It's the Leopard," that she realized that maybe something significant was about to happen.

To the outside world, the man Chichima saw standing outside was Festus Ratty Kumar, first cousin of Boko Haram leader Abubakar Shekau. To his men and followers he was known as the Leopard, for many reasons. There was the dirty, leopard-patterned bandana he always wore on his head to cover a nasty scar suffered in a knife fight at the age of twelve. There were also his skills: Festus was quick-tongued, quick-footed, and quick-fisted. Like a leopard, he operated on instinct, stalking his prey, attacking it unaware, and destroying it.

Now he bristled with almost inhuman energy, pacing back and forth in the jungle clearing and ordering his men to load the teenage girls into two trucks that had been stolen hours earlier from a local cement plant.

Festus Ratty Kumar's chief aide, a one-eyed northerner named Modu (which meant Mohammed in Kanuri), asked why. Kumar smiled out of the side of his mouth, looked at him askance, and answered, "Opportunity!"

Modu knew not to expect an explanation. When Kumar decided on a course of action, he did it whether people agreed with him or not. His bold decisiveness had led to many military successes and had attracted loyal recruits from Islamic radicals and criminals in northern Nigeria.

Ratty Kumar had been a wild, unusual boy from the beginning, born weeks after his father was arrested for stealing government property. He'd shot out of the womb carrying a sword, according to his mother. Possessed a crazy, relentless, uncontrollable energy that no one was able to curb or corral.

By age two, people in his village outside the northeast city of Maiduguri (capital of the northern Borno State) were already recommending that he be poisoned, drowned, or buried alive.

His mother and grandfather tried reasoning with the young boy and, when that didn't work, inflicted various forms of punishment. When his uncle beat him with a stick, Ratty responded by assaulting his older sister and pulling her hair out. When his uncle tied him to a tree outside for a week, Ratty managed to get free and set the house on fire.

In frustration, his mother went to the local tribal chief and asked, "What makes him like this?"

"Maybe you'll never know," the tribal chief answered. "Maybe you don't want to. The sky is wide enough for hawks and doves to fly without colliding into one another."

No school would have him because he was constantly making trouble and getting in fights. He was *nwa nwa* — loosely translated: a hell child. By the time Ratty turned ten, his mother remarried and her new husband gave her an ultimatum: Choose between him or me. The other has to leave.

A week later Ratty's mother dropped him off at the Christian Alliance Orphanage in Maiduguri. He lasted four months. An energetic, good-natured kid most of the time, he refused to follow rules or standards of good behavior. Had no respect for authority. Nothing — neither kindness and compassion, discipline, or lessons from the Holy Bible — seemed to make the slightest impression.

One night he was found fornicating in the pantry with a mentally deficient kitchen attendant. A month later he was accused of stealing money. A month after that, he was caught stealing brass religious objects from the chapel and selling them in the market.

The school's administrators expelled him.

If Festus Ratty Kumar felt any remorse, it didn't show. By age thirteen he was living on the streets of Maiduguri, scrounging for food and money. He used people, stole, lied, and learned that power was more important than money, knowledge, friendship, or sex. He derived his power from his strength, wits, and courage. No one or nothing frightened him—not the authorities, disease, loneliness, or even the wrath of God.

An unreal energy shone in his eyes, mesmerizing street kids and criminals. Some of them swore that sometimes, when he was excited, a blue light would emit from his hands.

At fourteen he was arrested for assaulting a girl. A month later he was detained by the police on suspicion of stealing a motorcycle. At sixteen he was sent to prison for possession of a stolen car, raping a girl while his girlfriend watched from the backseat, and then beating the girl and threatening to kill her.

Local newspapers called him a moral degenerate. Even though the victim refused to testify in court, Ratty was sentenced to nine years of hard labor.

His criminal activities continued in prison. He quickly developed a network of guards, and outside criminals, who smuggled food, cell phones, computers, DVDs, and drugs into the prison for cash. He even paid off the warden. A year in, he was approached by a recruiter from the Nigerian military who offered to commute his sentence in exchange for joining the infantry. Ratty signed up, and went AWOL two weeks into basic training.

A month later he was caught, beaten, and thrown back in prison. It was at that point that a visiting teacher and friend of his cousin came to talk to him about the Quran.

Rain started falling in big drops as the SEALs— minus Tiny Chavez, who had stayed behind because of his bad stomach—waited under the lip of a pre-fab aluminum structure that served as the AFSF base control tower. Thunder rumbled in the distance.

Thunder reminded Crocker of home, and summer nights on the front porch with his parents, sister, and brother.

He had instructed his men to strip themselves of anything that would identify them as US operators, including blood chits and dog tags. They were dressed in a combination of military fatigues and civilian clothes, armed with weapons borrowed from the Nigerians, mostly German-made MP5 submachine guns and Russian-made AK-47s, and their own SIG Sauer 226 pistols.

The rhythmic beating of the rain and his own physical exhaustion had lulled Crocker into a rare contemplative state. Like drawing a rainbow in his head, he retraced the arc of his life—son of a Navy veteran, rambunctious kid, gangbanger with the Flat Rats, motocross racer, girl chaser, marathon racer, Navy recruit, corpsman, BUD/S candidate, SEAL Trident recipient, husband, father, member of SEAL Team Two, divorcé, member of SEAL Team Six, long-distance athlete, husband, and divorcé a second time.

He started to wonder what lay ahead—travel, more marriage, more deployments—when Akil appeared at his right, water from the roof pelting the tops of his Merrell boots.

Crocker looked at his watch. 0136.

"What are we waiting for?" He'd forgotten about the boy in the hospital.

Akil shrugged. "Who knows."

He and his men hadn't seen action since Syria months ago. Crocker was looking forward to the burst of adrenaline, the thrill of unforeseen danger, and the synchronicity of men and machines moving together.

"What do you make of Lieutenant Peppie's intel?" Crocker asked.

"I trust him. He's a smart man."

Crocker was aware that the Nigerian lieutenant in charge of J-2 and Akil had struck up a friendship. What he didn't know was that Akil had spent the last couple of nights at Peppie's house, feasting on Peppie's wife's food, and discussing the problems with Islam. Akil, though born in Egypt and nominally Muslim, had never stepped into a mosque since immigrating to the US at age seven. He was curious about what a thoughtful, faithful Muslim man like Peppie felt about his religion.

Peppie had explained that all of the practicing believers he knew thought of their religion as one of love and tolerance. Even Sharia law, he'd said, had been misconstrued by fanatics.

Sharia, literally translated from Arabic, meant "a path to water where people can drink and seek nourishment." It wasn't intended as a set of laws, but rather a guidebook to how to lead a life pleasing to God.

It told Muslims how to become better friends, family members, and citizens.

"Then how does it result in the horror we see carried out in Iraq, in Syria, in the name of Allah?" Akil had asked.

"Paths can be tricky," Peppie had answered thoughtfully, "especially when they are meant to lead to God. Just as there are many paths to a well, there are many interpretations of Islamic law, and some paths lead people astray."

Crocker saw that the sky ahead had turned a very dark shade of red.

He turned to Akil and asked, "Where is the rest of the team?"

"Inside, keeping dry."

Crocker looked over his shoulder, through the window of the terminal building. Major Martins was standing and coolly smoking a cigarette in the company of some of his men. He wore a maroon scarf under the collar of his freshly washed jungle fatigues.

To his way of thinking, the major's nonchalance wasn't appropriate, not now, as they were preparing to launch a mission.

He reentered the tin-roofed shack, took a deep breath, and asked, "We doing this, Major?"

The major grinned. "When a cow hurries to go to America, it comes back corn beef."

Some of the officers around him chuckled. Crocker bit down hard on his annoyance.

"I'm not familiar with that saying."

"It means patience, Mr. Crocker. We'll be airborne soon."

"How soon?"

"Soon as the crocodiles are operational," the major answered. "Five minutes, maybe ten."

"Crocodiles? What crocodiles?"

Major Martins pointed outside where two Russian-made Mi-35P helicopters, with green camouflage bodies and noses painted to look like crocodiles, waited on the tarmac.

"Is there a specific reason why we're waiting?" asked Crocker, who was starting to boil inside.

"A minor fuel line problem in Crocodile One. The mechanics are patching it, and will be finished soon."

According to Lieutenant Peppie's informant, the Boko Haram trucks and cars were estimated to reach the Cameroon border by 0300. That gave them about a forty-minute window.

Around a corner, he saw Mancini and Gator sitting with their boots up on a table as CT adjusted the sights on his borrowed AK-47.

"We should be moving soon."

"Sure, boss," said CT.

Gator lifted his MP5 to his shoulder like he was ready for action, grinned, and said, *"Laissez les bon temps rouler."*

CHAPTER FOUR

*"I will not suppose that the dealers in slaves
are born worse than other men—No; it is
the fatality of this mistaken avarice, that it
corrupts the milk of human kindness and
turns it into gall."*

—Olaudah Equiano

AT THREE minutes before two, the SEALs were finally airborne with Major Martins and Lieutenant Peppie accompanying them in Crocodile One. Eight 72 AFSF operators rode in Crocodile Two behind them. CT sat on a bench across from Crocker and Mancini, an AK clenched between his knees and earbuds in to drown out the roar of the twin VK-250 engines.

Crocker imagined the big former University of Oklahoma wrestler was mentally preparing for the mission ahead. Instead, CT was considering the long and tortured history that had forced his ancestors out of Nigeria and had facilitated his return.

It was CT's older sister Alexis, now a high school civics teacher, who had traced their family's history all the way back to their Igbo forefathers who had toiled on subsistence farms not far from where he was now. And it was she who had urged him to read the book *Middle Passage* as a teenager. When he found out it was a work of fiction, written by a PhD in philosophy, he threw it aside.

His middle school English teacher in Compton, California, recommended *The Interesting Narrative of the Life of Olaudah Equiano, or Gustavus Vassa, the African,* a memoir, instead. It was written in 1789 after Equiano, who described himself as "neither a saint, or a hero," merely lucky enough "to be blessed by heaven," bought his freedom from his Philadelphia merchant owner.

"Blessed by heaven" to have experienced the horrors of slavery, and to have been one of the few who had escaped them.

He learned that Equiano came from a village in southeast Nigeria, a district where agriculture was the primary occupation, land was abundant, and people believed in one creator who lived in the sun and governed all of life's major events. Cleanliness and decency were esteemed, and music and dance celebrations were a weekly occurrence. Equiano had never seen the sea or a white man until age eleven when he and his sister were seized by members of a rival tribe, separated, and sold to European slave traders.

From Nigeria, he was transported with 244 enslaved Africans to Barbados—the horrific Middle Passage that was the subject of the novel that CT's sister had urged him to read. From Barbados, Equiano and some of his fellow slaves were shipped to the British colony of Virginia, where he worked in the fields of a plantation and observed many more horrible atrocities: overseers who cut and mangled slaves, and white masters who violated the chastity of the females, some as young as ten years old.

Equiano was sold several times, renamed Michael, forced to convert to Christianity, beaten, branded, and finally landed in the hands of an American Quaker merchant named Robert King, who was kind, patient, and gave him an opportunity to buy his freedom, which he did. Equiano subsequently moved to England, learned how to play the French horn, joined several debating societies, became deeply involved in the abolitionist movement, married a white British woman, and fathered two daughters.

CT had suffered his share of racial indignities, too, most dramatically when he was assaulted and beaten by a group of local toughs in Edmond, Oklahoma, one night while walking his white girlfriend back to campus.

Still had scar tissue over his left eye and partial deafness in his left ear.

Like Equiano, he'd moved on and learned that cruelty and bigotry weren't the provenance of any one race, tribe, or people.

Interesting how I'm back in Nigeria to complete the circle started by my ancestors, he thought, as he stared at the helicopter floor.

The Mi-35P helo reeked of fuel. The fuel line was probably still leaking. With "Alfie's Tune" by the great sax player Sonny Rollins playing through his earbuds, Crocker thought of alerting Major Martins, who was seated behind the pilot, snacking on pistachios. But ruled against that, because he didn't want to give him an excuse to turn back.

Wind buffeted the helo sharply left, then right.

Crocker had been through so many life-threatening situations with Mancini and Akil, he could often read their thoughts. The new guys, Gator, Tiny, and CT, were harder.

And yet every single SEAL he'd known over the

years had overcome intense physical and personal challenges to earn the Trident. Gator, Tiny, and CT were no exception. Like most guys on the teams, they were tough, energetic young men from poor and lower-middle-class backgrounds who had never been described as scholars. In Crocker's case, he'd barely made it through high school.

He knew that Gator was the product of a broken family from Concordia Parish, Louisiana. "Miles of rolling flatlands dotted with stinking swamps and populated with obese, drug-addicted white trash," was the very blunt way he described it. According to the US census, it was the poorest county in the country.

His dad had picked pecans before running his pickup into a telephone pole one night while drunk on bourbon. His sick, overweight mom wasn't strong enough to keep a job, much less support a family. He and his younger brother grew up in foster homes.

CT's childhood hadn't been a walk in the park, either. Raised in Compton, California, by his mother and stepfather, he'd never met his biological father. Spent his teenage years trying to dodge the Crip vs. Piru gang violence that gripped his neighborhood. Kept his head down and played sports.

Tiny Chavez's skin was lighter than CT's, but his background was just as difficult. No father, raised by his illiterate mother, who had crossed the border from Mexico while pregnant with his younger brother. Settled in East Texas where she got a job cleaning motel rooms. Tiny admitted that if he hadn't developed an interest in horses and bull-riding as a teenager, he would have probably ended up dealing drugs and serving time in prison.

All three men were highly trained now, likable, and positive.

Crocker reached his right leg across the floor and kicked CT's boot. "You good?"

CT nodded and smiled. "Ready, boss. You know it."

Farther down the bench, he saw Akil leaning into Lieutenant Peppie—an interesting cultural contrast— burly Egyptian-born former Marine and reed-thin Hausa tribesman, both from the continent of Africa.

They were huddled over a Garmin GPS mapping device.

Crocker cupped his hands around his mouth and shouted, "We close?"

Akil pointed to the screen on the device and gestured back with a thumbs-up.

Crocker slid in beside them. "How much farther?"

"About fifty klicks from the border. That's Cameroon, there. We're *here*..."

"Where's the road?" asked Crocker, pointing to the map.

Peppie shook his head. "No paved road. Only dirt path."

Akil gestured to the little square window behind his shoulder. When Crocker looked out, the view was obscured by darkness and clouds.

He nodded as if to say: Got the message.

Stepping past legs and weapons, he knelt next to Major Martins, seated behind the pilot and looking at something on his phone. Cupped his mouth to the major's ears and shouted, "The pilot needs to take this baby down."

"What's the problem?"

Crocker tried supplementing his words with sign language. "Can't see anything from this altitude.

The pilot needs to descend so we can find the column."

The major suddenly looked nervous. "Now?"

"Yes, now."

"Don't worry. We'll find it."

"We're not going to see shit unless we get below the clouds."

Major Martins leaned forward and said something to the Nigerian pilot, who responded by waving his arms and shouting.

"What's the problem?" Crocker asked.

"He said it's difficult because of the weather."

"Tell him to take it down another fifty meters."

"He doesn't want to."

"Order him to, Major. Aren't you in charge?"

As they drove deeper into the bush, Chichima's anxiety grew. She couldn't tell if the truck she and the other girls were seated in was moving north, south, east, or west. All she knew was that they were all dressed in matching black burqas, and the night was dark and without stars.

It reminded her of the terrible night two years ago when she, Navina, and other girls from her school had been carried away in a truck like this one. It started, she remembered, when she was seated under the light from the porch, her hair recently braided, rereading *Things Fall Apart* by the great Igbo author Chinua Achebe, who wrote about the clash between traditional Igbo culture and the influences of European colonization, a theme that resonated deeply in her soul.

She remembered how strongly she had identified with the book's protagonist Okonkwo, who rejected everything about his traditional Igbo father. Considered him backward, poor, cowardly, lazy, and interested in music and idle conversation. In the book, Okonkwo consciously made an effort to be different, and succeeded in becoming hardworking, productive, wealthy, and stoic. So stoic, in fact, that he rejected anything he regarded as soft and trivial, including music.

Chichima didn't think she could ever be as extreme as Okonkwo, but she did want to improve herself, her people, and her country. She focused so hard on schoolwork that behind her back classmates called her ITK (which stood for "I too know") and meant overserious student. She'd rather be called ITK than an *almy* (lazy person), or *ajebutter* (spoiled rich kid).

In the book, Okonkwo said, "If a child washed his hands, he could eat with kings."

Back then Chichima believed that one day she would eat with kings, too, and make her parents proud. She believed as Okonkwo did that the sun shined equally on those who stood before it and those who knelt under it.

Where is it now?

As she read that night two years ago, she heard loud voices from the direction of the front gate. They didn't alarm her at first. The local Igbo guards were often loud and demonstrative. But when the arguing continued, she put down the book and listened. Then she heard what she first thought were firecrackers.

She figured thieves or other undesirables had tried to gain entry to the school compound and were being chased away by the guards—a group of cocky guys who sometimes called her "Ching Chong" because of her wide, round face and droopy eyelids. She returned to the book.

> Perhaps down in his heart Okonkwo was not a cruel man. But his whole life was dominated by fear, the fear of failure and of weakness.

The passage troubled her, and when she looked up, she saw two bearded men watching her. They seemed to have appeared out of nowhere dressed in military uniforms with turbans on their heads and guns slung over their shoulders.

One of them asked in Igbo in a nonthreatening tone of voice, "You a student?"

"Yes, I am. What do you want?"

"How many girls are inside?"

She'd never seen soldiers wearing turbans on their heads. "Why do you want to know?" she asked back.

The man's expression turned ominous. "If you know what is best for you, tell them to come outside and wait," he threatened.

"Why?"

"Just do as you're told so we don't have to make you an example."

Example of what? she was about to ask. She stopped herself. The men meant business.

She put down the book, retreated inside, and joined a group of other girls gathered at the front window. Some were already sobbing and fearing the worst. Chichima scolded them for being weak.

"Instead of standing here, let's call Mr. Obindu," she said. Mr. Obindu was the school's assistant director.

"We did already. He's not answering."

"Then I'll call the police."

Five minutes passed and no policemen showed up, and the armed men entered the dormitory with guns drawn. There were six of them this time and some spoke Kanuri, which was alarming in itself because it was the language of the north.

The armed men roused the girls who were sleeping, and led them all outside where six more armed men were waiting. Approximately forty girls huddled together. The men refused to answer the schoolgirls' questions.

Chichima's best friend Navina whispered, "They are Boko Haram…"

Chichima had heard about the Islamic terrorists from the north province of Borno, but wasn't aware that they traveled this far south. She knew they had a reputation for targeting government officials for assassination.

"What do they want with our school?" she whispered back.

"Maybe they're looking for money…"

In Chichima's mind there was a reason for everything. She had seven thousand naira (the equivalent of twenty US dollars) that her mother had given her hidden in a shoe under her bed. She was planning to use it to buy a new skirt and blouse.

Should I offer it to them now, or should I keep quiet?

A second later the armed men were pressing the girls into a tight circle. It became so tight that Chichima had trouble breathing. A girl next to her fainted.

She and Navina knelt to help the girl up when she heard gunshots from beyond the ridge. Someone whispered, "That's coming from the boys' school across the road… They're shooting the boys… They'll kill us, too!"

It seemed unthinkable.

Why would these men, whoever they were, shoot the schoolboys? Why would they harm students? Most of us come from humble backgrounds. We aren't political, and are divided between Christians and Muslims, and different ethnic groups.

The whole situation didn't make sense to her. The shooting continued. As she imagined the terror the boy students must have been feeling, she started to feel light-headed. This wasn't what she expected would happen at a place where people acquired learning and wisdom. This wasn't how people were supposed to act.

She wanted to reason with the armed men, to explain to them that they were good, studious young women, but didn't know where to start. The armed men backed up a long truck and started to load the girls inside like cattle.

Where are the police? Why is no one stopping them?

The beatings, she remembered, started that night, inflicted with rifle butts on those who tried to escape. Girls screamed and bled. Others fainted and groaned in horror.

That truck wasn't big enough to accommodate all the girls. Still the men pushed and shoved them until the girls were sitting on each other's laps.

"Where are they taking us?" one very young one asked.

"Why are they taking us?"

The truck bounced and rattled out the front gate and entered the bush. It was a dark, moonless night. Some desperate girls jumped from the back of the truck and were shot. Chichima heard them call to their mothers in agony. Girls prayed silently. Navina wept.

She wasn't the same open, innocent, hopeful schoolgirl anymore. None of them were. Not after the beatings, rapes, indoctrination into Islam, and forced marriages.

She had wanted to be the strong, rational one like Okonkwo in *Things Fall Apart*. She wanted to challenge the armed men with arguments and logic. But how could she when she was constantly being pulled further into the dark unknown, like she was now? Pulled into the world of these strange, cruel men who didn't seem to care that the girls came from good families and had studied hard to be admitted to the Government Girls' School.

What was even more incredible to her was that no one stopped them. Three or four times in two years, she had heard helicopters overhead, but they had always passed like clouds.

Things like this aren't supposed to happen, she repeated to herself, resolving that she shouldn't expect anything different now, even though she imagined she heard the sound of a helicopter in the distance.

Or maybe it was her imagination, or a cruel trick her mind was playing on itself. She glanced up at the other girls, who sat numbly.

What new horror lies ahead? Chichima asked herself. *Where are they taking us now?*

CHAPTER FIVE

"Pretend you are dead and you will see who really loves you."
— African proverb

FESTUS RATTY Kumar sat proudly in the lead jeep, sipping from the bottle of purple drank (codeine cough syrup mixed with grape soda) clutched between his knees, certain that guns and supplies he had ordered from Russian arms dealer Victor Balt were up ahead, and convinced that his legend and influence would soon grow stronger.

So much had changed in five years. He remembered that he had been skeptical when his cousin and Imam Bello had first come to visit him in prison. Talk of the holy spirit and the messenger of God seemed like a lot of *yahoo* to him then. But the concept of a group of outcast rebels bringing society to its knees had a certain appeal.

So he listened over those next several weeks as Imam Bello explained the history of the Boko Haram movement, which he said dated back to the Sokoto Caliphate that ruled northern Nigeria, Niger, and southern Cameroon, and its resistance to British colonial control at the beginning of the twentieth century.

Kumar had never heard of any of it before. He learned that starting in 2002, an English-speaking Kanuri tribesman from Yorbe state named Ustaz Mohammed Yusuf, who had studied theology at the University of Medina in Saudi Arabia, founded a sect called *Jama'atu Ahlis Sunna Lidda'awati wal-Jihad,* which translated from Arabic meant "People Committed to the Propagation of the Prophet's Teachings and Jihad."

In the city of Maiduguri where Festus Ratty Kumar had grown up, Yusuf built a religious complex and school that attracted poor families from across Nigeria and neighboring countries. The center's political goal was to establish an Islamist state patterned on Taliban rule in Afghanistan. Coinciding with the rise of Islamic radicalism through the Middle East and Africa, the center became a recruiting ground for jihadists, who denounced the secularism and corruption of the Nigerian government.

Mohammed Yusuf's hundreds of followers, called *Yusuffiya,* consisted largely of impoverished northern Islamic students and clerics. Economic disparities between the country's north and south continued to draw recruits. Despite its vast wealth in natural resources, Nigeria had one of the world's poorest populations, particularly in the north where over seventy percent of the people lived in poverty and earned less than a dollar a day.

Before 2009, the group that became known as Boko Haram did not aim to violently overthrow the government. Instead Mohammed Yusuf criticized northern Muslims for participating in what he saw as an illegitimate, non-Islamic state, and Muslim leaders for taking bribes from the government in return for preaching compliance.

After years of tension and a series of minor incidents, things exploded in July 2009 when a group of Yusuffiya were stopped by police in the city of Maiduguri as they were on the way to the cemetery to bury a comrade. The officers demanded that the young men comply with a law requiring motorcycle passengers to wear helmets. The young men refused, and in the confrontation that followed, several were shot and wounded by police.

The Yusuffiya responded with violence, breaking into a prison, and attacking government buildings and police stations. Fighting quickly spread across five northern states.

The response from the federal government was severe. Federal soldiers were filmed summarily executing suspected militants in the streets. They stormed the group's mosque and school complex and took Yusuf into custody. Hours later he was killed. Yusuf's deputy and Ratty's cousin Abubakar Shekau was also shot by security forces and declared dead.

In total, more than a thousand people died in the fighting. Boko Haram was banned by the government, its mosques demolished, and its surviving members scattered and went underground.

Months later, Abubakar Shekau reappeared, saying that he had been in the mouth of the crocodile and was coming back to kill it under Allah's protection. Soon after that, he asked Festus Ratty to join the cause, form his own unit, and forge his own path.

His message: "A person knowing of the truth or the will of God does not need to believe in it. You are free to kill anything that God commands you to kill."

For five years now, since Abubakar Shekau had paid off officials and facilitated Festus Ratty Kumar's release from prison, Kumar had spread fear throughout northern and eastern Nigeria—killing Christians and government workers, blowing up churches and government buildings, and attacking school officials.

The idea of kidnapping schoolgirls had been suggested to him by the voice of Allah one night as he lay on a blanket in the Sambisa looking at the stars. His battle cry was spray-painted on walls throughout hamlets and villages throughout eastern and northern Nigeria: "I kill anything that God commands me to kill! I am God's Leopard!"

He and his men moved like leopards by night, attacking targets without warning. Sometimes they traveled by truck, sometimes they commandeered motorcycles. Often they seemed to appear out of nowhere dressed as policemen or soldiers.

Igbo people thought of him as the living embodiment of Ekwensu, the god of trickery and chaos. His companion was Death. The power of his rage was suffocating darkness that overwhelmed and destroyed everything in its path. It sucked all happiness and hope out of any living soul who opposed him.

By 2015, after one year under Ratty's military command, Boko Haram had the distinction of being the world's deadliest terrorist group, responsible for killing nearly seven thousand people, even more than ISIS had in Iraq and Syria. The terror they spread had forced approximately two million Nigerians to flee their homes.

Festus Ratty Kumar chose to believe what his cousin Abubakar Shekau had told him—that attacking civilians, killing unbelievers, beheading teachers, thieves, and homosexuals, and kidnapping schoolgirls were justified in the name of jihad.

*   *   *

Crocker rode in a helicopter approximately twenty kilometers west-southwest of the Boko Haram column. Leaning over Major Martins's shoulder, who was seated in front of him, he shouted, "Tell the pilot to take it even lower!"

Martins was speaking into a radio on his lap. Turned back to Crocker.

"I'm not sure that's safe."

"Look at the altimeter. We're at 308 meters. That's at least 200 meters over the tree line."

"The terrain isn't flat."

"According to my GPS, it's slightly hilly. There's room to take it down."

"Ill-advised."

Crocker pointed past him through to the darkness outside the bubble windshield. "Major, the point is, we still can't see shit."

"Okay, another fifty meters."

"One hundred, and tell the pilot to flip on the headlights."

The pilot didn't seem happy with the order, but complied. Now they were flying about seventy meters above the tree line. Dense foliage rose thirty meters. A dirt road, consisting of two muddy tire tracks, slowly became visible through the mist.

Akil shouted at Crocker, pointed down, and gave him a thumbs-up. Mouthed, "Look."

CT, Gator, and Crocker turned to the side windows simultaneously. Crocker straightened and raised an open hand—the ready sign. The men slammed mags into their weapons, and checked the gear on their combat belts and vests.

Minutes later, Akil, from the window farther down

the fuselage, shouted, "Boss! I see 'em now! Take a look."

Crocker chose the vantage of the large bubble window up front. Roughly 150 meters ahead, he made out a Hilux at the end of what looked to be a convoy of vehicles. Leaned into Martins and shouted, "There they are! There. Past that slope!"

"Yes!"

"Tell the pilot to buzz over them, so we get a better picture of what we're dealing with, but cut the lights first."

Martins nodded. Communications flew between Crocs One and Two. The pilot killed the headlights, banked, and slowly caught up with the column fifty meters to the right. From a parallel vantage, Crocker counted five or six vehicles.

Militants in the trucks responded with automatic weapons fire that started light and quickly built to a frenzy.

"Taking fire!"

"Hold on!"

Several bullets slammed into the side of the Mi-35P, causing Martins to lower his head into his lap, and the pilot to bank sharply right. So sharp that the strap holding Crocker to the bench broke, and he had to hold on to the lip with both hands.

Fuck...

The copilot opened up with the helo's twin 23mm chin-mounted articulated double-barrel guns. Made a huge fucking racket that pounded in Crocker's head.

All the while, he was trying to focus on the trail of sparks from the insurgents in the column so he could ascertain exactly what they were dealing with—two Hilux Toyotas armed with .50 cals carrying six militants each in back. Then a transport truck with more armed militants, several shouldering RPGs. Then an open truck with what appeared to be hooded figures on benches, then another Hilux and a jeep in front.

Couldn't be sure he was seeing the entire column because of the far-right angle, mist, and trees. Went forward past the major, crouched behind the pilot, and shouted, "Closer! Bank left! Come up behind it and rip the two Toyotas to shreds!"

The bleary-eyed pilot looked back at him like he was crazy. The copilot, with headphones over his ears, was still occupied with the twin 23mms.

"Closer! Closer, closer! Bank it in! Isn't this baby armed with Hellfires? Hellfire missiles! Direct your copilot to fire them. Fire them now at the rear two trucks before they seek cover!"

The pilot gave in slightly—another thirty meters max. When the mist cleared, it was enough for Crocker to see the open truck better. The hooded figures seated in the bed appeared to be unarmed.

In a split second, he put the image together with the intel about the arms exchange and what he had heard about Boko Haram's kidnapping of schoolgirls, which continued to be the talk of human rights activists in Nigeria, Europe, and the US.

Decided he didn't want to take a chance. Leaning over, grabbed the copilot's shoulder, and shouted, "Hold fire! Hold your fucking fire! They're carrying hostages! Women…Schoolgirls…*Ndi inyom!!! Ndi inyom!!!* Hold fire!"

Chichima heard the roar overhead and felt the excitement of the men in the pickup behind them. She lowered her head and held her hands in her lap. They'd been coarsened by months of fetching wood and water, cleaning floors and latrines, and other menial tasks.

Her hands took her back to her mother, who often said: "You must judge a person by the work of their hands."

She imagined her sitting in front of the outdoor stove making egusi soup. Her little twinkly eyes like precious stones. The gap between her front teeth making her look like a mischievous girl.

"Mother…"

The rain grew angry. A low roar came from the clouds.

Chichima watched as her mother started the egusi soup with palm oil poured into a cast-iron pot, then added chopped onions, and a large bowl of squash and melon seeds. She saw the wood fire burn, and flames lick the sides of the pot. Familiar smells that reached her nose. Blood rushed into her stomach.

"Mother?"

"However long the night, the dawn always breaks."

"Mother…You want me to add the locust beans?"

The truck bounced and jerked left and right. The girls huddled together.

Her mother turned back to her and smiled. Strands of dark hair peeked out from her green and yellow *dhuku*. Her mother's skin was more mahogany-colored than hers, but she carried no shame about that and used none of the popular bleaching products on her skin. In Igbo culture, yellowish and reddish complexions like Chichima's were considered more desirable.

"Ugliness with a good heart is better than beautiful."

"Yes, mother. I know that…"

She sat in front of a mirror, running a brush through her hair, appraising her features. Her cheekbones were too wide, her mouth too long, her nose too wide and flat.

The ugly black locust beans had been flattened, wrapped in shiny green moimoi leaves, and left to dry by the oven. Chichima slid the beans into the pot and the pungent smell that reminded her of dirty socks brought tears to her eyes.

"Why are you crying, girl?" Her mother smiled. "The beans mean no harm."

"It's silly, mother. I know."

The truck picked up speed and slid on the wet grass, flinging the girls off the bench and onto the floor. Chichima picked herself up. Tasted something familiar in her mouth.

"Chichima?"

She thought the popping sound she heard came from the beans bursting in the hot oil, and the whispering in her ear was coming from her younger sister.

"Ugoulo…Sweet Ugoulo, the stove is hot…"

Her sister was a daydreamer who amused herself by playing with dolls and making up stories. Their mother complained that she was too distracted to help around the house.

Chichima turned to shoo her sister away, and was surprised to see another familiar face.

"Navina, what are you doing here?"

"Chichi…Chichi…"

Her lips trembled and she couldn't get the words out. When Chichimi looked past her face, she saw that they weren't in a kitchen by the yard. They sat in the bed of a truck in the dark.

"Are you hurt, Navina?"

It was a ridiculous question. All of them had been violated in one way or another.

"My leg…It's numb…"

Things became clearer. She realized that pops weren't coming from the stove. The men were shouting, gesturing, and shooting at something in the sky. A roar filled her ears.

Her friend pointed up. "You hear that, Chichi?"

"I hear it, yes."

A smile spread across Navina's face.

CHAPTER SIX

"A friend is someone you share a path with."
—African proverb

THE WIND buffeted the lead Mi-35P helicopter left and right. Even though they were out of range of the rebels, and the helo could probably shred them to pieces with the 23mm and Hellfire missiles it carried, the excitement—verging on panic—of the Nigerians inside had not let up. Major Martins, the pilot, and copilot were shouting back and forth in Igbo and occasional English. Lieutenant Peppie was the only one who remained calm.

Crocker crouched beside Martins, trying to restore order.

"Listen…Major, listen…We're fine…More than fine. We've got the advantage…We need to stay calm. We need to rescue those girls."

Crocker had been briefed about the estimated three hundred schoolgirls that Boko Haram had kidnapped the past several years. According to rumor, many of them had been raped and then sold as sex slaves in neighboring Niger and Cameroon.

"Girls?" Major Martins responded. "What girls?"

"The girls we saw in the truck!"

"How can you be sure they're not rebels dressed as women?" the major asked. "The Boko Haram are clever. Very clever…We can't do anything without reinforcements, or orders!"

Somebody was shouting hysterically over the radio in one of the local dialects. Crocker assumed it was the pilot of the second Mi-35P.

"No, Major. Listen…There's no reason to panic. This is what we talked about in terms of maintaining situation awareness."

"We're outnumbered. I have assessed that now. We have to turn back!"

"No!" Crocker shouted. "No reason for that… We're out of range of their guns."

He could still hear occasional gunfire in the distance, and so far the terrorists hadn't fired any RPG missiles, which were a standard and ubiquitous part of any rebel arsenal. Maybe that had to do with the cloud cover, which was significant, or the difficulty of shooting at a moving target.

"Very dangerous," the major snorted. "Too much risk! We have orders only to do observation. We must turn back."

"Risk?" Crocker shouted, trying to control his anger. "We've got helicopters. They're armed with machine guns and Hellfires. We've got the advantage…"

"Dangerous. Too dangerous!"

"Those are your schoolgirls down there, Major. Nigerian schoolgirls."

The major seemed to take this as an insult. Turned and shouted over his shoulder, "We're turning back!" Meanwhile, a man was shouting hysterically over the radio in the major's lap.

All the lessons Crocker and his men had imparted about controlled breathing, mental focus, and effective decision-making seemed to have flown out the window.

Psychological and physiological tests performed on Crocker and the other members of Black Cell revealed that their pulse rates actually slowed when under extreme stress, their GSRs dropped and their EEGs quickly accentuated. Also, their brains responded by injecting liquid nitrogen into their systems, forming a blanket neural cull of all surplus feral emotion. They reacted the same as astronauts and serial killers when subjected to stress.

Unlike serial killers and other psychopaths, the SEALs also had something psychologists called "arousal control." Instead of killing their emotions, they kept them on a leash.

Crocker was practicing arousal control now, focusing on managing the Nigerians and looking at the bigger picture—figuring out how to free the hostages.

He was so tuned in that he appeared tuned out. "We can't turn around," he responded to the major. "That's not an option. We've got to stop the terrorists one way or another."

The helo pitched back and forth. The major, pilot, and Lieutenant Peppie were all screaming into radios at once. Crocker assumed they were communicating with the second helo and possibly AFSF headquarters in Abuja.

"Instruct the pilot to continue to the border," said Crocker.

"To what purpose?"

"We have to assume the men in the trucks are Boko Haram."

Major Martins nodded. "Yes. Boko Haram! Yes!"

"They're meeting someone near the border," he continued. "They're going where they're going with a purpose."

"Yes. Yes."

The pilot had taken the helo farther up. Shouting through the radio continued. Crocker glanced over his shoulder and saw Akil with a finger in Lieutenant Peppie's chest, as if he were in the process of making a point.

"Looks to me like they're going to exchange the women for weapons," Crocker said. "We don't want that to happen. Do we, Major?"

Major Martins seemed momentarily distracted by a message on his cell phone.

Crocker wanted to slap the phone away, but controlled the impulse.

"Major…Major, my role is to give you my best advice. That's what my men and I are here for. So let's proceed west and see what's up."

The major looked confused. "West?"

"Yes, west. Let's see where the weapons exchange is going to take place."

"Farther west, no! We are not permitted to cross the border. That's not good!"

"Major, I never said I wanted us to cross the border. We're going to proceed farther west and see what we find."

Lieutenant Peppie leaned and spoke into Major Martins's ear as he considered. Whatever he told him seemed to have an impact, because the major turned to Crocker and nodded. "Okay…" he said. "Okay…Let's take a look."

*　　　*　　　*

Festus Ratty Kumar sat in the passenger seat of the lead jeep, a pair of stolen Halcyon motorcycle goggles over his eyes, headphones on his ears, an AK clenched between his knees, bouncing up and down, and singing off-key to the song "King Kong (Remix)" by one of Nigeria's top rappers, Vector, featuring Reminisce and others.

"King of my city, kam bu King Kong…"

He rocked back and forth totally plugged into the song. Oblivious to the rain, the gunfire, and the beating of helicopters overhead. The Nigerian military didn't scare him. They never had. Should the helicopters attack from overhead, he'd shoot them down. If they landed soldiers, he'd wipe them out.

Vector and Reminisce had actually collaborated on the song to settle a longtime feud. It had risen to number one on the charts, and was a favorite on Festus Ratty's playlist.

"I can't lose…Competition should have known, right?"

Awon, the driver, wearing a camouflage hat, grinned out of the side of his mouth and, turning to Festus, said, "Run that mafia swagger. Believe the kingdom, brother! Never run away from a fight."

Ratty flung an arm overhead and snapped it to the beat.

"Fire! Papa, papa, papa…FIRE!"

A .50-caliber machine gun pop-pop-popped in one of the trucks behind him. Awon threw his head back and laughed. He was also high on purple drank, or sizzurp.

Ratty didn't need any more than the possibility of a mix-up to get him going. Didn't have a care in the world. Wasn't worried about any danger, or what lay ahead.

He buzzed with excitement, completely jazzed in the moment, raindrops spattering his neck and face, and totally believing in himself and God's will. Didn't care that the enemy had found him, and were circling in helicopters overhead, and could call in air strikes and reinforcements. They didn't have the power of belief that he had. They didn't have the magic coursing through their systems.

"Believe the kingdom...Shooting nonstop omo see machine gun..."

When the enemy struck, he trusted that Allah would be in his ear, advising him, and leading him to victory, or he wouldn't. Maybe God was a trickster, too.

Even if things should go wrong and he and his men were slaughtered, it would be God's will. And Festus Ratty was certain he would be greeted warmly at the fountain of paradise.

Allah in his white and purple robes would pat him on the head, wink, and say, "You're a gangster, Festus Ratty Kumar. You're my king."

The truck that Chichima and her fellow schoolgirls rode in slowed, turned into a small oval clearing, and stopped. As it did, her mind jostled, and slipped back in time to that night in April when the truck carrying her and the thirty other girls had stopped in the Sambisa Forest. All of them were sick and exhausted. Many of them stood in shock, their eyes focused on some awful thing in the future, as they were unloaded and forced to stand in a line in a clearing.

She was seated now. Raindrops pelted her face and water dripped down the back of her burqa.

Before there were stars glowing ominously overhead, monkeys howling from the trees, and a woman
in flip-flops and a dirty skirt and blouse offering them
water from a bucket.

Now there was just a truck sitting in a muddy
clearing, thick foliage, and rain. The shooting had
stopped.

Back then the water stunk and many of the girls
drank too much or too quickly and got sick. The smell
was so disgusting that Chichima had wanted to leave
her body.

She still wanted to leave it.

What is the difference between then and now? she
asked herself.

"Hope" was the answer that resounded in her head.

Two years ago in another clearing, she had willed
herself to stand and bear witness to everything, so one
day she would report what she saw, and her report
would make people angry, and inspire them to take
action.

Now she expected nothing. She sat still and listened
to the gentle ping of raindrops off the metal bed of the
truck. She wanted to wipe the water away from her
eyes, but her hands were bound behind her back.

Navina leaned in to her and whispered, "Why are
we here?"

"Why? I don't know."

She closed her eyes again and remembered how,
one by one, the girls had been led to a primitive latrine
to wash and relieve themselves. She was afraid to run,
scared that the armed men would shoot her in the
back, or should she escape, get lost in the bush and be
devoured by wild animals.

She thought that if she was smart she could outwit

her captors. Maybe out of the dozens of men she would find one who was sympathetic. Maybe a government plane or helicopter would spot them from the air. Anything could happen...

Like her father, she had been baptized a Christian. In the Bible, she'd read, "The Lord delights in those who fear him, who put their hope in his unfailing love."

Where was it? Where is it now?

She was amazed at how much she had been able to endure. In her memory, she stood in line again as a short, wiry man stood on a tree stump and lectured them in Kanuri, the language of roughly seven million Nigerians, and one Chichima didn't understand. It wasn't Navina's tribal language, either, but she'd learned a little from relatives, and translated as best she could.

He said, "You are the girls who insisted on attending school when we have said *boko* is *haram*. One day you will thank us because we have liberated you. You can't understand what I'm saying now, because you've been brainwashed. God has a destiny for all of us, and now that destiny can be fulfilled."

The words frightened her then, but no longer. The leader of the armed men, who was introduced as the Leopard, stepped forward and started gesturing wildly, and speaking in a fearsome jumble of anger and swagger. It reminded her of a video clip she had watched of Adolf Hitler addressing a rally.

When he finished, his men jumped up and down and shouted "Allahu Akbar!" Then the Leopard went down the line inspecting each girl as an aide with a submachine gun over his shoulder held a flashlight. When he stopped in front of Chichima, he ran a hand over the white braids on the top of her head. Then he made a comment, which someone translated into Igbo.

He said: "You look like something made in Japan."

His comment made her feel ashamed, which surprised her.

The Leopard spoke again and an aide translated: "Allah curses the one who attaches false hair and the one who has this done. Who has done this? Is she here?"

Chichima shook her head. She was protecting Navina, who had given her the alternating black and white braids.

The next morning Chichima had been awakened by two women holding her head down. A third sheared her hair off with a razor. Afterward, as she fought back tears, one of the women wrapped a turban around her head.

She asked, "Are you crying because you're upset, or happy?"

Chichima refused to answer.

"You should be happy because you have been rescued from a false life."

"My life isn't false."

"You will learn, and with Boko Haram you will enjoy more gifts, and good sex."

Chichima shuddered. The idea of sex with one of the killers and kidnappers made her sick to her stomach. She vowed to kill herself first.

The lead Mi-35P flew south to northeast along the Cameroon border. Crocker and the other SEALs crouched near windows peering through the dark swirling mist. Akil grabbed Crocker's shoulder and pointed to eleven o'clock.

"There they are, boss!"

"Where?"

Akil handed him a pair of Steiner 10x50 low-light binoculars.

Crocker made out a hill that sloped to a clearing and a line of trees to the west.

"What am I looking for?" he asked.

"Focus on the line of trees. Under the canopy you should be able to make out the sides of three trucks."

Crocker found them. "Check."

Then he leaned forward into Major Martins's ear and shouted. "There they are! There! You see them, Major?"

The major had his own pair of low-light binos hanging from a leather cord around his neck. But his attention was now focused on the handheld radio he held up to his ear. He was saying, "Sir…Sir…Yes, sir. Yes, of course…"

"Major, look. It's important."

He waved Crocker away.

"Who is he talking to?" Akil asked.

"HQ, probably," Crocker shouted back. He leaned in to Major Martins and spoke into his free ear, "Tell them, we need air support…reinforcements. Tell them to alert the Cameroonians. We've got the arms dealers in our sights. If we act fast we can trap both them and Boko Haram!"

Martins continued into the radio, "Sir…Yes, sir…"

"Major, please…"

"Boss! Hey, Boss…"

It was Mancini, his big paw on Crocker's shoulder, his dark eyes glowing red from the reflected lights of the instrument panel.

"What?"

"Crocodile Two has done an about-face!"

"What's that mean?" It was hard to hear clearly with all the noise.

"It's turned around and looks like it's headed west, back to base."

Crocker squeezed between the seats occupied by Major Martins and Lieutenant Peppie, both men talking excitedly into radios. The racket inside the helo was intense—wind buffeting the sides, men shouting, the engine roaring and whining.

Practically nose to nose with Mancini, he shouted, "What'd you say?"

Manny shouted back, "The second helicopter is turning back! *Back to base!*" He gestured with his arm.

Crocker turned back to look, but this wasn't a car with a rearview mirror. He scurried over on his knees to one of the side windows. "What the fuck…Why?"

He still couldn't spot the second helo. A flying branch glanced off the bulletproof bubble up front. The pilot shouted a warning in Igbo.

Mancini shrugged. "Maybe it got hit."

"Croc Two got hit?"

"Don't know. It turned around. That's all I know… It's going back!"

Crocker pivoted to the major to his left. Was practically in his face.

"Bad news," Major Martins declared. "Colonel Nwosu has ordered us to return to base!"

Colonel Ajala Nwosu was the commander of all of Nigeria Special Forces. Crocker and his men had met him briefly after they landed in the capital city, Abuja, roughly two weeks ago. A big man, tall, broad-shouldered, who carried himself more like a bank executive than a soldier.

"No!"

"It's an order."

"Let me speak to him," offered Crocker.

"Too late, sir...Too late."

"Call him back. Call him back now!"

"We live by rules, sir. In our military, orders from HQ must be obeyed!"

Crocker wasn't sure about that. Meanwhile Lieutenant Peppie was engaged in a big shouting match with the pilot. Seemed as though the pilot was ready to heed the Colonel's order, and Peppie had lost patience with his Nigerian colleagues and was having none of it.

Crocker heard him scream, *"Ee e!"* —(no!)—*"Gaa n'hi!"* —(continue forward).

The pilot banked the helicopter to the west.

Neither Crocker nor Akil nor any of the other SEALs could follow the argument between them, arteries standing out on both men's necks. Major Martins joined in, pointing a finger in Peppie's face and shouting.

A gust of wind hit the side of the helo, pushing the nose north and down. Out of the front, Crocker saw the clearing to the left. Felt the helo tilt right.

"Buckle in! Buckle in!" he shouted as the engines whined higher.

Akil was at the left window peering through Steiner 10x50 low-lights. Shouted, "Boss, there's a road up ahead. Must be the road in from Cameroon. Yeah...We can land along there and make an assault on the trucks. I make out three. Maybe four!"

Crocker wanted to see for himself, but needed to deal with Major Martins first.

"Major...Major! This is the moment...This is

what we came for! We've got the enemy where we want them!"

Akil shouted, "It's got to be the arms from Cameroon. If we do it right, we can grab them and the Bokos all at once!"

"Major! Listen, Major, this is your chance to stop them. You'll be a hero. Now is the time to act!"

"No! Impossible!" Martins shouted over his shoulder, then turned and addressed the pilot in Igbo. The engine grew louder, the rotors tilted, the helo nose angled sharply up and right.

Crocker couldn't help himself. He grabbed Martins by the arm. Was so in his face, he could make out the capillaries in his eyes. "You're making a big mistake!"

"Please, stop shouting!"

"I'm here to advise. I'm giving you my best advice!"

"No more."

Lieutenant Peppie was practically on top of the console, between the pilot and copilot, shouting hysterically at both of them. The pilot pivoted and used his right arm to shove Peppie back.

Crocker saw the pilot's elbow smash into Peppie's jaw, and then the entire helo jerked, and events seemed to unfold in slow motion. Maybe the pilot hit one of the instruments by mistake, or maybe Peppie did, but whatever the cause, the helo swooped sharply up and lost power.

Next thing Crocker knew it was looping down and sharply left. The pilot, copilot, and Major Martins were all apoplectic, screaming at the top of their lungs.

Crocker turned and shouted to his men, "Hold on! Hold the fuck on!"

The pilot was struggling to get the big metal bird

under control. Peppie wasn't strapped in, and lost his balance and crashed to the floor.

Crocker braced himself between the two seats, wishing he had a helmet, the helo pitching left and right. *Too late for that…*

The big metal bird spun sharply low and right. The pilot struggled to gain control and boost the engine's power at the same time.

Crocker saw the top of a tree appear suddenly through the mist. Shouted, "Watch out!"

Saw it smash into the bubble window. Heard the pilot scream. He finally lurched forward to grab the controls himself. But it was too late. The helo tumbled right, throwing Peppie against the side of the fuselage with a thud. Hit another tree—*bang!*—then another that threw the copilot out of his seat into the front of the bubble windshield.

Didn't he fucking strap himself in?

Struggling to hold on himself, Crocker shouted one more time, *"Hold on!"*

The right side of the helo hit the ground first. Crocker felt the tail break free, and the impact threw him into Peppie, sprawled over the center console, and he cracked his head into the lieutenant's back and passed out.

CHAPTER SEVEN

FESTUS RATTY couldn't believe his eyes and ears. He stood on the seat of the jeep with his hands over his mouth and his fighters gathered around the vehicle.

First, he had watched one of the Nigerian helicopters turn and run away like a frightened chicken. While he and his men had been celebrating that occurrence, the second military helicopter hit a tree, spun, and crashed into the brush ahead.

Like an awesome scene from an action movie, like the hand of God had flung the funny-looking metal bird out of the sky. Festus was now pointing in the direction of where the helo went down, jumping up and down on the seat, and screaming, "You see this. You see, my brothers!! You think that there are no miracles! You think that the great Allah is not on our side!"

He beat his chest over and over and felt a newfound power coursing through him, and his legend growing before his eyes. His face in the newspapers and on TV.

Heard his men shouting and waving weapons over their heads. "Leopard! Leopard! King of the jungle!"

Pointing to them, he shouted back, "Now you see the truth, my brothers. This is the power we have. *This is the kingdom!*"

They exploded in celebration, firing in the air and shouting, "Allahu Akbar!" In Festus Ratty's mind, God was already welcoming him into heaven and pointing to a place beside his throne for him to sit. Beautiful maidens with brass trays of food and nectars waited to serve him.

He was the unspoiled, untamed man of nature, brave enough to face the modern infidels and their machines. Victory was his destiny.

The downed helicopter sent pieces of hot hissing metal flying through the bush around them. Festus Ratty felt so invincible he didn't bother to cover his head.

His one-eyed aide, Modu, looked up at him and said, "Commander, this is the kingdom. And in the kingdom you are destined to lead us...Tell us what to do now and we will follow!"

Festus Ratty nodded and composed himself. Head in his hands, he considered the circumstances. First, he pointed to a thickly bearded fighter with a big belly. "Abu Sata, you will stay with four men to guard the girls in the truck."

"It is God's will."

"Modu, you will take four other men and go meet our Ambazonian brothers to make sure they have brought what they promised and the terms are still the same."

"Yes, Commander."

"The exchange prices have already been worked out with Russian arms dealer Victor Balt. One girl for every three-man portable air defense systems"—

MANPADS—"one girl for every crate of AK-47s; one for every crate of Russian-made RPG-7s. The Ambazonians give you any shit, you let me know."

"Yes."

"If everything is cool, you radio Abu Sata, and he will bring the girls."

"It is God's will."

"You got all that?"

The two sub-commanders nodded.

"The rest of you will come with me to hit the downed helicopter. We're gonna hit it hard, you know. Kill any survivors, grab anything of value— radios, binoculars, weapons, watches."

"Allahu Akbar!"

"The kingdom is ours!"

CT had strapped himself to the bench on the left side of the helicopter next to Akil, which helped him avoid the serious damage to the opposite side of the fuselage. He stared at it now, half conscious, steam curling past the ripped aluminum skin. The strong smell of aviation fuel made him focus and try to sit up.

The fuel tank is compromised. Gotta get out…fast!

Pivoting left toward the cockpit, he experienced an enormous jolt of pain from the back of his head. The underside of his ribs ached, too. Felt strange hands touching him there, started to push them away. "Hey…"

"Hay is for horses…Hold still."

Looked up at Mancini—aka Manny and Big Dog, Crocker's right-hand man and expert in all things technical. Blood streamed from a cut above his eyebrow.

"You're leaking, bro…"

"It's nothing. Hold still."

Manny sliced through the strap with his SOP knife. Held CT upright. "Stay still. I'm going to check for structural damage along your neck and back."

"Where the hell are we?"

"Quiet!"

Mancini felt carefully, but found no broken vertebrae or protruding discs.

"Now try moving your head and legs."

"Something's not right…But I think I can manage."

CT started to push himself to his feet.

"Easy, big guy…" Mancini helped hold him up, smoke rising from the instrument panel, red lights flashing. "You sure you can stand on your own?"

"Yeah…"

"Good…This sucker's gonna blow soon. The enemy is close."

"Where are the rest of the guys?"

Mancini wiped the blood away from his eye. "Romeo's outside with Gator. Crocker's in the cockpit trying to save Martins. I'm going to help him now. You think you can manage to set up outside?"

"Can do, brother. Thanks." CT stood in a crouch. Found his AK lodged under the bench. Managed to jimmy it out with Manny's help, who now pointed to the back of the helo. That's when CT realized that the whole tail section had been ripped away.

Heard someone moan from the cockpit and turned. Saw a mangled mess of metal and bodies, and Crocker kneeling over one. Took a step toward him, when Manny stopped him and pointing to the back opening. "Go outside! Now!"

"But—"

"Clear away as far from the helo as you can. We'll catch up!"

"Roger."

Mancini pushed around twisted metal and broken benches to the cockpit, where he saw Crocker working on Major Martins.

"You okay, boss?"

"Yep."

Crocker had been protected by Lieutenant Peppie's body, which had prevented him from being thrown sideways and forward, and probably saving him from serious injury or death. Peppie hadn't been as fortunate—his neck impaled on the center console. Through the mist that filled the cockpit, a strange relieved expression on his face.

Up ahead, Mancini saw that the pilot's head had almost been completely obliterated, and the copilot also lay in a mangled mess, his legs and twisted torso hanging halfway out the shattered front.

Fuck...

He turned back to Crocker. "We need to get the hell outta here, pronto."

"Just a sec."

The smell of aviation fuel filling his throat and nostrils, Crocker coolly attended to Martins, quickly working through the trauma medical progression. A for airway...Cleared. B for breathing...Good. C for circulation...Elevated pulse...Not good.

Not good at all...Gotta call for help...

The reason: a big slash to Martins's left chest, which he packed with QuikClot. Planned to clean and bandage the wound once he got him outside. It was the apparent trauma to Martins's back that alarmed him. Not only was the major as stiff as a board, even the slightest application of pressure to the area caused him to wail.

His spine?

Damage there could be worsened by moving him, and increase the risk of paralysis.

Mancini knelt beside him, blood trickling down the side of his mouth.

"Call for medevac," Crocker said.

"Boss, we need to evacuate first!"

Smoke was already starting to rise through a crack in the floor, and it was probably a matter of seconds before the helo caught fire and exploded.

Crocker reached under to try to feel the extent of the damage to the major's back.

Manny shouted, "No time for that, Boss! Let's go."

"You go ahead."

"Fuck that. You come with me, or we die together."

"Okay…Grab him by the legs, and help me get him out. Carefully…"

First they freed the major's tangled body, then Crocker lifted him under his right shoulder. That's when he noticed a flicker of flame through the gash in the floor.

"Shit…"

"Out the back," said Mancini, nodding past his right shoulder.

Crocker hadn't thought to inspect his own body, but became aware now of searing pain from his right upper thigh. Saw the gash in his black pants. Pushed through the pain and stumbled toward the back, an AK slung over his left shoulder, thinking that he should stop and look for a radio—they were going to need a radio—but there was no time given the fact that his entire groin was tightening, and blue flames were already crawling up the side of the fuselage to his right.

Took a deep breath and gritted through.

"Duck!"

The top of his head scraped on some metal on the way out. Rain pelted his head and back. He paused to take a breath. Smoke caught in his throat.

"Keep moving!" Mancini shouted. "Follow me."

Crocker remembered the medical kit and was about to say *stop* when in the golden glow of light, he saw that Mancini had it slung around his neck.

"Sweet."

"What's sweet?"

"Never mind."

Stumbled into the brush, and focused on the light that lit up his colleague's thick neck and shoulders to push away the pain.

"That's it, boss! Keep moving forward! Another fifty meters…"

Fuck…

Felt the heat on his back and realized where the light was coming from. Pushed as hard as he could. The major was speaking with someone who wasn't there. Seemed to be engaged in a serious conversation based on the frown on his face.

"Faster!"

Fuck you, Manny.

His boot had filled with water, or maybe it was blood. His heart burned in his throat.

"A few more meters!"

"Motherfucker!"

What Crocker would do now for a plate of spaghetti and meatballs at Il Giardino. A date with Cyndi. He imagined her tight bikinied body standing in shallow water.

What the fuck am I doing?

The light grew brighter to the point where it lit up the ground and he could clearly see where he was stepping—which was good and bad.

A loud whoosh, and he was shoved hard from behind. The thrust was so strong that it lifted him off his feet and forward, so he was literally flying.

Then he landed chest-first on the ground and lost consciousness.

Chichima dreamed that she was standing up to her knees in a river, drawing water with a bucket. Clear, fresh water. Something pressed into her shoulder and she opened her eyes. Saw a huge flash in the bush ahead as a column of fire rose into the night sky. The explosion that followed a split-second later hurt her eardrums.

She ducked her head and prayed.

When she looked up she saw a group of Boko Haram fighters running toward them. Recognizing the thickly bearded, heavyset man in front, she felt a pang of anguish rise from the pit of her stomach that almost caused her to pass out.

"Look," Navina exclaimed beside her. "It's Abu Sata."

"I see…"

"What happened? They look angry. Are they coming to kill us?"

If they were, to Chichima's mind, it would make a bitter kind of sense.

Because her and Abu Sata's fates had been bound together, though not through any free choice of hers.

Lowering her face into her hands, she remembered that a year into Boko Haram captivity, she had been presented with a choice: convert to Islam and take a husband, or be sold as a slave. She was barely seventeen at the time, and had never been with a man before.

She decided to perform the *Shahada* (testimony of faith), and to testify, "There is no true god but Allah, and Mohammad is the Messenger of God." The imam taught her how to repeat the words in Arabic.

He gave her a new name, Barja ("possessing beautiful eyes"), and prayed that none of the Leopard's men would want her. She considered ripping her hair out, screaming like an animal, and acting crazy. She even thought of using a sharp rock to ruin her face and body.

Then one day the imam introduced her to a woman who spoke to her briefly and carefully inspected her legs and hands.

She turned out to be the sister of a heavy, sour-smelling man named Abu Sata, who carried an automatic rifle and wore a belt of bullets across his wide chest and stomach. He seemed awkward and shy. Without looking her in the eye, he handed her a copy of the Quran, and said in Kanuri, "A man without a wife is like a vase without flowers."

Chichima had tried to pretend it was all a bad dream and that her mother would arrive with a glass of hot tea and wake her. She and Abu Sata sat in a clearing and drank tea. He had deep tribal scars on his face. As he read from a piece of paper, his sister translated, "The Prophet Mohammad advises the following…Go and see her, for seeing her in person is much better for having harmony between the two of you."

Chichima remembered looking down at the ground, hoping it would swallow her and magically transport her to another world. Meanwhile, Abu Sata's sister talked about her brother's bravery on the battlefield, how he was one of the Leopard's most esteemed fighters, and had already acquired two other wives.

She tuned her words out completely, reciting lines in her head from "Wrong Destination" by the Nigerian poet Mabel Segun, which she had memorized at school.

> *My thoughts strove ever so bravely*
> *To grow among the weeds,*
> *But they were choked to death…*

She didn't want to be with this man, but she didn't want to die, either.

They were married on a Sunday in Shawwal, the tenth month of the lunar Islamic calendar. Before the ceremony, Abu Sata's sister and another female relative spread a special mixture of sugar and lime juice over Chichima's skin to remove all body hair except for that on her head. They decorated her hands and feet with henna tattoos. Then, as they put special oils in her hair, and smeared perfumed oil over her skin, they read from the Quran:

> Righteous women are devoutly obedient, guarding in the husband's absence what Allah would have them guard. But those wives from whom you fear arrogance, first advise them; then if they persist, forsake them in bed; and finally, strike them. But if they obey you once more, seek no means against them.

But her hopes and expectations of a better life didn't go away. She clung to them even as she dressed in a white smock and a veil. The sun shone. Abu Sata appeared wearing a clean camouflage uniform. With the imam and some fighters watching, Abu Sata placed a ring on her right hand. Then Abu Sata was called away.

That afternoon, his sister led her to a hut higher in the mountains. There Chichima was introduced to Abu Sata's other wives, who showed her how to cook, wash his uniforms, and prepare herself for him the way he liked. Two nights later, he arrived very late, climbed on top of her, nearly smothering her, and entered her.

> Now I'm without my thoughts;
> They've given me new ones,
> But we do not get along—
> They're someone else's thoughts,
> Not mine.

Afterward she cried herself to sleep. To her mind, it was a fate only slightly better than death, and completely opposite of the future she had imagined for herself.

Once a week, her husband would arrive in the hut at night and climb on top of her. They exchanged no tender kisses or words. Afterward, Chichima would chide herself for not being brave enough to commit suicide by throwing herself off a cliff, or at least trying to escape as some of the other girls had tried to do.

Now she felt water dripping down her back and the girls around her trembling with fear. The back gate of the trunk creaked open and the men pulled them up, roughly.

She kept her eyes closed, because she didn't want to see Abu Sata's face and feel the shame again.

"What happens now?" Navina whispered. "Where are they taking us?"

Chichima didn't answer. She wasn't sure it mattered anymore.

The night had offered so many positive developments so far that Festus Ratty Kumar was almost giddy with excitement. He moved through the bush toward the downed Nigerian military listening to Lil Wayne through his headphones. "Look at you, now look at us…" His AK loaded and ready; a two-way radio tucked into his waistband.

"Rich as Fuck" was one of his favorite tunes. The same defiance and swagger ran through his veins.

"Look at you, now look at us…Money talks, bull-shit walks…"

More AK-47s, RPGs, and two-man portable air defense systems would soon enter his arsenal. The MANPADS alone would give him the ability to shoot down the Nigerian flying robots—his terms for military helicopters, jet fighters, and drones.

He'd assured Victor Balt that the girls were young and beautiful and worth their weight in gold—and a currency that to Festus's mind was in abundant supply.

Anytime he needed more, he'd just snatch them, like he snatched everything else.

Who is gonna stop me now?

He didn't trust the Ambazonians, either. The Ambazonians were Cameroon rebels who wanted to establish an English-speaking republic in Western Cameroon.

Sounded wack to him.

Should he have any hassle with the Ambazonians, he'd have no problems taking them out and stealing their cargo.

"Look at you, now look at us...I just wanna hit and run..."

He smiled at his own cleverness and took another sip of purple drank—like his man Lil Wayne—from the flask he carried in his back pocket.

As it burned its way down his throat to his stomach, he saw a flash of light behind him and to his right, and stopped. The explosion came a split second later.

He knelt behind a tree, grabbed his Standard Horizon handheld radio and shouted into it: "What the fuck was that?"

One of his men exclaimed back through it, "The helicopter exploded! You okay, Commander?"

"Haha! I'm good. They got what they deserved!"

"Yes, Commander."

"Any survivors?"

"We're looking now."

CHAPTER EIGHT

"To get lost is to learn the way."
—Nigerian proverb

CT HUGGED the warm ground, which felt welcoming, almost maternal. A stream to his right gurgled gently over the steady whistle of rain. He imagined his sister Alexis crouching beside him. Then a burst of AK bullets sailed over his head and tore into the trees behind him.

Where the fuck am I? What am I doing here?

His hand rested on a black AN/PSC-5 Spitfire radio. It helped him remember.

Yeah…Yeah…Gotta make contact before we're all killed.

He ignored the second stream of bullets, trusting that Akil, who he remembered was somewhere farther east along the embankment, would hold off the enemy long enough for him to manage the dials, which he was focusing on now. The back of his head hurt like hell. The pain beckoned him to a clean bed with white sheets and his wife, Nasima, holding his hand.

Baby…Oh, baby…

The will he'd developed as a wrestler came in

handy. The light from the burning helo helped him see the keypad. He punched in the code—72HH1.

"TOC-Alpha. This is Croc One. Do you read me? Over."

A voice with British-accented English came through the headset. "Yes…This is TOC-Alpha. Identify yourself. Over."

Lowered the volume as the shooting picked up. He lowered himself closer to the ground so he could feel his warm breath. Waited for a response from Akil, but heard nothing.

Intimate and dangerous. Gathered his thoughts. "I'm with 72 AFSF. 72 AFSF…based in Yola…One of the American advisors aboard Crocodile One. We just crash-landed near the Cameroon border. Suffered casualties. Incoming fire, require backup a-sap. Immediate medevac…Over."

"Crocodile One? Can you confirm that? Over."

"Crocodile One, that's correct. Over."

He removed the headset. The shooting had drawn closer. So near he heard voices of men speaking in a native dialect.

Where the fuck is Akil?

As a kid, he'd marveled at a shrunken head under a glass dome at the Natural History Museum of Los Angeles County. Wondered if he was about to die in this part of Africa. Made to bleed into the same soil his ancestors had bled into.

Alexis, what do you think of that?

"Crocodile One, you hear me? Over."

He was lost for a moment, replaying the shock of the helicopter crash.

Replaced the headset. "Crocodile One, this is TOC-Alpha. Do you read me? Over."

CT lowered his voice to a hoarse whisper. "TOC-Alpha. This is Crocodile One. I hear you. Yes...We've suffered casualties. Three at least. More injured. We're pinned down now near the Cameroon border. Crocodile Two has turned back. Need medevac and support...immediately. As fast as you can. Over."

Pushed the headset away from his ears.

The footsteps were so close he could hear them distinctly. CT reached for the AK on his back. Considered picking up the toaster-size radio and battery pack and retreating, when he was interrupted by a click and the whoosh of an RPG. Seconds later...an explosion, the sound of splintering wood, followed by heavy automatic weapons fire, and the anguished cry of a wounded man.

Akil?!

"Copy, Crocodile One," the man on the other end of the radio responded. "Crocodile One, message received at Yorba. Will report to my commanders and respond. Over."

"Respond quickly, TOC-Alpha! We're under attack. Situation is critical! Send support now! Over and out!"

He tore off the headphones, saw someone in the bush ahead near the embankment along the stream. Prayed it was Akil, but couldn't be sure. Went belly to the ground, readied his weapon, and took a deep breath and counted the seconds in his head.

One, two, three, four...

Waited for movement, scanned through the scope for a target. Heard something shift in the bush behind him. Turned abruptly and saw Akil crouched near the root on a fallen tree with a big grin on his face, casually giving him a thumbs-up.

Akil, you excellent motherfucker...

Wanted to shout, he was so glad to see him. Saw the RPG slung over his shoulder.

"You the one who did the shooting?" he whispered.

"Who else?"

"Wait..." Took a moment to send out an SOS signal on the MARS emergency military network. Then whispered to himself, "Hope someone responds..."

Crocker cursed himself for not being better prepared, and for failing to unload more gear off the helo before it blew. He stopped himself.

Got to focus on the present.

Quickly took stock—limited weapons, limited ammo, limited comms, and only one quickly dwindling medical kit. He'd lost much of his gear pulling away from the wreckage.

He wanted to blame it on the Nigerians, but that was useless, too.

Make the best of what you got.

No weapon or zone control. No control of immediate environment. No nothing.

A hot, ripe disaster, as his dad used to say. His dad always with a smile, a joke, and a sunny attitude.

The good news was that he had patched up the wounds to Major Martins's chest and back, and the major's vitals had stabilized. Wasn't sure how he'd managed, or how long Martins would last. He was shot up with morphine now and strapped to an Israeli litter that rested along the base of a nearby tree, quietly holding a conversation with someone in his head.

Crocker considered stuffing a rag in his major's mouth. For the time being it wasn't necessary even though the enemy was close, because no one could hear shit through the heavy rain. Couldn't see shit, either.

Wanted to huddle with Lieutenant Peppie, and then remembered that he'd died in the helo along with the pilot and copilot.

I hope they're in a better place…

In addition to attending to Major Martins, he also found time to set Gator's broken right leg and arm as best he could using SAM splints from the med kit, and wrapping them tight with bandages. Remembered he'd given Gator a handful of extra-strength (800 mg) Motrin (aka SEAL candy) to numb the pain.

Now Gator sat with his back propped up against the same tree Martins lay beneath with an AK pressed to his right shoulder, his whole body trembling. Crocker wished he had a Kevlar blanket to wrap around him, but there were none available.

As far as the gash to his own leg was concerned, all Crocker knew was that the QuikClot had stemmed the bleeding. He had no idea how far or how fast he could move on it. Didn't have enough ES Motrin to spare on himself, either.

Didn't really matter, because with the injuries to Martins and Gator, it was impossible to move. Temporarily, they had lost contact with Akil and CT, who carried the only radio. All he could do was hope that CT had reached the TOC in Yola and help was on its way.

The really bad news was that they were stuck somewhere between the Boko Haram column and a group of trucks that had arrived from Cameroon bearing Ambazonians, according to Lieutenant Peppie. He didn't know how many of them there were, but assumed they were well armed.

Which meant they were almost certainly fucked. Because, despite the darkness and rain, he knew that Boko Haram was searching for them at this very moment, and they wouldn't be that hard to find since they had only managed to move about three hundred meters away from the burning helicopter.

It was only a matter of time.

The Boko Haram were jostling them, and helping the girls to the ground with urgency. Rain was falling so hard now Chichima couldn't see more than five feet in front. The dirt had turned into mud.

Why are we here? What are they doing with us?

The men had fever in their eyes. One of them pushed Chichima's face down into the mud, as though he was about to bury her.

Please, don't bury me alive…

She imagined that she was immune to fear at this point, but the thought of being suffocated by the mud filled her with terror. She noticed that the men didn't have shovels. They were pushing and kicking her and the other girls under the truck, and shouting, "Ala! Ala! Ala!"

Why? Why is this happening? Gods and spirits, if I offended you in any way, I'm sorry. My only sin was pride. I was a normal village girl hoping to make a more modern life.

Thick mud entered her mouth and nostrils.

She lay still, overwhelmed again by memory. Her marriage to Abu Sata had lasted five painful, miserable months. Months she'd tried to block out, or excise from her brain. Still, the memories lingered like the stench of rotting locust beans.

There were some things Chichima hadn't been able

to fake, even when her life depended on it. They included showing any passion for her sour-smelling, crude husband. The nights he came to take her body, her mind traveled elsewhere, through the holes in the roof, to join the night birds in the trees.

She had gotten used to living simultaneously in different places, some so strange they only seemed to exist in her imagination.

The more distracted she had become, the more Abu Sata grew frustrated, until he slapped her face and shouted, "Where are you, woman?"

She stopped eating. It wasn't a conscious decision to stage a hunger strike. It was her body rebelling, saying: this is unacceptable.

It got to the point where the only thing she could keep in her stomach was water. She became so weak, she couldn't think clearly and couldn't remember if she was Chichima, Barja, someone else, or two different people at once.

The thinner and frailer she became, the more her husband beat her. Abu Sata wanted his young wife to get pregnant and bear him a son. To Chichima the thought of creating another human being out of some sense of duty made her crazier.

One day she wandered off into the bush, talking to herself. When Abu Sata found her, he tied her to a tree like a dog, and made her sleep outside. When she refused to eat even simple boiled rice, he pushed the food down her throat. When she spit it up, he beat her again.

After months of beatings, Abu Sata gave up and returned her to the prison camp at the base of the mountains.

He told the imam, "There is something wrong with

this woman. She still has an infidel spirit living inside her."

Her friends at the camp slowly nursed Chichima back to health.

Months passed before she was able to think clearly again. Though no one had informed her, she assumed her marriage was over.

She had asked herself then, *What's next?*

Now she realized that Navina and the other ten girls with them lying in the mud under the truck had also failed to satisfy their captors in some way. And she thought she had an answer to her question.

They're going to leave us here to die in the jungle.

CHAPTER NINE

"If you want to go quickly, go alone. If you
want to go far, go together."
— African proverb

BEHIND A clump of five-foot-high bushes, Manny crouched beside Crocker. He'd just returned from doing some recon and was breathing hard.

"What's the situation?" Crocker asked.

"The BH column has stopped roughly fifty meters east-south-east. They seem to have staged there, right off the path."

"Why?"

"Unclear. A group of 'em are sifting through the remains of the helo. Another group went to meet with the Ambazonians farther north, about another forty meters from here."

"So we're stuck between them."

"Basically."

"What is the Boko column waiting for?"

"Maybe they want to see if the second helicopter returns. All I know is they got guys out looking and it's probably a matter of seconds before they find us."

Crocker wiped the water from his eyes and forehead. "Miracle they haven't yet."

"Meanwhile, the four trucks from Cameroon are parked in a clearing about 150 meters north."

"Soldiers?" asked Crocker.

"Not exactly...Looks to be four drivers and another four to six guards. Lightly armed. I can't imagine why they would bother looking for us, but I could be wrong. The BHs will, and are."

"CT and Akil are back. That gives us four able men."

Mancini asked, "What are you thinking? Was CT able to reach the TOC in Yola?"

"That's an affirmative. Asked for support and medevac."

"On its way?"

"Hope so, but we haven't received confirmation. CT also sent out an emergency signal in case there are any military in the area."

Thunder cracked overhead.

Crocker looked at the thick bush surrounding them and said, "Even if relief helos do come, they'll have a difficult time pulling us out."

Mancini nodded. "What are you thinking?"

"I'm thinking that we leave a couple men here to watch Gator and Martins, and the rest of us outflank the Ambazonians and surprise them from the west. You know between here and the Cameroon border. How far did you say that is?"

"To the Amazonian trucks. Fifty meters. Sixty max."

"Close."

Mancini nodded again. "Yeah...But...why? Like I said before, they appear to be more guards than soldiers. But then again, what does an Ambazonian look like? Beats the fuck out of me."

"Listen...We attack 'em, then return for the others. That gives us trucks, ammo, a clearing for a rescue team to touch down. And it eliminates the possibility that we're squeezed front and back. Trapped."

"I say we take everyone with us."

"Won't work. They will only slow us down."

"Boss, it's the only thing that will work. Besides we're gonna have to move Martins and the others eventually."

Crocker considered. "You're right…We leave 'em here, they'll probably be killed."

"That's what I'm thinking…You okay walking on that leg?"

"Fuck, yeah."

Crocker, his mind shredded with pain and exhaustion from jogging through the bush, set down one end of the Israeli litter bearing Major Martins behind a group of tall trees at the west end of the clearing. Leaned against a palm tree for a minute to catch his breath.

"They should be safe here," he said to Mancini— who had taken the other end of the litter—CT, and Akil, who had hauled Gator on his back.

"Not for long," Akil cracked.

Crocker limped several meters with Mancini past the trees to get a better look at the Ambazonians. In diffuse moonlight that had started to peek through the clouds, he spotted the outlines of the four cargo trucks parked thirty meters south under a line of tall pines. They'd essentially circled to the other side of them, and were now stationed between the trucks and the Cameroon border.

"What do we do now?" Manny asked.

"Wait here for medevac."

They'd stopped on the way so CT could radio the TOC in Yola a second time. Yola informed them they were still waiting for approval from military head-quarters in Abuja, and headquarters was concerned about launching more helicopters in bad weather.

The rain had let up.

"Problem is the longer we stay here, and the lighter it gets, the greater the chance Boko Haram finds us," said Crocker, thinking out loud.

"You think the BHs have figured that there were some survivors of the crash and fire?"

"How would they have done that?"

"All the gear we left behind," offered Mancini. "If I'm them, I'm not gonna leave the area until I find sur-vivors."

"Agree. And the longer we wait for medevac, the slimmer the chance Martins lives."

Back at the hiding place behind the trees, Crocker asked CT to try the TOC again. He looked up a few minutes later and shook his head. "They're still wait-ing for approval from Abuja."

"You tell them about the improving weather and the wounded?"

"Yup. Also, sent out another SOS over MARS."

Crocker pulled his black T-shirt over his head and wrung out the liquid. Turned to Akil and Mancini crouched to his right and said, "They're not coming…"

Akil shook his head. "We're on our own."

"We either sit here and wait for the bad guys to do their exchange and leave, or we take the fight to them now and hope we can grab one of the trucks."

"Losers wait for motivation," Akil growled. "Win-ners get shit done."

"Where'd you hear that?"

"Some motivational speaker on YouTube."

"You need a checkup from the neck up, bro."

Mancini jumped in. "If we're gonna hit the trucks, we better do it now, before the BHs get there."

Crocker nodded. "Let's go."

CT stayed behind with Major Martins and Gator. Crocker instructed them to signal with two three-shot bursts should the Bokos spot them.

Now as he climbed the heavily forested embankment with Manny and Akil, he took stock. All they had were three AKs, six full mags, two grenades, and an RPG-7 armed with a single missile. Not an impressive arsenal. That's why it was vital to maintain the element of surprise, which they were trying to do now, taking a wide arc up, then climbing up through a thicket of banana trees until they faced the sides of the trucks in the clearing below.

Akil, at his right, was doing his best to keep Crocker's mind off his barking leg, whispering, "Boss, you hear the story of the two old men, Moe and Joe, who decided to make one last visit to a brothel?"

"Nope. Not interested."

"When the madam took a look at the two drunk old geezers she turned to one of her girls and said, 'Put some inflated dolls in the first two bedrooms. These geezers are so old and drunk they won't know the difference.'"

"Quiet."

"So the old guys are walking home, right? And Moe turns to his friend and says, 'I think my girl was dead.' 'Why?' Joe asked. 'Because she never moved or made a sound all the time I was fucking her.'"

"Not funny."

"Joe says, 'Could be worse. I think mine was a witch.' 'Why's that?' Moe asks. 'Because as I was kissing her all over her body, I gave her a little bite on the butt, and she farted and flew out the window.'"

Crocker held back a laugh, and punched Akil's shoulder. "You're two cans short of a six-pack."

Now that they had reached the top, the problem was that the vehicles sat under tall trees at the far edge of the open space, so to get to them they had to cross about twenty-five meters with no cover. Circling left would take them back in the direction of their teammates, which they didn't want to do. The right side offered less in the way of cover—lower shrubs and the road, or more like a path.

Also, the rain had completely stopped. They still had the cover of night.

"What do you think?" Crocker asked turning to Mancini, trying to ignore the warnings from his leg.

"Whatever we do, we better do it quick."

The trucks were parked back-to-back under a canopy of trees with the largest separation between the truck farthest right and the one next to it. As Manny had reported earlier there appeared to be four drivers, four armed men, and a ninth man with a big belly who seemed to be running the operation. Crocker saw them now through the Steiner binos gathered near the cab of the first truck on the left.

He said, "Here's the plan. Akil, you're gonna approach down the middle in line with that big tree over there."

"Got it."

"Manny and I will attack from the right. We'll take up our positions first. We've got nothing to signal with so you'll have to time it the best you can."

"Tick, tick, Chief. No problem."

"Okay, Mr. Timex," Crocker continued to Akil.

"You then set up at the bottom center where you're not too exposed and fire the missile at the truck farthest left where all the 'Zonians are. It appears to be sitting low on its suspension, which probably means that it's loaded with ammo. Take that sucker out."

"One and done."

"Once you hit it, the rest of them are either gonna run or jump in the trucks to the right. Manny and I will attack from a forty-degree angle. Akil, cover center and left."

"I can do that."

"Everybody clear?"

"Clear as fuck."

"Let's hit it!"

Nothing ever went according to plan, and this wasn't the exception. As Crocker started descending the slick incline, he slipped, jamming his leg. A massive bolt of pain traveled up his spine to his brain, and almost knocked him out. He tumbled down and landed in a heap at the right edge of the clearing.

The sound alerted the Ambazonian guards, two of whom took cover behind the truck farthest left. Meanwhile, the other two wandered out, weapons ready, to find the source of the noise. Crocker lay semiconscious, trying to overcome the intense pain from his leg, and crawl to the shrubs to his right.

He heard someone calling over the radio clipped to the top of his combat vest. "Boss...Boss?"

Akil, seeing the armed men approach Crocker, slid down the embankment on his ass, went to his knees, aimed the RPG at the truck far left, and fired. The missile hit behind the cab, inches from the fuel tank. It exploded—*boom!*—and the battle was on.

Light-green tracers zinged back and forth across the background of dark trees, flames from the truck licked the sky, and men shouted, ran, and fired in various states of panic and confusion. Seeing how exposed Crocker was, Manny ran down the embankment, AK blazing. He raked the two Ambazonians until his gun jammed and he tossed it aside. A round hit his chest, knocked him back and caused his feet to slip out from under him.

He landed with a thud a few feet from Crocker, when a secondary explosion from the truck lifted them both off the ground. It also roused Crocker from his mental haze. He blinked at what looked, at first, to be a spectacular Fourth of July celebration.

Until a flying shard of hot metal lodged in his injured leg.

Fuck this bullshit!

He pulled it out, singeing his fingers. Now he was fully alert. Took in the burning truck, Mancini, and an Ambazonian with a submachine gun going to his knees twenty meters away.

Crocker shouldered the AK, spun left, and fired. Saw the man twist and fall, with a scream of agony, followed by a few seconds of silence and a flash of white light, and a deafening crack of thunder.

What the hell was that?

The rain picking up again was a form of answer. Crocker slithered on his belly to Mancini as warm rain pelted his back, building to an angry deluge.

"Manny. Hey, Manny!"

He lay still. Crocker found a pulse on the common carotid artery on his neck. Ripping open Manny's T-shirt, he felt an indentation on his Dragon Skin vest, and burned his hand from the still-hot bullet lodged in it. He sighed with relief.

You lucky bastard…

The big man moaned, half-conscious, his head turned to the side. "Car…Hey, Car…" Carmen was his wife's name.

Knowing that a powerful impact to the chest could throw off one's heartbeat, which could result in a stroke, he rechecked Mancini's pulse. Another percussive blast sounded, muffled through the rain.

Sixty-five beats per minute. Still ticking…

He knew he needed to aid Akil, if they had any chance of succeeding. Slapped Manny twice until he opened his eyes, sat up halfway, and grabbed his chest.

"What happened?"

Crocker slid him on his butt behind a nearby shrub. "You got hit in the chest, but your vest stopped it. Rest here until you're ready, I'm going to help Akil!"

CHAPTER TEN

"Sticks in a bundle are unbreakable."
—Bondei proverb

THANK YOU," CT whispered to the rain pounding over his head, neck, and back.

He hadn't lost his mind. He was expressing his appreciation to the rain for the cover it provided, and for masking the groans from Major Martins, who lay to his left, buried up to his neck in leaves. Gator sat with his back against a boulder, eyes half-opened. CT was the only one of the three fully awake and capable of putting up any resistance, should Boko Haram or the Ambazonians approach.

The latter weren't likely to do that now, as they seemed to be engaged in a firefight with CT's SEAL teammates. CT couldn't hear the firing, but felt the explosions and saw the light from the burning truck. He wished he had NVGs or rain goggles to enable him to see better.

What he couldn't realize was that only fifteen meters separated him, Gator, and Major Martins from the Boko Haram terrorists, who had finished searching the helo wreckage and were now moving toward them.

He shivered.

"Yo, Gator?" he whispered.

A few seconds passed before Gator answered weakly. "What's up, *ami?*"

CT pressed closer. "You and me, we're going to Mardi Gras next year."

Gator shivered back. "We meant to be sitting by the bayou, bro...Think this shit Crocker gave me is messing with my head..."

"More messed up than it was before?"

"Yo...Just saw a waitress walk up to me and ask if I wanted onions on my burger."

"Do you?"

"Spanish onions, yo...Spanish red, if they got 'em."

Crocker ran toward the farthest-right truck, cutting through the driving rain, his leg cramping and screaming at him to stop.

Coming up along the far side of it, he saw Akil crouched behind the front wheel of the truck ahead, lining up something in his AK's sights.

His radio wasn't working, so he had no choice but to hurry up beside him. Akil didn't see or hear him till he was at his shoulder. This was the second time in all their years together that Crocker could remember seeing fear cloud Akil's eyes.

"Boss...What the fuck."

The first time had been on a raid to a rebel base in Libya, three years ago.

Akil slapped the stock of his AK. "I'm down to two rounds."

"Take mine." Crocker handed him the only remaining mag in his tactical vest.

Akil pointed and whispered. "They're huddled near the second truck."

"How many?"

Akil held up five fingers, then shrugged.

Crocker had no clear idea either. He'd counted nine before they launched the attack, less the one he'd wasted in the field, less maybe one or two who had died or were injured when the first truck exploded. Five sounded right.

Trouble was, he was short on ammo, too. But then he remembered: the trucks were rumored to be carrying weapons and ammo to resupply Boko Haram.

Whispering to Akil, "Wait here. I'm going to check inside," he pointed to the truck.

In the back, Crocker felt stacks of wooden crates, but couldn't see shit. Found the penlight on his combat vest, removed the SOG knife from its sheath—seven-inch AUS-8 metal blade with a partially serrated edge and black glass-reinforced nylon handle.

Holding the lit penlight in his teeth, he pried open one of the longer boxes. RPG-7s covered in Styrofoam beads. He removed one and set it aside. It was useless without rocket/grenade rounds to attach. Next, the smaller crate: AK ammo. He stuffed curved thirty-round 7.62mmx39mm mags in his belt and vest, eight in all, until they weighed him down.

Counting the seconds in his head, he pried another box open and felt inside. *Forty… Gotta get back to Akil.*

This crate held AK ammo in polymer twenty-round mags. Did he hear firing? He ducked just as rounds ripped through the canvas cover and slammed into the metal hood.

Akil…Fuck…

Crocker called into his chest mic, "Romeo, Romeo. It's Deadwood. Over."

No response. The radio was kaput.

He gave himself another thirty seconds to locate RPG rounds. Reaching into an open barrel near the cab, up to his elbow in straw, he found some.

Sweet!

Quickly, he removed four RPG rounds and tried to clutch them under his left arm. Clumsy fuckers were about six pounds each, and three feet long. He settled for three, and grabbed the even longer RPG launcher. Swinging out of the truck and to the ground, one of the AK mags dropped into the mud. He couldn't risk using the penlight outside, so he left it. Saw Akil on his stomach near the front tire. Crocker handed him four AK mags, mouthing, "Merry Christmas."

Akil grinned and pointed to the trucks ahead. Mimed someone firing.

Crocker gestured to the trees to the right, and then toward the lead truck. Mouthed, "Nice."

The sound of explosions had pulled him like a magnet away from the wrecked helo and through the jungle to the south. Festus Ratty ran in a trot, leading a column of thirteen men, all armed with AKs. Some also had RPGs and Russian-made PKM (Pulemyot Kalashnikova Moderniizirovany) belt-fed light machine guns.

A mantra repeated in his head: "You wreck my shit. You gonna pay…"

The smell of cordite and burning rubber excited him further. He didn't care about the thick sheets of rain, or potential danger. He was so high on adrenaline that he felt invincible.

The Leopard couldn't wait to face the enemy, which he imagined would be Nigerian Army soldiers, unmotivated and weak. He wanted to see the fear in their eyes as they threw up their hands and surrendered. And hear their pleas as he gunned them down and captured their souls.

They had no idea what they were up against, what it was like to be constantly hunted, moving from hiding place to hiding place, and fighting the forces of unholiness.

He hurtled ahead, no plan of attack, no strategy. Just righteousness and anger burning through his veins.

You will see, soldier boys, who the real warriors are. Who possess the hearts of leopards...Who has Allah on their side...

Crocker dragged his injured right leg, which had cramped up completely. The pain begged him to stop, but he had no time. He circled through the thick brush, the long thorns of kiame shrubs tearing his arms and legs. He took care not to slip and fall. If it happened again, he might not be able to get up.

When he figured he was roughly parallel to the lead truck, he turned and inched forward in a painful half-crouch until he heard the *pop-pop-pop* of AKs through the drone of rain. The water didn't hide the sparks from the enemy barrels.

The Cameroonians, or Ambazonians, or whoever they were, were trigger-happy. He guesstimated four shooters. Spotting a clear, narrow path through some eight-foot trees, and holding on to the trunk of a slender one, he slowly eased down to his left knee. His right leg shook as he loaded the spear-shaped PG-7VL round into the launcher.

You'll only get one shot. He rested the metal cylinder on his shoulder, lined up the truck in the sights, took a deep breath, exhaled, and pulled the trigger. *Whoosh!*

But the weight of the rocket caused Crocker to tip the launcher slightly forward. The rocket grazed the side of a tree, took a lower trajectory, and slammed into the left side of the front bumper of the truck, and exploded. He exhaled deeply, rainwater in his eyes and mouth.

Fuck…

He couldn't move anyway. Not without considerable effort. So he loaded another PG-7VL round into the launcher as re-directed AK fire flew in his direction, tearing into the leaves and bark, and fired again. This time the rocket hit within millimeters of the gas tank and the blast created a huge column of flames like an exploding volcano that blew toward Crocker.

He lowered his head to the ground. Hot metal zinged past. Bullets now were coming from both directions—from near the trucks and behind him, north.

Fucking Boko Haram! They're coming…

No time to fire the unused round. He tucked the RPG under his left arm, turned, and limped back to Akil's position as men screamed like banshees through the rain and bush behind him. The sound grew closer.

He'd heard that in Gaelic mythology the scream of a banshee meant that someone was about to die.

Rounds were coming thick and fast by the time he reached Akil, now crouched on the other side of the truck—the one facing the clearing. The flames from the two vehicles ahead danced in his eyes.

"Good work!" Akil whispered. "Who the fuck is shooting at us now?"

"Boko Haram!"

"It's a soup sandwich, boss! Soup fucking sandwich…"

They both knew they were trapped. Then gunfire came from the other side of the clearing near where they had descended. For a second Crocker thought they were being surrounded. But the shooter wasn't directing his fire at them.

"Where's Manny?" he asked.

Akil shrugged. The shots from Boko Haram in the eastern foliage now redirected toward the shooter at the right-center of the clearing.

Crocker and Akil took this little window of opportunity. Crocker pointed left toward the road. "Let's go!"

They proceeded fifteen meters, just beyond the penumbra of the light from the truck, when his right ankle buckled and he started going down. For a second, he figured he'd never be able to get to his feet again—his right leg felt completely frozen from his foot to his upper thigh. Ready to tell Akil to leave him, the former Marine Akil dipped and came up under Crocker's right shoulder, in some graceful semi-ballet motion.

Enough weight was taken off Crocker's bad leg so he could hop.

"Thanks!"

"Semper fi…"

Crocker glanced over his shoulder as they went. Boko Haram fighters were nearing the trucks, and the Ambazonians continued to direct heavy fire to the center and north side of the clearing. They hadn't spotted him and Akil yet.

Mancini had saved their asses. Now they had to find a way to return the favor before their teammate was ripped apart.

The pair of them managed to build up to a good

pace, both sucking hard for air. Crocker dragged his right leg like it was made of wood. They made it two-thirds of the way to the south end of the clearing, into the cover of darkness and rain, when Akil stopped.

"What's a matter?"

"We're fucked," Akil said as he tried to catch his breath. "Look."

About thirty meters ahead and to the left, near the mud road, he saw a strange gold rectangle through the slanting rain. A windshield, reflecting light from the burning truck.

"What the hell is that?" Crocker was totally confused.

Until he made out the partial outlines of an armored Toyota Land Cruiser with gun turret in back.

"Can't be the QRF." Quick reaction force. "It's coming from the wrong direction."

"More Bokos," groaned Akil. "Now what do we do?"

Crocker took another glance back and saw the shadows of at least a dozen fighters swarming around the trucks. It was only a matter of seconds before they located all the SEALs—himself, Akil, Gator, CT, and Mancini, and systematically finished them off.

I screwed up.

A high, taunting voice echoed through a megaphone behind them. "How you gonna pay, soldier boys…You gonna pay the Leopard!"

A shiver ran up Crocker's spine. "We can't stay here."

He saw no one moving near the Land Cruiser ahead. Their only chance was to reach cover near it, fifteen meters away.

"Go!"

"You sure, boss?"

"Yes!"

They altered their course to the left. Pushed hard and were within five meters of the bush, when the dark silhouettes of four armed men emerged from the shadows of the trees, fingers on triggers, AR-15s aimed at them.

Crocker felt the red dot laser scope burning into his forehead. *God have mercy…*

Akil grunted low, "We're toast!" Just loud enough for the armed men to hear.

A two-second pause, then one of the guys wearing NVGs asked, "You the Yanks?"

"Yeah, yeah, we're Yanks…Who are you?"

"Brit Shell security workers. We picked up your emergency signal!"

"Thank God…"

The armed Brits lowered their weapons and waved Akil and Crocker forward. Two got on each side of Crocker, lifted him off the ground, and quickly carried him into the bush.

Mancini was using an AK he had recovered from one of the dead guards. And was grateful he had it—it was the most dependable weapon he knew, especially in shit conditions like this. The trouble was he was down to a third of a mag of ammo. And he was running back the way he had come, up the embankment, with a half dozen Boko Haram savages on his tail, whooping and hollering "Allahu Akbar!"

He paused ten meters up, his chest still aching from the stopped round earlier. As he caught his breath, he saw that the BHs had already reached his side of the clearing and were starting to climb. To add to his most serious dilemma, he had no comms and no way of knowing if any of his teammates were still alive.

Minutes earlier, he'd seen Akil and Crocker kneeling beside one of the Ambazonian trucks, but, based on the shouts of celebration he'd heard from the other side of the clearing, he feared they'd been captured or shot.

It was a strange, funky feeling, and especially ominous for this fit bear of a man, the veteran of hundreds of combat missions. This exact situation had always been his biggest fear—alone in a hostile land surrounded by the enemy. Two things he was sure of: he wouldn't stop until he'd done everything he could for his teammates, and two, he would never allow the enemy to take him alive.

Not happening…

He would spare his wife and family the horrible ordeal of his filmed torture, beheading, or other brutal treatment. He pictured them for a split second, sitting solemnly at the dining room table.

Gotta find my teammates and get back home one way or another…

Imagining his wife, Carmen's, warm, smiling face, he gritted his teeth and took a quick assessment.

Aside from the AK, he had two grenades, a SIG Sauer 226 pistol with one full twelve-round mag, and a SOG knife. No way he was going to blast his way out of this, or outrun his pursuers, who knew the terrain a hell of a lot better than he did and were climbing up the incline like goats, and probably had food and water, when all he had was a single energy bar tucked into a pouch of his combat vest.

Gotta find my teammates first…

Best thing he could do was to keep the BHs guessing, and throw them off his trail. Then find a way back to that road and try to get a ride to base. He'd walk back if he had to.

How long can I elude the enemy, when there are six on my ass now and more coming?

His best chance would be to draw them into a trap, or fool them into thinking they were pursuing a larger force.

Gotta find my teammates...Gotta find a way.

Promising himself that he would live to enjoy another plate of his wife's manicotti, Mancini surveyed the terrain as best he could in the dark. No binos, no NVGs, no comms. Scanning the shadows, he remembered a little gully about a third of the way up the embankment to his left. Nice place for a picnic in drier, less perilous times.

Gotta find a fucking way.

Panic wasn't an option. If he went down, he'd go down fighting.

Gotta find a way...

Breathing hard, he picked through bushes in a northerly direction, thorns and low branches ripping at his clothes and arms. Ignored the scratches, wiped the rain from his forehead. Proceeded low to the ground, his thighs burning until he spotted the gully ten meters below. Knelt and listened to the Bokos climb at two o'clock.

There's gotta be a way out...

A worthy opponent, he thought. The tougher the better.

He was building up a head of steam. Picking up rocks and branches from the ground, he tossed them into the gully, counted to twenty in his head, and waited. It was allegedly an old Mohawk trick he'd learned from reading James Fenimore Cooper in middle school.

He could hear one of the Bokos hooting through

the hissing rain, trying to disguise himself as an owl. Another Bokō hooted back. Mancini loosened a big rock with his foot and pushed it in the direction of the gully. It rolled and smacked a tree trunk hard, which threw it off course. Picking up momentum again, it ripped through the brush.

This time the Bokos responded with blasts of AK fire in the direction of the sound.

Go ahead…

Mancini waited until he heard them clamoring up, hooting and whistling to one another. Pressed low behind the base of a tree, he pulled an M26 fragmentation grenade off his vest, and waited. Weapons fire thudded in the distance and tore into the trees to his left.

The sound of branches shifting at one o'clock. He looked and saw six heavily armed dudes in camouflage fatigues, a variety of turbans and scarves on their heads. Two of them seemed to be silently arguing, slapping their chests and pointing in different directions. He waited until they huddled together to look into what appeared to be a primitive handheld GPS device. A little blue glow, in the dark.

Mancini pulled the pin on the M26 and counted *one-Mississippi, two-Mississippi* in his head.

On five, he rose and threw, then scurried left and higher, diving behind a tree and covering his head.

Ka-blam!!!!

The blast lifted him off his belly. He heard groans as he gathered his feet under him and, without waiting for the smoke to clear, turned and humped farther up the embankment and south.

Crocker imagined he was sitting in a chair on the little balcony of his Virginia Beach apartment. Cyndi was walking toward him with a pitcher of lemonade. Her sundress patterned pink and white. Her toned legs glistened gold from the setting sun. Her finger- and toenails were painted red.

"Babe…"

Instead of pouring the liquid into a glass, she fed it to him direct from the pitcher, so that he gulped, choked, and the liquid splashed over his chin onto his chest.

He started to laugh and pushed her away. "Stop…"

"Boss…"

He blinked and saw Akil feeding him water from a bladder, while seated on the running board of a truck. A matching dark-green Toyota Land Cruiser was parked beneath trees behind it.

He couldn't remember where he was. Blinking again, he spotted three armed men drift into his periphery. He started to reach for the SIG Sauer on his belt. Akil stopped him.

"They're friends…Mil contractors from the UK… Moxie, Brian, Rufus, and Scott. Good guys."

"What?"

"Remember? The Brits. Work for Shell Oil as security consultants."

All he could recall was that they had been in danger. "Where…"

"You that fucked up? Nothing to worry yourself about, boss. Relax."

Crocker nodded; he still wasn't sure it wasn't a dream.

The tallest of the contractors grinned and saluted. "Cheers, mate…Feeling better?"

"Cheers."

Akil fed him more water and two painkillers borrowed from the Brits, and explained, "They work security for Shell Nigeria at a natural gas plant farther south. They were not far from the Cameroon border checking another Shell plant nearby. Heard the MARS broadcast. When they heard we were Americans, they came to help…"

"Hey, thanks…"

"Anytime, mate."

Crocker looked up at Akil and asked, "Where are the rest of the guys? We gotta find 'em."

A tall Brit with red hair said, "Lead the way."

Akil warned, "One problem…We're gonna have to kick some Boko Haram ass first."

The Brit winked to one of his teammates. "Why is that a problem?"

CHAPTER ELEVEN

*"Ears that do not listen to advice, accompany
the head when it is chopped off."*
—Nigerian proverb

AS INTENSE as the sudden firing from the other side
of the clearing had been, with .50-cals and automatic
weapons, Festus Ratty Kumar was surprised that any
of his men had survived. Now, as he ran through the
bush, questions pounded in his head. Where had the
armored trucks and reinforcements come from? Had
the Ambazonians and Victor Balt betrayed him? Had
they attempted to screw him over and steal the girls?

He didn't have time to answer now, because the enemy was coming hard like rats running from a fire.
But he would. And when he did, someone would have
hell to pay.

It was time to fade into the jungle like leopards and
regroup. No shame in that. He wasn't stupid. Like a
leopard, he was sly and nocturnal. No one could ever
hit him and escape his revenge.

What did the infidels know? They had always
judged against him, and would never stop trying to
get him to judge against himself. But God's will made
him strong.

It told him that the schoolgirls he'd kidnapped, the people he'd killed in bombings, the soldiers he'd slain, none of them would ever weigh on his conscience. Guilt was a hoax. Anything that caused you to question yourself was a trick.

"Pull back," Ratty shouted in Kanuri as he and his remaining five fighters ran through the brush, the soldiers on their heels. "Pull back and live to fight another day!"

Hours ago, when they had felled the enemy helicopter, the mission had seemed like a big success. Now they were running for their lives, their lungs and muscles straining.

Ratty turned, went to his knees, and fired. Then got up and continued picking his way through the bush.

To his mind this was a minor skirmish in a very long struggle. They would fade back into the Sambisa and while the enemy was resting, thinking they were safe in their beds, he and his men would strike again. Next time they would be even more clever and terrifying, killing more infidels, and maybe kidnapping more girls.

He wouldn't stop until the bodies were piled all the way to the sun, and the oceans turned red with blood.

This was his mission. It was how he chose to live. He harbored no dreams or illusions of a comfortable life and family. Those were for weak men, who were afraid of death and refused to bow in reverence to God.

Crocker rode in the passenger seat of the lead Land Cruiser with Moxie at the wheel, Akil on the bench behind him, and another Brit, Rufus, manning the .50-cal in the turret in back. They were in pursuit of the Bokos, who zigzagged through the thick foliage to their left, stopping occasionally to drop and fire. Rufus complained that it was hard to fix a target with the continuing rainfall and darkness.

The .50-cal reverberated in Crocker's ears. Concerns swirled through his head, and though his mind and body begged to rest, he was trying to separate the trivial from the most important. First priority was to recover the wounded. Second, to gather his men.

He'd be more than happy to take out more Boko Haram insurgents if the opportunity presented itself. Punish the bastards. No QRF or medevac was coming. That was clear.

More incompetence, and lack of will…And politics, maybe…

He didn't know. The .50-cal clamored again. Shouts of anguish emerged from the bush.

"Got one!" Rufus grunted.

Crocker struggled to make sense of everything that had happened since they'd left the base. The jeep hit a pothole and lurched right.

Lack of will is a theme here, he thought, trees and shadows flying past. *You can't let religious fanatics and sociopaths hurt good people and get away with it.*

Every time he'd seen that happen, something worse followed. He'd try explaining that to Nigerian military leaders if he got the chance.

Then he remembered his daughter, Jenny, back in Virginia, and the promise he had made to her to watch her college graduation via Skype. It would be taking place tomorrow. He wanted to, of course, and was supremely proud of her accomplishment, but couldn't think about that now.

He had teammates to recover and injured men to attend to. And he only had the foggiest idea of where they were.

Akil, in the backseat, was trying to reach CT on the radio. "CT...CT, this is Romeo. Can you hear me? CT, CT, can you hear me? Respond!"

Hearing CT's name reminded him that they had come by helicopter, and Boko Haram had arrived in jeeps and trucks.

"They came in trucks..." he said out loud.

"Who, mate?" Moxie, from East London, asked. "The Bokos?"

"Yeah. Parked 'em near here, I think." He was trying to mark time traveled and bends in the road. "A clearing off this path. I'm pretty sure it's ahead."

"How far?" Moxie shouted from behind the wheel.

"Feels close. That's probably where they're headed now."

"How many?"

Trying to focus. "Vehicles? Four or five trucks and jeeps."

"Four jeeps, two trucks," Akil corrected him.

"What about you Yanks?"

"What about us?"

Akil leaned over the seat, and cut in. "We came in a Nigeria military helicopter that crashed about 150 meters to the left. Three casualties...Some wounded."

"Wounded...they make it out?" asked Moxie, taking his eyes off the road for a second to glance over his shoulder.

The vehicle hit a puddle, bounced hard, and sent up a thick stream of water and mud that doused Crocker through the open window.

Crocker held on, and tried to remember...They

had left Gator, CT, and Major Martins hiding near the clearing. They were missing someone…

Mancini! Fuck…

He turned back to Akil.

"Where's Manny? Where's Tiny?"

"Tiny stayed back in Yola."

"What about Manny?"

Akil leaned close so that his face was inches from Crocker's. "Last time I saw him, he was firing on the other side of the clearing. Covering our asses… The terrorists were chasing him…"

Big emotions gathered in Crocker's chest. "We gotta turn back! Our teammate is back there!"

"Now, mate?"

"Yeah, now. Turn around!"

Chichima had remained so still that her body was practically frozen. She'd listened from under the truck as a battle waged in the distance, as things exploded and men shouted, and her friends moaned and wept around her. Now she wanted to yield to the mud, and let the earth take her away to another place. But a part of her resisted and vibrated with a kind of incandescence and buoyancy that filled her entire being.

God, why won't you receive me?

The resistance was like an energy deep inside her telling her to remain alert and listen, and if she did, she would heal and evolve. It spoke in a woman's voice like her mother's.

Heal and evolve to what? I'm practically dead… I have nothing left…

Her mother had told her about the female energy that was part of Odinani, the source of all things.

She imagined Odinani speaking to her now, telling her to remain calm. The future would be what Chichima determined it to be. Whether she chose to live in the body her spirit occupied now was unimportant. In this life she had called to herself the experiences that she needed to learn and evolve.

"Let go, child. Relax…"

These were ideas expressed by her mother that she had judged as primitive and had rejected. They clashed with the concept of a redeemer God she had embraced as part of Christianity.

Chichima heard the voice again, gentle and reassuring.

"Let go, child…Let go of all thoughts and fears…"

It was easier to do now that she had been stripped of everything—pride, vanity, chastity, and even a sense of identity.

So she surrendered, and instead of sinking into hopelessness she experienced the buoyancy of something else. A fighting, almost defiant, force that burned deeper than her personality and education.

It told her that the father spirits had pushed her into the mud, and now it was up to her to fight her way out, resuscitate the female spirit, and restore a balance that could only be reached in the heart.

She listened as the Boko Haram fighters returned to the clearing. Their agitated voices, and their boots plied the ground. She heard them whisper to one another as they formed some kind of plan. Then she saw one fighter with a long, black beard poke his head under the front truck, heard him cock his weapon, and she intuited what would come next.

A voice in her head commanded simply, *Run!*

She propelled herself on her belly toward the rear

of the truck, whispering to her friends along the way. "Follow me, now! Come!"

Some followed, others didn't. The guns went off like little explosions. She squirmed under the drive shaft, poked her head out the back, gathered her feet under her, and started hurrying toward the trees. The mud made it impossible to run. She kept pushing. A bullet tore into the flesh of her shoulder, feeling like a dozen hornet stings at once.

She continued pushing, clawing at the mud with her hand, and reached the trees. Then she tumbled over a fallen stump and hit her head. When she looked up she saw girls gathered around her.

She distinguished Navina's voice like a prayer. "Chichima, I'm with you."

"Navina, I'll always be with you, too…"

Hands helped her up onto her knees. The girls huddled together like one quivering mass.

All their voices whispered at once: "Are they coming? Have they stopped? Why did they bring us here? Will they make sure we're all dead?"

Navina said, "You're bleeding. I'll tie my scarf around it to stop the blood. I hate this scarf anyway."

She smiled inside.

"Chichima…"

"Chichima, is it bad?"

"Shh!" she said. "They will hear us."

Minutes of silence passed and the only sound was their breathing and the beating of their hearts. Then she heard a truck engine start, tires slipping in the mud and gaining traction, and the truck and the other vehicles departing. Then silence. A long silence like a sigh. The rustling of leaves. The plaintive call of a dove.

Beside her, Navina whispered, "Did they leave? Did they abandon us in the jungle? I don't trust my ears anymore...Is that what you heard?"

"Quiet...It will be okay..."

Silence returned. The rain and shooting had stopped. The clearing ahead started to lighten. The sun was rising and its light obliterated the darkness like it always did.

Relief filled Chichima's chest. "Wait here..."

Ignoring the pain from her shoulder, she inched forward toward the clearing, hid behind a bush, and looked. The trucks were gone. So were the men. She counted to twenty before she poked her head out and saw tire tracks leading back to the road, and the bodies of half a dozen girls. No men.

Chichima covered her mouth and stepped back behind the bush, pausing for a moment as her mind bounced back and forth between the polarities of relief and horror. Then turning, she called to the other girls. "Come...The men are gone! The men have left! Come see..."

Navina was the only one with the courage to join her. She lowered her eyes when she spotted the bodies of their friends.

"Why?" she whispered.

Chichima hugged her, and Navina spoke the same sentiment Chichima was experiencing, but couldn't put into words. "Is it over? Is it really over, Chichima? Will it ever be over?"

"One day...Yes."

They found Mancini near the wreckage of the Ambazonian trucks, covered with scratches and bruises, mumbling to himself. "There was a road...I can't

seem to find it…I turned the corner and got lost…"
He was still hugging the AK to his chest.

Crocker pulled it away. "Easy, big guy…It's
Crocker. You can chill now. We got your back."

Manny seemed to be in a mild state of shock, turning this way and that, a confused look in his eyes.
"Cherry Lane…Cherry Lane…was here…I saw
it…Now it's gone. How'd that happen?"

Crocker put his arm around his shoulder. Cherry
Lane was the street in Dam Creek where he lived. "It's
okay, Manny. We'll get you home."

"You will?"

"I promise."

"Tonight?"

"Not tonight, but soon."

The scene around them was grim. Smoldering car-
casses of trucks. The bodies of twelve men, some
burned, some so torn apart that it was hard to recognize them as human.

Manny, seated on the running board of one of the
Land Cruisers, claimed to have killed six on the embankment, and another three or four as they escaped
into the bush.

"You did good, Manny. You saved our asses,"
Crocker said as he helped him up and into the backseat of the truck.

"I…I gotta call Carmen," Manny whispered, "let
her know I won't be home for dinner. You see my cell?"

"No, but it won't work here anyway, big man. No
service."

"AT&T sucks…"

"Sure does…Watch your head."

Akil cleared a place for him and handed him an
MRE and bottle of water. "Drink up, bad ass…"

Manny gulped it down and asked for another. He seemed to be suffering from dehydration.

"Bloody mangle…" Moxie commented as he walked beside Crocker, surveying the damage around the trucks. All that was left of the first three were chassis, melted rims, and empty metal boxes. It appeared as though the BHs had dragged away some of the ammo. Most of them hadn't gotten very far into the bush thanks to the .50-cals on the Land Cruisers.

Bodies, discarded rifles, machine guns, and belts of AK rounds lay scattered in a long oval.

"They Bokos?" Moxie asked, nodding toward the bodies.

"Some Bokos, some Ambazonians…" muttered Crocker.

"Strange bedfellows…"

"Some remaining AK ammo in the last truck," redhaired Rufus reported.

"Probably best to light it up."

"Let's wait on that until we find our men…" Crocker remembered CT, Gator, and Major Martins waiting on the west side of the clearing.

Just twenty seconds later, the second Land Cruiser radioed that they'd located them. Gator was alive but in bad shape, and Major Martins hadn't made it.

"I'm real sorry to hear that."

"Ironic that his own military never bothered to help him," groaned Akil.

"How bad is Gator?" Crocker asked through the radio.

"He's in a lot of pain."

"You try reaching the TOC in Yola?"

"They're not responding."

"Fucking cowards…"

CHAPTER TWELVE

*"He who fears the sun will not become
chief."*
—Ugandan proverb

S'MORES ANYONE?" Akil asked as new flames rose from the wreckage behind them.

It wasn't a joyous time, but Crocker couldn't help but crack up. It was a way of relieving tension, and soon laughter reverberated throughout Land Cruiser One as it proceeded west on the dirt road—now deep puddles and mud. Then the fireworks started outside, rockets igniting, rounds exploding.

"East African version of a ten-gun salute," Akil commented.

"Not funny," Crocker said as he reloaded his long gun and pistol. "Major Martins had a wife and family. Stay alert."

He imagined how they would react to the news, and wondered whether the Nigerian government would take care of them.

Moxie and Scott—the drivers of the two Toyota Land Cruisers—arranged to rendezvous at a bend in the road up ahead. And Scott, in Two, reported that it looked like the Bokos had fled.

"Can you confirm that?" asked Crocker.

"From the little promontory we're on now, it looks like two jeeps, two trucks speeding northwest... Maybe fifty meters ahead...Should we make pursuit?"

"That's a negative...Gotta get the wounded back to base." Gator, in truck two, needed a hospital.

"Copy..."

Before they left the area, Crocker, in truck one, wanted to inspect the clearing where the Boko Haram vehicles had staged. See if they'd left clues to the location of their hideout or future plans—maybe a laptop, notebook, phones, etc.

"You sure we have time for this?" Moxie asked as the Land Cruisers continued and the sound of the exploding ordnance faded behind them.

Crocker held up five fingers. "Five minutes." Adrenaline coursing through his system again, he told Moxie and the others, "Keep an eye out for stragglers...or surprises."

Scanned the rain forest through the bulletproof glass for moving shadows, the flash of a muzzle. Before they reached the rendezvous location, Moxie spotted the top of a vehicle in a clearing to the left and applied the brakes.

"Ten o'clock!"

It looked like a tan SML Isuzu transport truck with *Pepsi* stenciled across the hood. "What the bloody hell is this? Soda delivery out in the sticks?"

"Stolen, most likely," replied Crocker.

"How come Cruiser Two didn't report this?"

"Scott is daft. Might have seen it and didn't think it was important. Probably in a hurry to get home and Skype some chick."

"Wait here, and cover," Crocker said, stepping out. Akil followed.

They approached carefully, weapons ready, and stopped at the entrance to the clearing. Signaled back to Rufus in the turret. Continued through thick mud sucking at the soles of their boots, scanning left and right, up and down.

Akil pointed to something ahead—the body of a woman facedown in the mud.

Crocker's heart sunk. Steps closer, he leaned in, and saw that she'd been shot multiple times in the back. Took her pulse. Nothing. Followed the same procedure with five other female bodies near the truck. All dead.

Fucking savages…

It reminded him of photos of Jonestown after Reverend Jim Jones and his followers drank poisoned Kool-Aid. Add this to the list of things he'd seen but hoped to forget.

Akil shook his head. "What a waste…"

"Disgusting…" Groaned through gritted teeth.

Crocker assumed these bodies were the remaining kidnapped schoolgirls that Boko Haram was going to use to trade for the arms and weapons. Were there more in the nearby bush? He remembered seeing about a dozen women from the air.

They did nothing to deserve this.

It pissed him off that the Nigerian authorities hadn't done more, or responded quicker. Crocker had a daughter, too. He saw a pink plastic sandal stuck in the mud, watched Akil poke his head in the cab of the truck and come out holding a key and a walkie-talkie.

Akil held the radio up to Crocker. "Look…"

Crocker waved his hand up and down to indicate

quiet, without knowing why specifically. Either from concern about Boko stragglers hiding in the trees, or out of respect for the dead. It was time to move on.

As he turned back to the Land Cruiser, he had an eerie feeling he was being watched. Sniffed the air and surveyed the foliage at eleven o'clock. Gestured back to Rufus at the .50-cal to cover and saw him swing the big gun around.

Froze for twenty seconds and heard nothing. Soon as he took a step, he saw something move in his periphery. Went to one knee and held up a fist to indicate to Akil to stop.

Shadows shifted and a shape slowly emerged from the foliage. The mud-covered form looked like an apparition. When it reached the sunlight, he recognized it was a woman, half bent over, wearing a dark robe.

"Careful," Akil whispered, "she might be wearing an explosive vest."

Crocker sensed she wasn't a threat. Held up a hand to signal her to halt. "Stop right there."

The young woman obeyed, and replied in English, "I don't have a bomb. I don't have a weapon. I'm a Nigerian student. I was kidnapped by Boko Haram twenty-two months ago. Who are you?"

"We're Americans. American soldiers. We've come to rescue you. To take you back to your family," Crocker said. "Are you alone?"

She looked confused. "Americans?"

"Yes. What's your name?"

"Chichima Okore."

He saw a dark spot on the burqa near her shoulder. It could be blood. "Are you injured? Are there any other girls still alive?"

She stammered, "I was shot…" She pointed to her

shoulder. "There are five other girls behind me. The others are dead…"

"It's over now, Chichima," Crocker said gently. "Tell your friends to come out slowly with their hands over their heads."

They had left the deep foliage and were on a two-lane dirt road traveling over an undulating savanna. Cattle and ostriches grazed in the distance. The sun burned through the morning haze.

As Crocker bandaged Chichima's shoulder, a smaller girl beside them on the backseat hummed to herself, a sad melody that she repeated over the growl of the engine. Her voice reminded him of Emmylou Harris, who he'd heard perform at a roots festival in Charlottesville several years ago. The same haunting quality, and a far cry from the hard rock he'd listened to as a teenager or the fifties jazz he had loaded on his iPhone now.

They were packed in truck one with Moxie at the wheel, Akil beside him, and Rufus and CT in back. The other four girls rode in truck two with Gator, Manny, and Major Martins's body, which lay under a Kevlar blanket.

Crocker regretted they didn't have time to recover the ashes of the pilot, copilot, or Lieutenant Peppie from the incinerated helicopter. They had families and loved ones, too.

The bullet that passed through Chichima's shoulder had avoided major bones and arteries. He was applying a triangle bandage when Scott's voice came over the radio from truck two.

Crocker couldn't hear him over the roar of the engine.

Akil turned back to him. "Boss?"

"Yeah…"

"You finished with her? Because you're needed in the other truck."

"Why?"

"Gator isn't doing well."

Crocker was the team corpsman or medic. They stopped and he changed places with Mancini in truck two. The mood in the second truck was grimmer. Gator lay slumped on the middle bench next to a Brit named Brian, who had received trauma medical training while in the Royal Marines, and was checking Gator's blood pressure with a cuff.

Crocker slid in the other side. "What is it?"

"Low, mate…and falling…Ninety over sixty-five… He's been slipping in and out of consciousness the last several minutes."

"Let me see…"

The obvious injuries were his broken right arm and leg that were complex and would require surgery.

Crocker asked, "What'd you give him for the pain?"

"Extra strength ibuprofen. That's all we've got…"

Gator was having trouble breathing and his skin was clammy, so Crocker used four fingers on his right hand to check if his airway was clear. It was. Then he quickly searched for signs of trauma to his neck and chest. Negative.

Felt his way down to Gator's abdomen, which was severely swollen—a sign of internal bleeding, along with the lowered blood pressure and shortened breath.

Crocker whispered his prognosis to Brian, who nodded back.

All they could do for him now was feed him fluids, monitor his blood pressure, and hope the bleeding stopped on its own.

"How far to the closest ER?" Crocker asked.

"Rufus is checking now," Scott, at the wheel, answered. Then a minute later: "Yola is about forty minutes away."

"That's the closest hospital?"

"Affirmative."

"Any chance Yola can send a rescue helicopter now that we're out of danger?"

"I'll check again."

One of the girls in the backseat saw them attending to Gator and started to recite the Lord's Prayer.

This moved Crocker, who continued monitoring Gator; cleaned his face and neck. Wiped away a tear from his cheek.

Sometimes people did the most amazing things, even if they seemed little.

The girl was nearly killed, is still in shock, and yet she prays for one of us?

His mind was operating on two channels at once. "Any luck?" Crocker asked, leaning over the seat ahead.

"Yola's still not responding," Akil answered.

Crocker knew he'd be extremely pissed off if Gator succumbed to his injuries. In fact, the way he felt now, he wasn't sure if he could handle it. The death of a teammate was one of the hardest things he'd ever had to endure—right up there with losing his elderly mother in a fire.

He blinked away the image of the coroner's wagon and her charred remains. Still suffered guilt over that.

"Useless guilt, son," his mother had told him in a dream.

As they drove and he continued monitoring Gator's blood pressure and temperature, Crocker started to blame himself for not being better prepared, for allowing the Nigerians to lead the mission... Then he stopped himself.

What fucking good will that do now?

Maybe what his mother had said about guilt being useless was right.

Chichima sat by the open window and let the warm air caress her face. The Americans and Brits seemed friendly, and the movement felt liberating. But she wasn't ready to declare victory yet.

Like she had done every several minutes since they had left the bush, she looked back to see if trucks filled with Boko Haram were following them. Again the road behind was empty. They passed carts loaded with yams and people on bicycles. Signs of normal life.

This new reality was hard to accept. It was almost shocking when the men in the truck smiled at her, helped clean her face and arms, and gave her a bar of chocolate and water. Seeing that her water bottle was empty, the bearded man in the seat in front of her took it, filled it from a bladder on his lap, and handed it back.

He didn't look that different from some of the lighter-skinned Boko Haram rebels. Only larger all over.

Akil saw the suspicion in her eyes. "You don't like me?"

She smiled back at him, and as she did realized that she hadn't smiled in months.

"I'm very nice. I promise. You need anything, just ask."

She wasn't used to kindness, either, and took a few seconds to answer, "I'm fine. Thank you for everything."

"My pleasure. We'll get you back to your family soon."

It was hard to believe. She didn't know how to prepare for that.

So she looked out the side window where even the foliage seemed welcoming. They moved faster now, passing stalls and huts, and children in colorful shirts and sandals walking to school with their parents. Some things hadn't changed.

The sight of young schoolchildren holding hands and looking happy brought tears to her eyes. And it wasn't just her friends who had died in the clearing she was crying for. She wept in part because she remembered that it hadn't been so long since she'd been a carefree child herself. She felt like an old woman now, and wondered if she could ever go back to school to finish her studies, be accepted, and have a normal life.

Then Chichima remembered she was only eighteen years old.

CHAPTER THIRTEEN

"Peace is costly but it is worth the expense."
—African proverb

CROCKER HEARD a rustling sound, turned abruptly, saw muzzle flashes coming from the darkness ahead, and bolted awake. Sweat coating his neck and chest, he reached for his weapon, but couldn't find one. He tried to shout a warning to his teammates hiding in the bush behind him, but no sound came out.

Something hissed and he sat up in the dark. Seeing the silhouette of an unplugged medical monitor in the corner and a ribbon of light under a door, he realized he was in a hospital room. Shadows crisscrossed the linoleum floor, light peeked through the curtains.

How did I get here? Where the hell am I?

He wasn't in Virginia, judging from the lizards crawling up the lavender walls, and the wood carving of a giraffe hanging near the window.

Wherever he was, he needed to get up and locate his men. Lifted the sheet and saw he was wearing nothing under the light-blue hospital gown.

Where the fuck are my clothes?

As soon as he shifted his weight and tightness

gripped his leg, he remembered. The long night and morning; the helicopter crash, fighting, and the schoolgirls; how, when they had arrived in Yola, he had insisted on assisting the surgery on Gator, which had offended the Nigerian doctors. All kinds of alarms went off in his head.

Where is Gator now?

He remembered how close Gator had come to dying. And how his pulse and blood pressure had slowly stabilized after an emergency blood transfusion. And the relief he had felt when that finally happened.

Last thing he remembered was staggering down a long hallway to the front door, stopping to ask a nurse what day it was, and thinking that he needed to call his daughter because it was the day of her graduation.

What's today's date? The fifteenth? The twenty-first?

He didn't know what happened after that, or how he ended up in the hospital bed. Now he had to find his clothes, and check on Gator, and make sure Manny and CT were okay, too.

Concerns rushed back. There were reports to file with headquarters and things to settle with the Nigerians. Major Wally Martins was dead!

Oh, fuck…

He'd Skype Jenny later.

What would he say to Martins's wife and children? Was it even proper protocol for him, as an American advisor, to reach out to them?

Screw that…

Then he flashed back to the concentration on the doctor's face as he stitched the gash in his leg, and the doctor informing him that they had attended to the wound just in time, as it was starting to get infected.

He'd forgotten about his leg, and remembered thinking they could have sawed it off as long as his men were okay. Now he took a mental roll call in his head.

Akil, check…Manny, check…CT…Tiny?

As he slipped back into unconsciousness, he pictured Jenny's angelic face. She was a young woman now with a job and boyfriend. But she still had a special smile for Crocker.

Wives and girlfriends came and went, but she was all he had.

Dr. B, as he called himself, was a handsome man in his fifties with a smooth, high forehead, and remarkable amber-colored eyes. He looked like a movie star in his white medical coat, and sounded like one, too. A deep, resonant voice like a big cat.

Crocker had come to his office to apologize for his behavior the night before, but Dr. B was having none of it. "I'm sorry, Mr. Crocker," the doctor said, "but I can't accept your apology."

A large wood carving of a gazelle stared at him from the corner. A ceiling fan stirred the humid air. Crocker took a beat to register what the doctor had just said.

"I'm embarrassed, Doc. Was I as rude as they say I was?"

Between sips of coffee, Dr. B explained. "This morning it was quite obvious that you were under considerable mental and physical stress. What was remarkable to us members of the medical staff was your very deep concern for your colleagues."

Crocker breathed a sigh of relief. "If I insisted on being there for my teammate's surgery, I hope you understand." He sipped from a cup of sweet coffee.

Dr. B said, "You might think a liberal African nationalist like myself would be negatively predisposed to an agent of a colonialist power. But in my particular case you would be incorrect."

Crocker sat up, expecting to have to verbally defend himself.

But no verbal attack came. Instead Dr. B showed him a photo of his Chicago-born wife and their two good-looking children, then explained that he had met his wife while attending St. George's University medical school on the Caribbean island of Grenada. They were there in 1983 when hard-line communists took over the government and threatened to take the medical students—including the doctor, his future wife, and several dozen Americans—hostage.

US President Ronald Reagan launched Operation Urgent Fury to rescue the students, prevent a communist Cuban-backed takeover of the government, and restore democracy.

Crocker was in grade school then, but he knew that had been the first SEAL combat mission since Vietnam. Four members of SEAL Team Six had died during the initial assault on the island when they got tangled up in their parachutes and drowned.

Dr. B remembered the relief he had felt when he saw the US soldiers.

"They were so young," he said. "And very brave."

"It's a small world," said Crocker, silently saluting the men who had perished.

"This morning I finally got a chance to return a favor," Dr. B responded. "One good deed deserves another, as you might say."

Now Dr. B reported on the condition of Crocker's men. Mancini and CT were receiving fluids and would be released later in the day. Gator had already been medevaced to a US carrier off the African coast and would then be flown to Ramstein Air Base, Germany.

This was the first Crocker had heard about this. "How bad is he?"

"Don't worry…Severe, but not critical."

"What are the chances he fully recovers?"

"Ninety-eight percent," the doctor responded, and then seemed to be checking something with himself. "Physically…that is."

That was good enough for now. "What about the other member of my team…Akil?" asked Crocker.

"Akil?"

"Big Egyptian-born guy. Considers himself a lady-killer."

"Oh, yes…He's fine. Charming chap. Entertained the nurses with jokes and stories. Chose to sleep at the base."

"Good." He was happy to receive any piece of favorable news. Hoped there was more.

"The schoolgirls we recovered…you saw them, too, correct?" he asked, wanting to make sure he hadn't imagined it.

"Me, personally, no, I didn't treat them. But the staff did…" He consulted some papers in a folder on his desk. "One rather minor bullet wound sewn up, some symptoms of malnutrition, one case of dysentery, other minor female problems. Physically, they should recover quickly. Psychologically is another matter."

Festus Ratty Kumar and his men had returned to their hideout in the Sambisa to heal and rest. He was already out and about in the mid-afternoon, visiting

with surviving fighters and handing out thick stacks
of hundred-naira bills featuring a portrait of Chief
Obafemi Awolowo on the front and the slogan, "One
Nigeria, One Promise." Due to rampant inflation, one
hundred naira was roughly equivalent to twenty-eight
cents US.

Festus laughed as he gifted the money. Not only
had it been stolen from a bank in Mayo Bani, but
also Chief Awolowo was credited with helping secure Nigeria's independence from Great Britain in
1960. However, to Festus's mind, Nigeria wasn't
really a country, and many of its people still weren't
free.

Chief Obafemi Awolowo had admitted this himself, stating, "Nigeria is not a nation. It is a mere geo-
graphical expression."

Idiot and double-talker, Festus thought.

If he had been chastened by the beating last night,
it didn't show.

As energetic as ever, he addressed his men standing
in line for a breakfast of akara (deep-fried black-eyed
peas with spices), green tea, and bread. "We lose one
battle, we win three others."

They all responded, *"Jes, aur leped. Jes!"*

Festus Ratty was seated on the stump of a tree sipping water with lemon juice and making plans, when
his chief aide, Modu, walked over to him carrying a
satellite phone. On the other end was Victor Balt, the
Russian-born, Emirates-based arms dealer who had
provided the weapons that had been destroyed last
night near the Cameroon border.

Balt wasn't someone Festus Ratty took lightly. Not
only was the arms dealer an important supplier of
weapons, he also had many very powerful and

dangerous friends throughout West Africa, Europe, and the Middle East.

Now Balt demanded the $150,000 he was owed for the ammo and weapons that had been lost and destroyed. Ratty had already paid him $150,000 up front. In addition to the second payment, the Russian also wanted another $120,000 in recompense for the four trucks he had borrowed from the Ambazonians.

"To hell with the Ambazonians," Festus Ratty replied. "They betrayed me."

"No, they didn't betray you," Balt explained. "They were attacked by the same forces that attacked you."

Ratty had never met Victor Balt face-to-face, and didn't know where he was calling from. But he knew his reputation as someone not to be double-crossed. Now Ratty explained again that he had planned to pay him with twelve beautiful young Nigerian girls who they had previously negotiated as worth at least $15,000 each.

"Yes, I remember," Balt said in heavily accented English, "but where are the girls now?"

"Gone," Festus Ratty exclaimed, "due to unforeseen circumstances. But don't worry. I can get more anytime I want."

"I admire your confidence," remarked Balt. "But you still owe me $270,000."

"Not a problem. I also want a new shipment of rockets, guns, and ammunition. Same as before. Same price."

"That can be arranged," Balt responded. "When?"

"As soon as possible. Tell me where you want to meet."

Balt suggested that this time the arms be dropped from a C-130 to a secure location in the Sambisa Forest. Festus Ratty had a perfect spot. He suggested the drop occur at dawn before any Nigerian Air Force drones were deployed.

"I can arrange that."

"The Nigerian Air Force never send the drones out before ten o'clock," said Festus. "The men who fly them like to sleep late."

Balt laughed. They negotiated a deal whereby Kumar would send his couriers to the Cameroon town of Kontcha with $350,000 in stolen US dollars and gold to be stored in Balt's safe-deposit box in the Afriland First Bank. This would serve as compensation for the lost trucks, the final payment for the arms that had been shipped and destroyed, and an advance on the future shipment. Following the drop in the forest, Ratty also promised to send an additional ten girls to another location inside Cameroon.

"Do we have a deal?" Festus Ratty asked.

"Yes, but there's one condition. First, you have to punish the men who staged the attack."

"You want me to blow up a Nigerian military outpost? I'll do it right away."

"No. The attackers weren't Nigerians," Balt cautioned. "I'm hearing that they were either Americans or British."

"British?" Festus Ratty knew the stories about the almost fifty years of British colonial rule: how the British had imposed Western education and Christianity on the Nigerian people, had profited from the cultivation of cacao, and peanuts, and had even pumped Nigerian oil out of the ground to run their buses and cars. "Who told you this?"

"I have it on good authority," Victor Balt answered. "Before we do any more business, I want you to punish them."

*　　*　　*

Crocker was trying to stay calm. It had already been a challenging day and it was only two-thirds over. He'd spent the last two hours trying to get Tiny Chavez released from a Nigerian military police prison cell.

In all the confusion and exhaustion, Crocker had forgotten that they had left Tiny behind in Yola. Only this morning had he learned that after Crocker and team had left last night, Tiny had been detained and arrested for recruiting a small group of Nigerian soldiers and commandeering a Nigeria helicopter against the orders of AFSF 72 commander Colonel Nwosu in Abuja and the officers in charge of the TOC in Yola.

It had been Tiny's intention to rescue the wounded men near the Cameroon border and aid his teammates—understandable and admirable to Crocker's mind, but a decision that had grated against the political and cultural sensitivities of the Nigerians.

Needless to say, Nigerian military officers were severely pissed off. Today it had taken several calls to the Nigerian military command in Abuja, and apologies by Crocker to Colonel Nwosu, to secure Tiny's release.

Now he was on the phone with his own commander, Captain Sutter, at DEVGRU headquarters in Virginia, who also sounded annoyed.

Holding the phone in one hand and a bottle of mineral water in the other, Crocker explained: "No, sir, the mission wasn't planned. It was a spur-of-the-moment decision to accompany the Nigerians, and one for which I take full responsibility."

"Then you've got a shitload of explaining to do, Crocker."

He wanted to say, "I don't feel like explaining anything now," but decided against it.

Instead, he asked, "Can I call you back later, sir?"

"No, you cannot!"

He was about to explain that he was missing his daughter's graduation, which he had planned to follow via Skype, but Sutter cut him off.

"Washington is demanding answers now!"

Crocker took a deep breath. His relationship with Captain Sutter—who he had considered a tough but sympathetic commander and a Kentucky gentleman—had been severely strained by the mission to Syria four months ago. Since then they had maintained a respectful standoff, avoiding each other except when absolutely necessary.

Crocker still couldn't forgive Sutter for not supporting him and his men at a critical time during the mission to Syria, and for even betraying them by approving the drone strikes that had nearly killed them, and had resulted in the death of his friend Séverine.

He exhaled deeply. "Sir, what do you want to know?"

"You can start by telling me who authorized this godforsaken mission, and why I wasn't informed?"

Frustration with himself and anger over what had happened in Syria rushed back, and Crocker imagined grabbing the captain by the neck and lifting him off his feet.

With great restraint, he answered. "Sir, all I can report with certainty are the sequence of events. They went like this...At around 2200 hours last night, the fourteenth, 72 AFSF received intel from a local source about Boko Haram forces moving toward the—"

Sutter cut him off. "The Nigerians?"

"The Nigerians, yes. They're the ones who received the intel. It came from a source of theirs."

"Who specifically are you dealing with there?"

Crocker took another deep breath. He preferred not to do this now, not when the feelings were so raw, not when his daughter Jenny's boyfriend was expecting his Skype call, but tried to tell himself why it was necessary from ST-6 HQ's perspective.

"Okay...The officer in charge here is a man named Major Wally Martins."

"I've heard he has a good reputation..."

Crocker ducked that comment, reporting instead, "One of the major's junior officers received intel from a source about a column of Boko Haram fighters moving toward the Cameroon border for a possible weapons exchange. Because of potential problems an influx of arms into terrorist hands could cause, a decision was made by Major Martins to see what Boko Haram was up to. He invited us to tag along in an advisory capacity."

"He invited you?"

"Yes."

"As advisors?" Sutter asked.

"That's correct."

"Jesus Christ, Crocker. I wasn't born yesterday."

He took a swig of water and waited for his anger to fade.

"Sir, our brief was to train 72 AFSF to function as a quick-reaction antiterrorist force. This was the first opportunity to test our training in a possible live-action situation."

"Your training, or theirs?" Captain Sutter asked, sarcastically. "This was supposed to be a soft mission, not a goddamn smashup with downed helicopters and multiple casualties."

"Believe me, captain, none of that was intended. The Nigerians invited us along and we went. It's as straightforward as that. If you want to criticize me for not being better prepared, or for expecting a more robust response from the Nigerians here at Yola after we were attacked, go ahead."

"First I want to know why your chain of command, which includes me, wasn't briefed prior to the mission."

Crocker took a swig of water and a deep breath. "There was no time, sir. And since we were acting within the precepts of our mission, I didn't think it was necessary."

"Which one is it?"

"Like I said before, we complied with our ROEs. We didn't go expecting to engage in combat, nor did we expect the level of resistance we encountered, or the terrible weather, or the bad piloting, or the second helicopter deciding to turn tail and run."

"I get that, Crocker, but—"

Crocker's emotions continued rising. "We basically got caught in a major shit storm, captain. And I can assure you it wasn't fun. In fact, if it hadn't been for a group of British military contractors who showed up unexpectedly, we'd probably all be dead now, or be held by Boko Haram. But, thank God, we caught some luck and in the process were able to rescue the schoolgirls, which was a real big plus, in my opinion."

"A real big plus in a lot of ways," Sutter replied. "Because those schoolgirls are likely gonna save your ass as far as Washington is concerned."

"Sir..." He was about to add, "I could give a shit about that," but stopped himself.

"I note for the record that this is the second time this year this has happened."

Crocker gritted his teeth to hold back a scream.

Captain Sutter was referring to the recent Syrian op, which had similar circumstances when Black Cell's rescue of an American nurse held hostage by ISIS had helped them avoid charges of disobeying orders.

He said, "You really want to rub salt into that wound again, sir?"

"That's not my intention... All I can say is that you better hope this Major Martins backs up your story, because otherwise you're likely to find yourself neck-deep in horseshit."

Crocker waited a beat before he said, "Major Martins died in the encounter."

"He's dead?"

"Yes. Died when the helo went down."

A long pause followed. "You're a lucky man, Crocker."

"Better lucky than good, right, Captain?"

CHAPTER FOURTEEN

*"If you close your eyes to facts you will
learn through accidents."*
—African proverb

CHICHIMA DREAMT that she was back sitting on the ground in the Sambisa Forest listening to the strange little imam in the purple prayer hat. He spoke into a microphone, which he held in his right hand, which was missing two fingers and looked like a hoof.

"Obedience to Allah is a form of worship."

The three rows of girls around her, all wearing matching dark-green hijabs, repeated his words in unison.

The heat felt extremely oppressive. The trancelike lifelessness of the girls made her feel alone.

The imam's strange speech, long hair, and shrunken body and face reminded her of Dre Head from Harry Potter. Wanting badly to escape, she wished she had the powers of an Animagus—a witch or wizard capable of changing into animal form—like Sirius Black, and could transform into a large black dog and trot off into the forest.

In a high, whining voice the imam explained the process of *ghusl*, or washing the body with water—

obligatory for women after menstruation and recommended before performing Friday prayers. Each word felt like a little drop of poison.

He said: "You always wash the right hand and wrist first, making sure to rub between the fingers. You wash it three times before repeating the same process on the left hand. Then you cleanse all impurities off the private parts with clean water. Then you wash the right hand and left hand each three times again."

The girls sat frozen. None of them protested. Not a groan, a whisper, a glance, or a raised eyebrow. Their indifference made Chichima feel more frustrated and alone.

"Next you form a cup with your right hand, fill it with water, swirl it inside your mouth, and then spit it out. Again, using your right hand, you fill it with more fresh water and inhale it into your nose. Then, covering your left nostril with your left hand, you blow any remaining water out of your right nostril. You do both procedures three times."

She couldn't tell if the extreme heat she was feeling was coming from the sun or inside herself. The girl to her right started to tremble. Waves of heat came off her body, and then very slowly her head started to melt, dripping onto her shoulders and over the front of her chest.

Chichima opened her mouth to alert the imam, but no words came out.

He continued: "Next you wash your face from hairline to chin three times. Then you pour fresh water over your head three times and rub the roots of the hair with your wet fingers. Next, you pour water liberally over the entire body, starting with the right side and moving left."

The head of the girl in front of her started melting, too. She tried to stand, but her legs were frozen. She raised her hand instead.

The imam closed his eyes and spoke so quickly that his words ran together. "Finally, you move away from the area where you performed your *ghusl* and wash your feet three times up to your ankles, starting with your right foot, making sure that no parts of the feet are dry."

Heat ran up and down Chichima's arm. Her fingers lost all feeling, and she woke in a panic, bathed in sweat. Shook her right hand to restore the feeling, which slowly returned.

And sat up, realizing she was in her bed back home.

Crocker's Suunto Traverse Alpha watch read 2212 as he trudged from the gym to the barracks, covered with sweat, his arms heavy and limp by his side, scolding himself for being a bad father, son, and husband.

Why do I always let down the people I love? My mother, my wives, now my daughter... What is wrong with me?

Imagining what he was going to say to Jenny when he called her and explained why he had failed to Skype her graduation, he looked up and saw three Nigerian soldiers hurrying toward him, MP5s slung over their shoulders, and stiffened for a second.

Now what?

"Mister Crocker?" one of the soldiers shouted.

He stopped. "Yeah. That's me. What's up?"

One of them shone a flashlight in his eyes.

"You are Chief Crocker?"

He shielded them with his hand. "Who wants to know?"

He thought that the next thing they were going to try to do was arrest him, or take him somewhere to face more annoying questions. His mind was already quickly running through his possible excuses—I can't talk now, I'm needed at the hospital, any questions should be directed to my commander back in the States.

"You come, Chief…" one the Nigerian soldiers barked as he lowered the flashlight to the ground. Crocker recognized him as one of the more disciplined and sympathetic members of 72 AFSF. A tall kid named Chuk who was a fan of American baseball. Watched it streaming on the internet when he could. Admired Aaron Judge of the Yankees.

"Where you taking me, Chuk?" Crocker asked. "Is there a problem?"

Chuk waved him forward toward the front gate. His English wasn't good. "You come quick. You see…"

"What?"

"Come now, Chief…You see. Please!"

"Maybe later. I've got to clean up first."

"No. No, later no good. You come now!"

Crocker didn't know how to interpret Chuk's insistence. Decided to trust him. With the tall Nigerian leading the way and the other two soldiers on either side of him, he accompanied them at a brisk pace past 72 AFSF HQ to the front gate. Saw a group of people waiting. Mostly solemn-looking men dressed in dark colors.

Looks like a lynch mob…

He was very aware he was unarmed, carried no phone or ID, and was only wearing a sweaty T-shirt and shorts. Thought about turning and beating it the hell back to the barracks.

Before he had a chance, a thickly built man wearing

an ill-fitting suit and a strange bowler hat stepped forward, opened his arms, and wrapped Crocker in a hug. Crocker, who had never seen the man before, froze for a moment. Then the other dozen or so people closed around him and patted him on the back and head.

They chanted, "Crocker, Crocker, Crocker…"

He was totally confused until he saw the boy standing on crutches behind them. It was Azi, who smiled and waved the same little hand that had been playing with a lizard last night by the fence.

The boy pointed at Crocker and shouted, "Thank you."

Crocker waved back.

Chichima and her mother and sister had been cooking for two days—plates of fried plantains and samosas, bowls of garden eggs (eggplant) stew and jollof, and cassava cakes with a creamy custard topping. She had enjoyed it because it had taken her mind off herself and what had happened, and it made her feel she could still do something useful.

Now, she and her parents were seated in her father's old white Toyota 4-Runner on their way to the 72 AFSF base for the memorial for Major Martins and the fallen pilots and soldiers. Her hair had been conditioned with shea butter and jojoba, and newly braided, and she was dressed in the same white blouse and black skirt that she had often worn to class. No *gele*—head covering—on her head.

Her mother had asked her to wear purple or gold, but she refused. Why, she didn't know. In a childish kind of way, she enjoyed the ability to make decisions for herself.

This was the closest Chichima had been to Yola since her return, and familiar sights passed outside — traffic circles crowded with cars, motorcycles, and three-wheeled taxis, shops and stalls selling electronic products, furniture, and medicine, women and men with baskets on their heads hauling vegetables and fruit to the market.

She noted the changes, too. A new, modern three-story building, new-model cars, posters for movies and music she'd never heard of. Feelings of displacement grew, reminding her of the cartoon version of Rip Van Winkle she'd watched on Lagos Weekend Television as a little girl.

Seeing a young woman sweeping the front of a store with a palm frond broom, she remembered the character Sharru Nada in the book *The Richest Man in Babylon,* who, when he arrived in Babylon as a slave, saw some poor workers toiling near the gateway to the city. Forty years later, when he returned to Babylon a wealthy man, he noticed the same men working in the same spot.

I know how he felt…

They were traveling on Yola Road, and had just passed the turnoff for the airport. The entrance to the Government Girls' School lay ahead. Chichima started to ask her father to take another route, when her mother took her hand and held it.

Her mother said, "When the roots are deep there's no reason to fear the wind."

Chichima expected the sight of the high ochre-colored wall and the large iron gates to revive the horror of that night two years ago. They filled with warm memories instead—of her teachers, friends, and the discussions they had about books, clothes, and favorite movies.

Once she was an enthusiastic young student looking forward to an exciting future. Now she wasn't sure who she was, or what she wanted. Inside she felt like the same strong person. She would find a way back to that, somehow.

Crocker had finally reached Jenny to congratulate her for graduating from junior college, and apologize for not being able to Skype. "I got caught up in something and couldn't call in time."

For the umpteenth time in her life, she forgave him. "I understand, Dad." She'd learned that although his work often didn't allow him to be at family events in person, he was always supportive.

Now she was telling him about the job she'd started as assistant manager of the Hilton Hotel in Virginia Beach and how much she was enjoying it. She had talked about how she was thinking of transferring to a four-year college to pursue a degree in hotel management.

"It all sounds wonderful, sweetheart. Listening to you fills me with pride."

"I love you, Dad."

He bid her goodbye, thinking about how it seemed like months ago he had been holding her—a newborn—in his arms. Now she was a young woman with a boyfriend and a promising future.

His own felt more uncertain. The Navy and SEAL teams had been his salvation and way of life. Many of his old friends back in Methuen, Massachusetts, hadn't found a positive path, and ended up lost in drug addiction, alcoholism, and lives of crime.

Whatever frustrations he had with his superiors, he would never forget the value of discipline and service to country and others that the Navy had instilled in him.

Now he was Skyping with the Colombia-born widow of ex–SEAL Six teammate Cole Nathans. Cole had died three years ago in a helicopter crash in Afghanistan, and had left behind a wife, young daughter, and teenage son. Crocker had recently met Cole's widow, Manuela, at the ST-6 reunion and had agreed to keep in touch.

They had gone out to dinner twice, and had slept together for the first time. Now she was telling Crocker that her fifteen-year-old son, Nash, was having trouble in school and she was worried.

Crocker remembered Nash as a personable, good-looking boy who had been deeply impacted by his father's death.

"What do you think is bothering him?" he asked.

He'd seen many similar situations of sons and daughters of SEALs who had drifted off course while their fathers were away on missions.

"I don't know," Manuela answered. "He doesn't talk … He stays out late, he never tells me where he is, or who he's out with."

She was a fit, attractive woman who coached soccer and volleyball at the local high school. Desirable, and familiar, too.

"Is Nash there now?"

"No, he's at a friend's house working on a project for school, but he isn't answering his phone. I don't know what to do."

Akil was at the door, dressed in his best casual clothes and clean-shaven, signaling to Crocker that it was time to go.

"Hold on a sec…"

Akil whispered. "The colonel is waiting…"

Crocker turned back to the screen.

"Manuela, I have something to take care of now, but I'll call you back."

"Sorry to bother you with this. I know you're busy."

"Don't be sorry. It's not a problem. Tell Nash that I want to take him fishing when I get back. Does he still like deep-sea fishing?"

"I think so."

"He's a good kid. Let him know that you believe in him and you trust him. He'll be okay."

They had many common friends, history, and interests. He could easily see them together, but knew that if he got involved, it would be complicated for a number of reasons. He hadn't been there for his wives and daughter, and didn't want to repeat the pattern again.

He wasn't sure he was ready to face Colonel Nwosu, either, who had flown in from Abuja. Crocker met him for the first time as he entered what had formerly been Major Martins's office on the second floor of base HQ.

Colonel Nwosu was taller than he had imagined, with a severe face, and salt-and-pepper hair. Akil had warned Crocker to be careful, since he was a second cousin of President Muhammadu Buhari.

Framed photos of Major Martins standing with various African dignitaries, including Nelson Mandela, former Libyan strongman Colonel Muammar Gaddafi, and former Nigerian President Goodluck Jonathan, lined one wall.

After greeting him warmly, the colonel gazed at Crocker with sad, heavy eyes.

"Chief Warrant Officer, at a time like this I have to

express what I feel in my heart," he said in a deep, rich voice. "The loss of Major Martins and our pilots and soldiers has been a serious blow to us, in this part of Nigeria, and we haven't received one word of condolence, or support from your country. Not a single text, email, or call from any US official."

Crocker was at a loss for words.

The colonel continued, "I'm not blaming you, Chief. I know this has been very difficult for you as well...But as we say in Africa, silence speaks the loudest." He held up a finger for emphasis. "Not one call."

Crocker's emotions were complicated, wavering between loyalty to his country and displeasure with his captain, and guilt over his role in lobbying for the mission and anger at the Nigerians for not sending reinforcements and medical rescue.

He stood simmering in place as Colonel Nwosu moved behind the desk and read off the names of the dead and injured men starting with Major Martins and Lieutenant Peppie, and the approximate value of the lost helicopter and other equipment.

Despite the colonel's relationship to the Nigerian president, Crocker decided to speak his mind.

"Colonel, my teammates and I had grown close to Major Martins, Lieutenant Peppie, the pilots, and the other soldiers who died. I know they have families who must feel their loss profoundly. I hope I get a chance to express my condolences to them today."

"You will, Chief Crocker. You will..."

"As I told my commander, I take full responsibility for my part in the action. I regret that my men and I weren't more fully prepared. We could have done better."

Crocker took a deep breath before he continued.

"But since we're being honest, there's one thing that troubles me, and it's this… After the helicopter crash, we called the TOC here in Yola repeatedly to send re-inforcements and medevac. Had those units arrived, I'm confident that we could have saved some of the lives of the men who were lost."

Colonel Nwosu fixed Crocker with the same heavy, sad look as before. Turning to the window, he said, "Thank you, Chief, for speaking honestly…"

"Thank you, Colonel."

Assuming he had been dismissed, Crocker crossed to the door, feeling as though he'd gotten something important off his chest. He didn't know if the training mission would be suspended and he didn't care…

Colonel Nwosu's voice stopped him. "Chief, for your information, I want you to know that I did order a medevac team and a Special Forces unit to the battle zone. Unfortunately, all four helicopters were forced to turn around because of the very difficult weather."

Crocker took a beat to let this news sink in. Then he replied, "This is the first time I'm hearing about this, Colonel. Thank you. I hope you'll continue to aggressively pursue Boko Haram."

"We will, Chief. I can assure you of that."

Crocker saluted and left.

CHAPTER FIFTEEN

*"If there is no enemy within, the enemy
outside can do us no harm."*
—African proverb

FOURS DAY after their return to Yola the sunlight
continued to bother Mancini's eyes. The name for it
was photophobia, and in his encyclopedic mind he
knew the main causes, which include corneal abrasion
and uveitis (inflammation of the iris).

The bear-chested SEAL suspected something more
serious. He hadn't told Crocker or any of his teammates that he was still having trouble sleeping and
his head wasn't right. Normally after a rough op, he
bounced back mentally and physically, and each day
brought improvement. But this time was different.

For one thing, his senses weren't working right. At
strange and inappropriate times he was experiencing
strong, almost overwhelming smells, dreams, and vi-
sions breaking into the normal waking consciousness,
and sudden obnoxious tastes in his mouth. All weird
and disconcerting.

His personal prescription after a difficult op had
always been to rest and focus on mundane things—
cleaning gear and weapons, cataloging everything,

catching up on emails, working out—a form of meditation, which enabled him to track the random thoughts passing through his head.

Some of them, since the mission two nights ago, were highly paranoid and violent in nature, and ended with him living alone in the woods away from the teams, his family, or any form of civilization.

Now Mancini stood looking down at the reviewing field thirty-five meters away and wondering if he should report his concerns about his mental health to Crocker, knowing that if he did, he would probably be sent back to Virginia to see the team shrink, which could result in him being retired from Black Cell.

Long white tents and canopies had been set up with tables and chairs. Hundreds of people—women in white blouses, long colorful skirts, and matching headdresses, and men dressed in long white tunics—occupied the field. At the center, dancers in matching red and gold outfits were performing a choreographed dance accompanied by drummers and musicians.

Mancini's immediate concern was base security, and what he saw in 360-perspective alleviated some of those concerns. A long line of relatives at the gate waiting to be inspected by armed soldiers, all the towers manned by soldiers with machine guns, guards ringing the circumference of the compound, and tanks and APCs at the gate and in the corners. If they weren't enough to stop a Boko Haram attack, he had his AK and pistol by his bunk, fully loaded, and ready.

He spotted Crocker, CT, and a woman from the local university standing at the edge of the crowd and joined them.

"I thought this was supposed to be a memorial service for Major Martins and the other deceased men,"

Mancini remarked, trying to sound confident. "Looks more like a celebration."

"It's both," CT replied, a big smile on his face. He appeared fascinated.

"In Igbo tradition, death is not an end to life," Ndidi Collins explained. She was the British-born teacher at the nearby American University, who Crocker had met during a trip into town. "It's simply a transition to a new world."

An attractive woman, dark skinned with a little British nose and mouth.

"So this is a rite of passage," Mancini remarked, proud to be standing with teammates who had an interest in local culture. "What happens when you pass to the other side?"

"You enter a different, more spiritual realm," she replied.

Mancini had been raised a Catholic and believed God was infinite and divine and could only be known by the properties and natures of the things he had created. According to Catholicism, immediately after death, God judged the soul of a person based on their sins and relationship to his son, Jesus Christ, after which the soul would enter three states of afterlife— heaven, purgatory, or final damnation.

"In your culture is the spiritual realm split between heaven and hell?" he asked.

"It's complicated," she answered. "We have a saying: He whose brother is in heaven does not go to hell."

"I'm not sure how to interpret that."

"Spirit for us is deeply tied to family and society, and that relationship doesn't end when the spirit leaves the body," she explained. "This celebration, for example…In the local language it's called *ikwa ozo,* which literally means 'celebrating the dead.' If the families don't organize it, they believe the deceased will torment them with disease, disasters, and poverty. So they're basically making a sort of tribute to the dead and sending them off with good wishes."

CT pointed to a group of men and women seated under one tent all dressed the same—the females in white dresses with purple headdresses and big coral necklaces, and the males in immaculate white robes. "Who are they?"

"Those are the relatives," she answered. "Toward the end of the ceremony, you will see them gather in a circle and shave the heads of the widows."

"Why?"

Someone set off a firecracker that produced a loud bang. Mancini went into a crouch and covered his head.

"You okay, Manny?" Crocker asked as he extended a hand to help him up.

Ndidi pretended not to notice. "Those towering figures in the middle of the dancers are called masquerades. The men behind the masks never show their faces and are believed to be from secret societies who are able to receive the spirits of the dead."

"Interesting…"

"So the spirits of the dead are believed to play a part in the celebration?" CT asked.

"Yes… The people from this region, the Igbo people, have very active spiritual lives. Some of them are Christians, but for the most part they honor traditional beliefs and rituals."

She smiled at the three Americans and said, "Come, let's get closer and try some of the food… I think you'll like it."

Mancini stopped Crocker and whispered, "We still planning to return the equipment we borrowed to the Brits this weekend?"

"We're leaving first thing in the morning. You're coming, right?" asked Crocker.

Mancini looked confused. "Don't know."

"Tomorrow is Rufus's birthday. They're planning a party. Give us a chance to get away and blow off some steam."

"Yeah. Could be good."

Two hours after the ceremony had begun, it was still in full swing, fueled by copious amounts of food, alcoholic beverages, and drumming. And Crocker was literally trembling from the dozens of handshakes and hugs he had received from the many relatives of the slain Nigerian commandos—brothers, parents, sisters, grandparents, aunts, and uncles. Some spoke English, some didn't. They all wanted to express their grief, appreciation, and friendship.

The feelings were overwhelming and Gator still weighed on his mind. He wanted to call Germany again. Halfway to the barracks, he was stopped by two Nigerian girls in matching white loose-fitting blouses (called *bubas*), and colorful long wraparound skirts (known as *iros*). The smaller of the two girls also wore a purple head wrap (*gele*) that matched the fabric of her skirt.

"Remember us?" the taller of the two girls asked. She had wide, high cheekbones and a rounded forehead. Not beautiful in a traditional way, but attractive and beaming with intelligence.

Crocker's mind was on other things—specifically Gator, and whether he should check with the command to see if the training mission would continue—so he didn't recognize the girls immediately, and covered that by saying, "Hello…Good to see you."

"It's very good to see you again, too," the taller girl responded.

He looked again and the first thing that struck him about them was their youth; and the second thing was that, unlike most Nigerian women, they appeared gaunt. Then, something about the Asian cast of the taller girl's eyes struck him as familiar.

"Oh, my God," he gushed, turning to Chichimi, "you look so much better that I didn't recognize you at first."

"I look a long hot shower and washed my hair. This is my best friend, Navina. You remember? She's a survivor, too."

"Yes, of course. Chichima and Navina…Of course! It's wonderful to see you again. You both look terrific. How are you getting along? How's your shoulder healing?"

He took her hand, and she leaned closer and rested her head against his chest.

"Much better, thank you. I hardly feel it anymore. It's strange being back with all these people, but it's good, too, because they make me feel safe."

"I'm so glad to hear that. Navina, I don't think we were ever introduced. My name is Tom Crocker. Please call me Crocker. Everybody does."

"Thank you, Mr. Crocker. Thank you for everything…When we were in the forest we started to think that no one cared. That was the worst part, really. We never expected to see Americans, did we?"

"No…Never."

"God's messenger is a trickster, you know. We call him Eshu."

Crocker smiled. When he asked the girls about their plans, both said that they had decided to return to school—which he considered a brave decision. When they told him that they had been attending the Government Girls' School in Yola when they had been kidnapped, he offered to introduce them to Ndidi Collins from the American University.

After that the girls took him to meet their families, who offered him hugs and thanks.

Crocker was wrung out by the time he reached the barracks and called the Ramstein Medical Center in Germany. The nurse he spoke to had an update.

"Your friend just came out of surgery, and is resting. The doctors say that his prognosis is good."

"How good is good?" asked Crocker.

"They cleaned out the infected tissue, and if all goes well tonight, he should be available to talk to you in the morning. He asked us to tell you that he's anxious to get after the coo-yawns, whatever that means."

Crocker smiled. "Thank you. That is good news. Thank you very much."

The drive south to Utorogu was an opportunity for Crocker, Akil, Mancini, CT, and Tiny Chavez to get away from the base, chill, and see some more of the countryside. Most of the roads they traveled were paved, but a few were so badly damaged that cars and trucks chose to create their own path on what would be considered the shoulder. The scenery definitely made up for any difficulties they had. Beautiful savannas and vistas, lakes, salt flats, and sightings of zebu and species of birds they'd never seen before. A couple times they stopped for souvenirs, and pulled over at a private zoo, where they took pictures of themselves with baboons, antelope, flamingos, goats, and water buffalo—all native to eastern Nigeria.

They snacked on ipekere (plantain chips), peanuts, potato chips, and a hard brittle candy called chin-chin, made with nutmeg, eggs, flour, and sugar.

They followed the A13 to the A4, along the savanna-covered foothills of the Shebshi Mountains. Amusing themselves as they drew farther south, they sang along to tunes on Akil's playlist, including "You Belong with Me," by Taylor Swift.

Mancini actually knew some of the lyrics. After they finished severely busting his balls, they started with the jokes. Akil began by asking: "How can you tell a soldier is a redneck?"

CT: "His nameplate reads Billy Bob."

Mild laughter.

Tiny: "His ACUs have cut-off sleeves."

Same response.

Crocker: "He has a gun rack on his backpack."

A big laugh from CT.

Akil: "He fixes deer antlers to the front of a tank."

Groans.

Tiny: "You find live bait in his footlocker."

The most popular so far.

Akil: "He tries to design a new beret, out of a hub-cap."

Groans and some laughs.

Akil said, "Come on, Manny. Don't you have something?"

Mancini thought for a minute and responded, "He refers to the field latrine as 'modern technology.'"

His elicited the biggest laugh.

Crocker asked, "You hear the one about the Army general, Marine general, and Navy admiral?"

"No," answered Akil, at the wheel. "You make this up yourself?"

"No, smart-ass. Heard it from an SF master sergeant I met in Iraq."

"Is it funny?"

"Judge for yourself...An Army general, a Marine general, and a Navy admiral are all sitting around discussing whose service is better and whose troops are braver. The admiral, well into his third beer, says, 'My SEALS are the best in the world and I can prove it.'

"'How?' the Marine general asks.

"'I'll call one of my guys right now and, I'll get him to do the impossible. You'll be amazed. You'll see.'"

Akil broke in, "Tiny, stop farting."

"My stomach's still messed up. Can't help it."

Crocker cleared his throat and said, "Crack open a window." Then he continued, "So, the other commanders took up the challenge, and soon all three of them were on their phones summoning their best operators—a SEAL, a Force Recon Marine, and an Army infantryman.

"The Admiral said, 'Since it was my idea, I'll go first.' Turning to the SEAL, he said, 'I want you to rappel down that cliff, swim across those ten miles of shark-infested waters, climb up that sheer cliff and return with two bird eggs...unbroken of course.' The SEAL, being the highly trained mofo he was, turned and immediately started running toward the cliff.

"'Hoo-yah!'

"After performing a triple-lindy into the water, he swam across the ten miles, while fending off sharks with his bare hands, reached the far cliff, and began climbing. Near the top of the cliff, he grabbed two eggs and started back down, fighting off the pissed-off birds, reached the sea, swam back, again fighting off sharks, climbed back up the first cliff, ran back over to the admiral and handed him the two unbroken eggs.

"'Fuck yeah.'

"The Marine general turned to the admiral and said, 'That was nothing.'

"'Fighting words…'

"He turned to the Force Recon Marine guy and said, 'I want you to go down that cliff, swim across those waters, climb that other cliff, then trek through four miles of unmapped jungle, and bring me back two eggs from the mountain on the other side of the jungle.'

"The Force Recon guy saluted and moved out, rappeling down the cliff, swimming across the sea, climbing the far cliff, moving through the jungle, and upon reaching the two eggs, he heads back, all the while fighting off lions, tigers, bears, and sharks. Finally he reached the Marine general and handed him the eggs.

"'I don't believe it.'

"The Army general then leaned back and said, 'Very nice, gentlemen, but now I'll show you true bravery,' and turning toward his best Airborne Infantryman, he said, 'I want you to go down that cliff, across that sea, up the far cliff, through the four miles of unmapped jungle, over the mountain and bring me back two eggs from the forest on the other side.'

"The paratrooper looked at the general, then the cliff, and again back to the general, and he said, 'Screw you, sir!,' rendered a proper hand salute, and walked away.

"Then the general turned to the other two officers,

whose jaws were on the table, and said, 'Now gentlemen, that's true bravery.'"

Before they reached the capital of Taraba State, they turned left at a Total filling station onto another asphalt road and over a bridge, where they stopped at a sign for the Utorogu gas field and processing center.

"It's close," Akil announced.

"Close to what?" asked CT.

"Dinner, I hope," answered Mancini.

The sun was starting to set as they slowed to a stop alongside a sleepy-looking Nigerian army compound. Two very thin soldiers with rifles slung over their shoulders signaled them to stop.

Akil lowered the side window. The soldiers took a casual glance inside their SUV, saw that they were foreigners and waved them through without asking a single question.

"Top-tier security," Mancini remarked. He was feeling better.

The road bore sharply right, and past a patch of tall trees they saw the complex, which was larger and more elaborate than they had expected with dormitories, administrative buildings, and storage tanks and high cooling towers in the distance.

"Nice…"

The plant stood out because it was situated on a cleared patch of land in the middle of nowhere. Moxie, in a khaki uniform and maroon beret, met them at the gate with a cooler filled with cans of Foster's beer.

"Here's something to wash the grit out of your mouths."

"If you've got anything for stomach gas, hand it to Tiny. Quick."

"Which one's Tiny?"

Soon as they parked the Suburban that 72 AFSF had lent them, Moxie and Scott showed the SEALs around, explaining that Utorogu was a wet-gas field, and the natural gas processing plant operated in partnership with the Nigerian National Petroleum Corporation and Royal Dutch Shell produced over several billion cubic meters of natural gas a year, which made it the third largest in Nigeria and one of the top twenty in the world. Elaborate pipelines connected it to three separate gas fields, one of which was thirty-five kilometers away.

"Billions?" Tiny asked.

"Yes, billions."

"That's a lot of beans."

The gas treatment plant had a capacity to process thirty million cubic meters of gas a day and consisted of three parallel trains for gas processing and condensate stabilization. The treatment plant was equipped with CO_2 removal, mercury removal, molecular sieve dehydration, LPG recovery, residue gas re-compression, and power generation facilities.

All of this was Chinese to Crocker, who was more impressed by the fact that the plant employed more than two hundred people, split between Nigerians and foreigners—engineers, managers, cooks, nurses, and security officers from the UK, Japan, the US, Australia, Norway, and the Philippines.

Moxie pointed out that the plant contained separate dormitories, dining facilities, and gyms for locals, foreigners, and VIPs, which struck Crocker as odd.

"What makes someone a VIP in a place like this?" he asked.

"You're either a top engineer or a plant manager."

Mancini was more concerned about the threat level and security arrangements, which Scott readily explained.

"There are six of us Brits responsible for training and supervising the thirty-person security detail. It's made up of Nigerians, mostly former military and policemen, and a few Peruvians, and includes four females. The locals tend to come and go, which keeps us busy. The threat level is low. It was higher four years ago when local bandits were stealing liquid gas. Now most of what we deal with is internal. Breaking up fights, lovers' quarrels…Petty shit like that. Nothing major. You're safer here than feeding the pigeons in Piccadilly Square."

CHAPTER SIXTEEN

"A hunter with only one arrow does not
shoot carelessly."
—Nigerian proverb

CROCKER COUNTED fifty-eight men and twenty-two women seated at nine large round tables in the expat dining hall. It was a habit called "situational awareness." In any public gathering, in any part of the world, he always considered how to defend it in case of attack.

They were in a large room, modern, rectangle-shaped, and multipurpose with a small stage. The walls had been decorated with blue, red, green, and yellow balloons and streamers—the official colors of the Royal Marines, where Rufus had served. The foods on offer included fish and chips, bangers, fresh peas, mashed potatoes, herbed Yorkshire pudding, and ice cream—his favorites.

Rufus was dressed casually with a West Ham United cap worn backward. His fellow Brit security officers were taking turns at a microphone at the front of the room telling jokes and making tributes.

When it was Scott's turn, he said, "Rufus may look like a ponce, but he's one of the toughest blokes I've ever met."

Rufus shot him the middle finger to jeers and laughter.

"He doesn't say a hell of a lot, or brag about his exploits, or complain. But I can tell you that as my former sergeant in the Royal Marines, he's an ornery SOB and an ancient fucker. Most of you don't know that before he took this job with Shell, he tried his hand at being a high school teacher. Poor kids, right?"

"Poor fuckin' sloggers!"

"It was a tough school in East London where Rufus was assigned. He taught British history, which he knows fuck all about. Thinks the Magna Carta is a volcano in France."

Rufus replied, "It ain't?"

"A week before his first day at the school, Rufus injured his back playing rugby, and was required to wear a plaster cast around the upper part of his body. Fortunately, the cast fit under his shirt and wasn't noticeable. The Brit version of what you Yanks call 'don't ask, don't tell.'"

The Americans in the room cracked up.

"Because Rufus was a former Royal Marine, he was assigned to the most difficult students in the school. The smartass prats were leery of our boy Rufus and he knew they would be testing his discipline in the classroom."

Scott's voice deepened. "That first day, all eyes were on him as he strode like the brave soldier he is into the rowdy classroom, opened the window wide, and sat down at his desk. When a strong breeze made his tie flap, he picked up a stapler and stapled the tie to his chest. All the rowdy kids watched in silence. Rufus never had a problem with any of them after that."

*   *   *

After dessert was served, they lowered the lights, and a DJ, who in real life was an intake engineer from Trondheim, Norway, played Motown tunes and EDM.

Crocker, like the rest of his teammates, gravitated from the security team's table to one of the ovals filled with women. Even though he was a lousy dancer, he'd asked a little self-possessed brunette named Zoe to dance as a way of breaking the ice. She accepted.

The song was "My Girl," by the Temptations. Light reflected off a disco ball on the ceiling, and she felt warm in his arms. Her thick, wavy hair reminded him of his ex-wife.

"I assume you're from the States, correct?" she asked in an Aussie accent.

"Born in western Massachusetts, live in southern Virginia. You?"

"I was born in south Australia. A city named Adelaide. Ever heard of it?"

"I've been there, actually."

"Get off…When?"

"Ten or eleven years ago." He couldn't tell her why he was there, so he lied. "Passed through on vacation. Beautiful beaches."

As they swayed to the beat, he traveled back to Methuen, the place where he'd first become familiar with the song and a girl named Leslie, who had been short and slim like Zoe. Leslie died after they broke up, when she was driving with her drunk new boyfriend who slammed their car into a tree.

His entire body shuddered, and Zoe pulled back.

"Something the matter?" she asked.

"A back spasm, sorry…Old injury…"

They sat outside on a concrete bench, where he was

surprised to see the central parts of the Milky Way directly overhead, from horizon to horizon like a giant bruise. Reminded him that he was in the southern hemisphere where the night sky boasted the brightest external-eye galaxies, largest diffuse nebula, and some of the brightest stars in the night sky.

He had located some of them and was trying to remember their names, while Zoe explained that she had studied anthropology at Melbourne University with her sights set on becoming the next Margaret Mead.

When she couldn't find employment in her field, she decided to pursue her interest in other cultures by taking a series of jobs in countries overseas. So far, she'd taught English in Brazil and Costa Rica, worked briefly for Qantas Freight, which had taken her all over Asia, and for the last eight years she'd been working as a freelance journalist.

"What are you doing here at Utorogu?" he asked.

"I'm actually visiting a friend for the weekend. I'm in Nigeria researching a story about Borno State for the BBC."

She reminded Crocker of a series of strong, independent-minded women he'd met various places overseas. Like the legendary Polish climber Edyta Potocka, who he'd climbed with in the Himalayas. Séverine also came to mind.

"What have you learned so far?"

"A lot of the discord in the north derives from environmental factors. A drought specifically, which is the result of global warming. I don't know if you're aware of this, but Borno is the home of Boko Haram."

"I've heard that. Yes…"

"I've learned that most Boko Haram foot soldiers

aren't Muslim fanatics, they're poor kids with no opportunities, up against a corrupt central government that pretty much ignores the entire northern section of the country, which is generally underdeveloped and uneducated."

He thought that she could say the same about a whole host of violent movements in other countries, including Yemen, Iraq, and Syria, but kept that observation to himself.

"Different perspectives call for different kinds of responses," he remarked.

"What do you mean by that?"

"When someone is shooting at you, or has kidnapped your daughter, you really don't care if they're a poor kid or not."

"What brings you here?"

"I'm working as an advisor to the Nigerian government."

"What sort of advisor?"

He was looking for an evasive answer when he heard what sounded like a truck backfiring in the distance.

"Security," he answered.

She smiled and took his arm. "You want to go inside. I have a good bottle of Aussie wine in my room."

"Sure." His attention was divided now between the look in her eyes and a place in the distance, not far from the gate. He calculated the sound of the gunfire he heard was coming from the direction of the military outpost they had passed earlier.

He stopped.

"Is something the matter?"

"You hear that?" he asked. The OODA loop, devised by United States Air force pilot Colonel John

Boyd, was processing in his head: observe-orient-decide-act. Boyd had developed the loop to assist fighter pilots in directing their energies to defeat an adversary and survive.

Crocker paused at "orient," and turned back to Zoe. She didn't appear alarmed.

"Probably the Nigerian boys acting up," she said. "They're a rowdy lot…"

He let her pull him in the direction of the expat dorm, hoping she was right.

Festus Ratty Kumar was dressed in military fatigues and a Nigerian security forces black beret and riding in the first of two technicals (Toyota Hilux pickups) painted with Nigerian military symbols and colors speeding toward the Utorogu gas plant gate. Days of hurried planning and coordination were beginning to pay off, and he was psyched to the max.

The idea for the attack had originated with Victor Balt, the Russian-born arms dealer, who wanted to strike back at the people who had destroyed his arms shipment. Balt had matched Ratty with a detachment of AQIM (Al-Qaeda in the Islamic Maghreb) jihadists operating out of Niger, who would represent his interests and share fifty percent of any ransom. The other fifty percent would go to Ratty Festus and Boko Haram.

Balt promised that it would be a very healthy amount, given the value of the world-class natural gas processing plant. But Festus Ratty didn't care about that. The audacity of the attack and the shock it would create in Nigeria and the rest of the world excited him.

Both he and the AQIM commander, Umar Amine,

had agreed to contribute fifteen of their most experienced fighters and operate under the name "Written in Blood."

Last night, Festus Ratty and Umar Amine had met in the Sambisa. Ratty was intent on attacking the AFSF base in Yola, but Umar Amine, who hailed from Mali, had larger aims than revenge.

A serious, taciturn man, Amine's thinking had been deliberate and carefully organized. The choice of target to his mind had to be based on four factors: economic impact, political impact, ideological message, and audacity. While the base in Yola met the last three in his opinion, they didn't answer the first, namely critically damaging the enemy's critical infrastructure and destabilizing its economy. To Umar Amine's mind, attacking the Utorogu gas plant did. Furthermore, as he had explained, the Utorogu compound would be much easier to overrun and hold.

Festus Ratty had no argument with that. He was pleased to be collaborating with a highly motivated and intellectually vigorous militant. From a strategic perspective he understood any action against the gas plant had to be lightning fast, unexpected, and possibly suicidal.

In addition to their usual AKs and pistols, Balt had armed both groups with 60mm mortar shells to serve as explosives, RPG rockets, PK and DShK machine guns, and sniper rifles.

The combined force of thirty had left the Sambisa in the late afternoon and traveled over heavily obscured roads along the Cameroon border in six technicals (chariots of modern warfare) bearing the symbols and painted in the colors of Nigerian security forces.

The plan called for Umar Amine's men to attack

the army outpost, taking hostages and seizing the barracks, which Festus Ratty's BK force would simultaneously hit and penetrate the front gate of the gas plant compound itself.

Festus Ratty heard automatic gunfire behind him and looked at his watch. It was 2258. The AQIM unit wasn't supposed to strike until midnight. What he didn't know yet was that Umar Amine's force had run into a van filled with eight Nigerian soldiers leaving the plant, and had engaged them, hitting the van with rockets and gunfire.

That had alerted the remaining twenty or so soldiers on the base, some of whom were firing back at them now.

Ratty was so hyped up on adrenaline he didn't care. He stuck his arm out the passenger window of the first technical and raised his fist. Both vehicles stopped twenty meters from the main gate, throwing up a wall of red dust. The militants inside them got out and immediately started firing rockets and machine guns at the guards around the gate. A number of them ran for cover. Those who remained were quickly mowed down.

Their moans pierced the night sky and were soon drowned out by the sounds of the Toyota trucks roaring into the compound. Festus Ratty fired his AK into the "Welcome to Utorogu" sign past the gate, then screamed excitedly into his handheld radio, "Rambo One. Rambo One. Entered compound. Front gate taken!"

Four of Festus Ratty's men jumped out of the second truck to mop up the area around the gate, drag away the bodies, and assume the position of guards. He and the others proceeded directly to a concrete plaza in front of the second grouping of buildings in the compound—an area known as "expat town," where most of the plant's foreign workers resided—and started firing at anyone they saw.

When the shooting reached the gate, approximately thirty meters from the front of the expat plaza, Crocker turned to Zoe and said, "This sounds serious...Run to the living quarters. Alert everyone to hide and barricade themselves in...I'm going back inside to find Moxie and his men."

Zoe stammered back, "I—I...want to stay with you."

He pulled her close. "Go inside and warn them...I'll catch up with you later."

Now he was hurrying through the side entrance of the dining hall. As he stopped to look back at the headlights of vehicles hurrying in his direction, a very queasy feeling took over his stomach. He entered the kitchen, pushing around confused, panicked people running out toward the rear of the building. They had apparently already heard the shots, and maybe received a warning from the gate.

He saw a man shove into a Japanese woman, who slipped and hit the side of her head on a metal counter. Crocker caught her before she hit the floor. In the multipurpose room ahead the sound system was still playing "I Heard It Through the Grapevine," which now sounded like a warning.

I bet you're wondering how I knew
'Bout your plans to make me blue...

The woman was unconscious and bleeding from a gash above her ear. Crocker grabbed the next man who ran past—a guy with a big gray mustache—and exclaimed into his face, "Take her. Help her out the back!"

The man looked at him numbly.

Crocker tightened his grip around the man's forearm. "Help her out the back. She needs medical attention. I'd take her myself, but I'm headed inside the dining hall."

The man nodded, took her from Crocker, and looked back in fear. The gunshots sounded like they were right outside the door now. Then a rocket exploded near the front, shaking foam tiles loose from the ceiling.

Crocker pushed the mustached man. "Go!"

With screams reverberating off the walls, he continued through a hallway, into the dining hall—a scene of chaos. Chairs turned over, spilled drinks and ceiling tiles on the floor, the body of a collapsed man holding his throat, people hiding under tables. Fear was electric. Another rocket exploded outside.

"This man needs medical attention," Crocker shouted, pointing to the man on the floor.

A woman crawled out from one of the tables over to the fallen man as Crocker scanned three-sixty for the Brit security officers and his teammates, taking in dozens of impressions, and matching faces. Failed to find them in the red confetti-like colors off the disco ball.

Called, "Moxie? Has anyone seen Moxie, Brian, or Scott?"

No one answered.

"Moxie?" he shouted. "Rufus? Brian? Scott?"

A second later the lights went off and people in the room moaned with a kind of morbid resignation. Crocker couldn't tell if someone had turned them off deliberately. Reached the front door, which was hit by a volley of bullets, and went to the floor. That's when he realized he was unarmed; wasn't even carrying the SIG Sauer pistol he had brought with him.

Left it in the fucking dorm…

Gathered himself, harnessed his massive energy. Hazarded a look out the metal front door. Saw a medley of muzzle flashes in the plaza outside, the dark outlines of the technical painted to look like a military truck by the concrete bench where he and Zoe had been sitting minutes earlier. A Browning or DShK mounted in back. Confused him at first because it was directing fire at the corner of the sand-colored building to his right. Saw sparks zinging off a large trash compactor, then shadows behind it, the outline of an automatic rifle.

What the fuck is going on?

Whoever was behind the compactor was pinned. Spotted two dark shapes in the foreground—a man on his back resembled Moxie. Saw Rufus's body beside him. They were both still and bleeding out.

Sons of bitches…On his friggin' birthday…

No way the attackers were Nigerian soldiers, or something was very wrong. Instinctively tried to locate the weapons of the fallen Brits, in the chaos and muted light. Calculated that he didn't have a chance of reaching them before the big guns on the technical ripped him to shreds.

His survival instinct was turned up to eleven. Observe-orient-decide-act.

The firing in the plaza in front of the dining hall was relentless—PK machine guns, rockets, AKs, even

DShKs. They seemed to be shooting at anyone that moved.

Fuck…

Figured he had about a minute to warn the people in the dining hall before the DShK ripped apart the metal front door, and the attackers swarmed in. Turned back and started to spread the message.

"Fast! Fast! Everyone out the back!"

Some frightened expats didn't respond. He went to his knees and pulled them out from underneath tables.

"Get the fuck out of here now, or you're dead!"

As he scurried from one to another, he ran into two Indian men; one of them was carrying an armful of pistols.

"I need one of those," he said, grabbing a Glock. "Help me clear these people out the back. We gotta get them out!"

When he peeked out the front this time, he saw a tremendous roar of fire directed toward the men hiding behind the trash compactor. Violent sounds of rounds clanging off the metal and tearing apart the wall. Watched as someone who looked like Brian dashed from behind the compactor toward the back of the building. Halfway there he was lit up by a spotlight from one of the trucks. Then a DShK ripped his legs out from under him, and continued firing—*bang*—clang of the recoil—*bang*.

Lost another shape following Brian in his periphery, but doubted he'd managed to escape. His doubts confirmed by a shout of "Allahu Akbar!" How he hated to hear that.

In a split second he noticed the shadow of a figure staggering around the corner toward him, sandy hair splotched with blood. Took him in his arms and recognized Scott's anguished face, bleeding from a fist-sized wound to his jaw. Crocker was amazed he could even breathe.

Scott wheezed, "Help...Help me...ge..."

"I don't understand."

Crocker leaned closer so his ear brushed Scott's mouth.

Scott said with great difficulty. "The alarm...Help me...to the alarm." Then he pointed toward the left side of the compound.

Crocker pivoted immediately and carried Scott through the back of the dining hall, his left hand holding what was left of Scott's jaw in place, blood flowing down his arm. Running full-tilt out the back.

Scott wheezing, "Left, mate...Turn left..."

Reached the rear of the building next door—the one Moxie, Rufus, and Brian had been hiding alongside of. Scott no longer had the strength to lift his arm.

"Where, Scott?" Crocker whispered. "Tell me..."

Shouts of chaos and anguish amid the continued firing coming from the plaza. Echoes of people running.

"Glass...ba..."

"What?"

"B...ox..."

It was so dark Crocker couldn't see. Saw a glint of light reflected off a four-inch-by-four-inch piece of glass. Scott was using his last bit of energy to try to make a fist. Crocker got the message. Hit the glass so hard it shattered. Reached in and pushed the button that activated an alarm that rang sharp and loud throughout the compound.

When he looked down at Scott, his eyes had rolled up in their sockets. He wasn't breathing. As Crocker set Scott's body down at the back of the building, he caught a glimpse of the satisfied look on his face.

CHAPTER SEVENTEEN

*"When two elephants fight it is the
grass that gets trampled."*
—Swahili saying

TINY CHAVEZ was in bed in the expat dorm playing *Oddworld* on his laptop, when he heard something in the distance that sounded like an explosion. Left the fictional world of Mudos and returned to Earth, where he quickly confirmed that what he heard outside was real.

Thinking that it could be fireworks or some kind of salute related to Rufus's birthday celebration, he slipped out of his bunk on the second floor of Building A in the expat living quarters to see what was going on. First thing he noticed was that Akil and CT weren't in their room next door. When he looked across the hall where Mancini and Crocker were bunking, he saw that it was empty, too.

Party monsters… They got lucky…

Tiny loved women, but was trying to avoid temptation. Lately, his marriage was on the rocks. One wrong step and it would be over, and he didn't want that. Not with a two-year-old son and infant daughter he was dying to spend more time with.

On the table beside one of the bunks, he found a push-pull radio with a RadioShack logo on it. Thinking he'd get better reception in the hallway, he hurried out wearing only his underpants and called into the radio, "Deadwood, it's TC. You read me, bad boy? Over."

No answer.

He decided to try Akil. "Romeo, it's TC…Put your dick back in your pants and answer…Romeo…Hey, Romeo…"

Tiny stopped when he heard footsteps hurrying up the stairs. Turned and saw what he thought was a Nigerian soldier in a black beret and olive uniform. Grinned.

"Hey, dude, you speak English? You know what's going on?"

Instead of grinning back or answering, the soldier stepped forward and pulled the walkie-talkie out of his hand.

"Hey…I need that!"

Tiny reached to take it back.

When the soldier hid it behind him, Tiny cocked his head and butted him in the forehead so hard he fell backward and hit the cement floor.

"That's what you get for trying to steal a radio from a Chicano."

As Tiny bent to retrieve the push-pull, two other soldiers ran up behind him with automatic weapons.

"Yo!"

Tiny turned as one of them fired and hit him in the foot. Felt like a red-hot poker passing through it top to arch.

"Motherfucker! Why'd you do that?"

The soldiers jumped on him. Despite his injured

foot, he put up a ferocious struggle, elbowing one soldier in the eye, and slugging the other. When the soldiers finally got him to the ground, they roughly handcuffed his wrists behind his back.

He continued to protest, shouting, "You stupid idiots…You don't know who you're dealing with. I want to talk to your commanding officer, now!"

One of the soldiers used the butt of his AK to smash him in the face. Tiny's world went dark.

Akil and CT were three quarters of a mile away on the other side of the 32.2-acre compound in the VIP section called Company Town, which sat on a little ridge overlooking the gas plant at the south end of the compound. Consisted of a crescent of single-story bungalows that housed the plant's top administrators and managers, around an office building, combination canteen and rec hall with an outside patio, a Jacuzzi, and a clinic.

The two big men were drinking bottles of local Trophy beer and playing pool in a back room of the rec hall with two nurses—one light-skinned and Irish, the other darker and Algerian—when the alarm went off.

CT, who was lining up a bank shot to a corner pocket, stopped and covered his ears. "What the hell's that?"

"Don't tell me it's a fire drill at one a.m.," Akil remarked, looking from the clock on the wall to the dark-skinned nurse Saliha.

They couldn't hear the fighting from the expat section, which was nearly a mile away. It didn't help that they were in a windowless room with Akil's iPad playing "Sexual Healing" by Marvin Gaye.

Akil turned the music off.

"Could be a problem with the electrical system, or a fire in one of the other sectors," offered Sally O'Rourke, the older and taller of the two nurses, as she sniffed the air. She didn't want the party to end, but felt a strong sense of duty.

"I'd best check it out," she announced.

CT, covering his ears to muffle the piercing sound, said, "I'm coming with you. Make sure you don't get lost."

Sally smiled, "Invitation accepted," and pushed her long hair back.

She currently ran the emergency center and on-site ambulance. Having served as a medic in the Kosovo war, and having worked across Africa in a variety of petrol and forestry sites, she considered herself hardened to crisis.

CT was setting down his cue stick on the table when the lights went out.

"Now I can't see where I'm aiming," said CT.

"He's soft," Akil joked. "Can't take the slightest bit of adversity."

Sally said, "Give me your hand. I'll guide you."

Akil and Saliha chose to stay behind, both hoping that once they were alone, they'd get a chance to slip into the Jacuzzi.

Sally took charge leading the way along the wall to the rear exit, where she offered CT a pair of hooded chemical-resistant coveralls to wear over his blue polo shirt and khaki pants, and noise-canceling headphones.

"No, thanks."

"Come on, you'll look sexy."

He took the headphones and left the chem suit behind. Soon as they got outdoors, they heard gunshots and explosions in the distance. "You hear that?" she asked, pausing near the ambulance.

CT had just removed the headphones when a Gulf Oil 4x4 skidded up and a blond-haired engineer got out, shouting, "Terrorists! Terrorists! Fucking hell… It's a terrorist attack!"

"Where?" CT asked.

"Front gate. The expat section! Holy shit! They're killing everyone!"

Keeping a cool head, Sally initiated the appropriate protocol. With CT's help, they pounded on bungalow doors, rousing sleeping administrators and engineers, and instructed them to lock themselves in and hide under their beds.

Moving to the rec center, they did the same to the half-dozen expats they found there. That's when Akil and Saliha appeared, pulling on their clothes.

"What's going on?"

"While you're jonesing one another, the compound is being attacked," CT explained.

"Where?" Akil asked.

"They hit the expat section where our buddies are," answered CT.

"Who?"

CT turned to Sally. "We need weapons."

"No weapons," Sally answered. "Protocol is to sit tight and contact the duty officer at Shell headquarters in South Holland. They'll notify Nigerian authorities and handle everything."

"Fuck that," exclaimed Akil. "We're trained for this kind of thing."

"He's right!"

"You don't understand. The plant is particularly vulnerable because of—"

Akil cut her off. "Where are the weapons? Our teammates are under attack!"

Sally reluctantly obliged, unlocking the security locker, where the SEALs armed themselves with automatic weapons, shotguns, pistols, armored vests, and flares.

Now the debate between CT and Akil was whether one of them should stay and guard Company Town and the gas plant next door, or both hightail it to the expat dining hall. It was over quickly, with Akil insisting, "You stay here and do what you can, I'll go!"

"Roger."

A half-minute later, Akil and Saliha climbed in the ambulance and sped north on the paved road that paralleled the eastern fence. As he drove, Akil saw military vehicles parked in front of a cluster of buildings on a promontory to his right.

"What's that?" he asked, pointing.

"That's the LN section?" Saliha answered, craning her neck.

"LN?"

"Local nationals?"

"Those military vehicles normally parked there?" CT asked.

Saliha shook her head: "Never seen that before, but I'm not sure."

Mancini had left the party early and returned to his room in the expat dorm Building A—an airy, sand-colored three-story building. He'd seen Crocker go off with some Aussie babe. Crocker was single, so good for him.

Manny had decided to read for a while, two chapters of Stephen Hawking's book *The Grand Design*.

Trying to grasp the concept of a multiverse—the idea that our universe is one of many that had appeared spontaneously out of nothing—he stood in the shower and let the warm water calm his head and body as he considered the idea that another version of him existed in a separate universe or dimension.

Mind-blowing stuff, he decided, as he toweled himself off in the paneled locker room. Since boyhood, he had a sense that the past was still alive somewhere in the universe, and had never understood where that idea had come from.

He was curious to read more, but decided to hit the hay, and continue in the morning. Maybe try to contact Carmen via Skype or Viber. She was five hours behind in Virginia, and probably cleaning up after dinner.

Mancini, with a towel around his waist, took a step toward the door when two men rushed in, one with red hair holding a bleeding wound on the side of his head, the other an Asian man whose eyes were practically bulging out of their sockets.

"What happened to you?"

He barely got his question out when the Asian man pointed behind him and spit out the word "T-t-terrorists!"

"What terrorists? Where?"

"Outside…They're swarming all over the plaza shooting people!"

What had been a peaceful night so far for Mancini was now interrupted by the sounds of men in the hallway, breaking down doors and shouting.

"Any idea how many?"

He was trying to remember where he'd left his pistol, when the bleeding man leaned into him and said in a panic, "Lots. We'd better hide. They're targeting foreigners."

"You sure about that?"

"One of them saw my red hair, and ran after me and bashed me in the head! So, yes!"

Mancini wrapped an extra towel around the man's head, grabbed his shorts and shirt, and started looking for a means of escape. Behind them stood a sauna and shower; neither had a window or offered a route out of the building. Exiting into the hallway would put them in the path of the terrorists.

"You know another way out?" Manny asked, trying to override the panic signals from the lizard part of his brain.

The freaked-out men shook their heads.

His mind was operating at warp speed now, quickly calculating that the three of them had no way of overpowering or fighting their way past even two armed soldiers. Turned to the lockers, which were too narrow to accommodate a small person.

One of the men said, "The only thing to do is give ourselves up. Beg for mercy."

"Not happening," Mancini responded, as he stood on a bench and climbed up to a four-foot space between the tops of the lockers and the ceiling. "Follow me…"

From there, he removed a panel of the white foam ceiling. Looked toward the wall and saw an aluminum ventilation tube wide enough to accommodate a large human being. Pulled away the curved L section that connected to an exhaust vent in the ceiling, and pushed it out of the way.

Now with access to the vent, he crouched down and offered his hand to the Asian man. "Come!" he whispered. "Come quick!"

"I'll never fit…"

"The fuck you won't! You'll see…" Manny pulled him up and helped him into the vent. He reached down for the red-haired man, who was shaking from head to toe, coaxed him up, held him, pushed up and in.

The sound of men at the door, conferring in a foreign language. He hoisted himself up and climbed into the vent as boots entered the small room.

Shit!

He'd left his shorts and tee on the bench, and his cell phone in his room. More importantly, he hadn't replaced the ceiling tile. Reaching down to do that now, he nearly lost his balance.

AQIM leader Umar Amine and his men had crashed through the unguarded side gate and quickly overrun the LN dormitories. Many of the 138 Nigerians housed there in two buildings—one for men, one for women—worked as chefs, cleaners, and restaurant workers and were employed by a local subsidiary of the French catering firm CIS.

The terrorists went room to room through the men's dorm hunting for expats. When the locals learned that, they secretly texted warnings to their foreign friends in other sections of the compound. In fact so many texts were being sent back and forth between people in different parts of the compound that the local network became oversaturated and shut down.

One of the cooks ran to the female dorm and alerted the women that the terrorists were coming to inspect their rooms. Suspecting they were Boko Haram, many of the women tied scarves over their heads to try to pass as Muslims.

Ultimately, Umar Amine and his men found no foreigners. So they herded all the Nigerians in the lobby of the men's dormitory, where tall, bearded Umar Amine stood on a table, quieted the assemblage, and announced, "We have nothing against you Nigerians. You can take your things and leave out the side gate."

Somewhere in the confusion, someone had handed Crocker an AK and two extra twelve-round mags, which he'd stuffed in the waistband of his black pants, along with the Glock he took earlier. The terrorists seemed to have moved their attention to the expat dorms farther south. He'd spent the last ten minutes with other volunteers retrieving wounded men and women from the plaza and carrying them to a makeshift triage center that had been set up in the kitchen behind the dining hall.

It was grisly, bloody work as many of them had been shot in the head. Others had tried to scale the three-meter-high security fence topped with rolls of barbed wire, and gotten stuck, and had to be helped down.

The kitchen was a mess of blood and organs, nurses and medical volunteers trying to do the best they could with very limited resources. There was no one in charge. Men and women shouted back and forth, and others were on phones and radios in an adjoining room, trying to alert Nigerian officials and Gulf headquarters. That room, a pantry area, had been turned into a de facto emergency operations center.

Occasionally one of the people in the pantry would stick his or her head in the kitchen and shout an update.

"Colonel Nwosu is sending a squad of soldiers!"

"Gulf headquarters says we shouldn't resist. It's a hostage situation. As soon as we identify the leader or spokesperson, we're to put him in touch with them!"

Crocker ignored most of what he heard. Certain things were clear: the terrorists were gunning down innocent, unarmed people, and targeting foreigners. The Utorogu plant security team had been overwhelmed and most of them were either dead or had disappeared into the night. As far as Crocker knew all Brits in charge had perished.

It was a desperate situation. Literally nothing and no one stood between the surviving expats and the heavily armed terrorists. And the two dozen or so expats that remained in the dining hall didn't have the resources to organize any sort of defense.

All Crocker could do now was what he had been doing—trying to rescue as many of the wounded as possible, and hope that some sort of rescue force arrived before the terrorists returned.

He took a second to wonder about Zoe, then the lights came on. A Moroccan man who was one of the plant's Electrical and Instrumentation Atex engineers explained that the previous blackout had been caused by a bullet that hit a high voltage transformer. Now a backup generator had automatically kicked in, but only had sufficient fuel to last for several hours unless the tank was refilled via fuel truck, which wasn't likely to happen.

Male and female managers in the crowded pantry debated whether it was better to disable the electricity again. A moot point, in Crocker's mind, because the sun would rise in a few hours.

He was trying to sort through the chaos, and painfully aware that he wasn't in touch with any of his teammates. It didn't help that he'd left his phone behind in expat dorm Building A, which was probably inaccessible now.

This time when Crocker went outside to look for more wounded, lights lit up the perimeter fence and plaza, and at least in this northeast section of the complex the situation appeared stable. He saw no terrorists or technicals nearby.

He found a Nigerian man in a white shirt and black pants slumped behind the front tire of a bullet-riddled Gulf truck. The man had been shot in the stomach and teetered on the edge of consciousness.

Looking north, he saw several militant trucks parked in front of a building seventy meters away. He assumed it was one of the expat dorms, but wasn't sure.

"What's your name?" Crocker asked the wounded man.

Instead of answering, he pointed to his throat.

Crocker turned the man's head sideways and used his fingers to empty blood out of his mouth.

"My name's Uzoma," he moaned.

"You've worked here long?"

"Two years...Food service, sir..."

"You from near here?" Crocker asked. Hearing the sound of helicopters in the distance, he gathered the man in his arms.

"I love...my family..."

"Of course..."

"My wife and baby girl..."

Crocker hurried around the corner and turned to maneuver Uzoma headfirst through the open door.

When the light from inside hit the man's face, he saw that his eyes had rolled back into his head.

"Uzoma, stay with me…Help is near."

Set him on one of the aluminum food counters, and tapped the shoulder of an Indian man wearing a surgical mask and a blue polo splotched with blood.

Said, "Doc, this one is critical."

"I'm not a doctor. I'm a dentist," the man whispered back. Without saying another word, he leaned over Uzoma and went to work, inserting a tube into his throat to help him breathe.

Crocker, light-headed from dehydration, grabbed a water bottle off one of the counters and drained it as a very tall, blond-haired man hurried in from the other room.

Seeing the AK slung over Crocker's shoulder, he leaned into him and asked, "You with security?"

"Not officially, but what do you need?"

"We have a situation," the man spoke with a Scandinavian accent. "Very critical…The terrorists have taken three of my engineers and are attempting to restart the plant. We need to stop them…My name is Alf Knutsen, I'm one of the operation managers. We also need to get members of the JOC and the GM over to the 50 Main office so they can communicate with HQ."

Crocker didn't know what JOC, GM, or 50 Main stood for. "I thought your guys were talking to your headquarters already."

"Cell reception is bad…Terrible, really…The important thing we need to establish is whether the gas is flowing into the plant."

"How do you determine whether the gas is flowing?"

"From the gas burn-off stacks. If they're burning the gas is on."

"I'll check."

Out of the corner of his eye Crocker saw the dentist cover Uzoma with a long sheet of waxed paper.

Damn…

CHAPTER EIGHTEEN

"Character is like pregnancy. It cannot
be hidden forever."
—African proverb

TINY'S FACE, arms, and chest pulsed with pain from the beating he'd taken. He looked through the swollen slits around his eyes to the very energetic man at the front of the room delivering an impassioned harangue in a language he couldn't understand.

He made out certain familiar words like "United States" and "crusaders," and kept thinking of his wife, two-year-old son, and infant daughter in Virginia and what he would need to do to see them again. Despite their arguments over his long deployments and his wife, Eleena's, infidelities, she was the person closest to his heart.

They had traveled a long road together, from the church mixer where they had met in El Paso twelve years ago when he was a nineteen-year-old world top-fifty ranked bull rider with a promising career and she was an undocumented Mexican immigrant working as a receptionist for the customer management company Alorica. In quick succession he had suffered a serious accident, his mother died, and he spent all his savings on doctor bills. Eleena stuck with him through his long recovery, his joining the Navy, and going through BUD/S.

He'd bid goodbye to her three weeks ago, knowing that their marriage was in trouble. She hugged him, wished him well, then returned to the sofa with their two-year-old son and five-month-old daughter and continued watching *Stranger Things,* her favorite TV show.

Tiny admitted he wasn't clear about a lot of things. He didn't know the identity of his father, and he wasn't sure he wanted to identify as Mexican-American or Hispanic. He'd chosen a career that brought him face-to-face with violence and tragedy, but cried openly at funerals and teared up when watching romantic movies.

The thing he was most certain of as he sat on the linoleum floor with a C4-packed suicide ring around his neck wired to a remote detonator was how much he loved Eleena and wanted to see her again.

The ambulance was driving with its headlights off, Akil at the wheel, a Colt AR-15 assault rifle in his lap, speeding toward the expat plaza and specifically the expat dining hall where he'd last seen Crocker, Tiny, and Mancini. He spotted more technicals parked in front of two buildings ahead and to his right.

Saliha sat beside him with her eyes closed.

He touched her shoulder and pointed. "What's that?"

"Those are the expat dorms."

"Is there any other route to the dining hall?"

"Not without exiting the compound and circling around to the front gate," she answered.

"That will take us longer, right?"

"Yeah, yeah. Of course." Seeing armed men dressed like soldiers standing outside the expat dorms, which they were fast approaching, she grabbed his shoulder, and shouted, "We'd better stop!"

Akil pushed the accelerator to the floor. "I can't do that."

Saliha looked at him like he was crazy. "Why not?"

They were within twenty-three meters of the dorm now, and the speedometer had crept past a hundred and fifty kilometers per hour (approximately ninety-three miles per hour). With one hand on the steering wheel, Akil checked to make sure the mag was locked tight into the AR-15 firing chamber and the safety was disengaged.

He handed it to Saliha. "Take this."

"What am I supposed to do with it?"

He calmly lowered the passenger-side window. "If they start firing at us, shoot back."

"Me?!" she screamed. "Are you out of your mind?"

"Maybe! Just squeeze the trigger."

Festus Ratty Kumar was almost delirious with excitement. His men had taken the entire north end of the complex, from the main gate to the security office, expat dining hall, expat dorms, and expat recreation center. He had personally gunned down more than a dozen foreign workers, and his men had killed scores more. Currently, they held twenty-six foreigners hostage in the expat dorm, and hoped to find more.

The violence had unleashed a dark energy inside of him, but the complexity of the operation confused him. From his perspective, he had inflicted the revenge he wanted, and now he could inflict more, and then end it.

Standing outside the front entrance of the expat dorm, his aides Modu and Banjoko were trying to talk him out of executing the foreign hostages and blowing up the building.

"My brothers in Allah, if God wants the infidels to be executed," Ratty shouted, pacing back and forth and waving his arms like Mick Jagger, "the infidels will be executed!"

"Commander, we have been victorious," Modu said, trying to calm him down and listen to reason. "We can't act without conferring with Sheikh Umar Amine first."

"Why? Where is he? We're invincible now. This is the moment of victory! What are we waiting for?"

"But we agreed to a common strategy, Commander," Banjoko argued. "We gave our word to use the hostages as leverage."

Ratty continued pacing, squeezing the sides of his head. "It is wrong to wait. This is not what Allah wants…I know…It only gives the infidels time… Time to plan…and get inside our heads…where they don't belong."

"The sheikh is coming…Look." Modu pointed south, in the direction of the FN center and gas plant, and Festus Ratty stopped pacing and focused on a vehicle speeding toward them. He couldn't remember what kind of vehicle Umar Amine had arrived in.

"This is Amine?" he asked.

The vehicle was traveling through a dark section of the compound and its headlights were off. Modu tried the radio, but Umar Amine didn't respond.

He was trying Amine's top aide, Abu Abbas, when

Banjoko interrupted him by shouting and pointing at the sky to the north. "Look, look! A helicopter!"

"A helicopter?" Festus Ratty asked. Things were happening too fast for his brain to process. The operation was too complicated.

He and Modu tore their eyes off the approaching vehicle and turned their focus to the night sky in the opposite direction, and watched with growing concern as the outline of a South Africa–made Rooivalk attack helicopter traveling low to the ground came into view.

Festus Ratty shouted at his gunners in the back of the technicals to fix the aircraft in their sights and prepare to fire.

The helo, known as a Red Kestrel and based on the French-made Aérospatiale SA 330 Puma, zoomed in sixty meters off the ground and engaged its twin 20mm canons.

Festus Ratty knelt behind a column in front of Building A and shouted into his handheld radio, "Open fire!" The DShKs (Dushkas) and Browning M2s (Ma Deuces) started up and the tremendous noise they made obliterated every other sound.

He didn't notice Banjoko pointing to a second Rooivalk swooping in from the west, cannons booming and catching the BK gunners off guard. Men shouted and ran for cover. Festus Ratty aimed his AK-47 and yelled, "We're invincible! They can't stop us! Shoot the evil robots out of the sky!"

Akil drove pedal to metal as Saliha lowered her head behind the dashboard and prayed out loud, "In the name of Allah, the Gracious, the Merciful, I seek refuge—"

"Do it silently!" Akil shouted. "You're making me nervous!"

Saliha continued the prayer in her head even though she hadn't stepped inside a mosque in five years. Petitioning for intervention from a celestial power seemed like the only option left.

Akil's eyes remained locked on the road ahead. He was aware that the Ford E350 ambulance was moving too fast for him to take any kind of evasive action without losing control. He quickly calculated that the critical window lay a few seconds ahead when the ambulance passed within fifteen meters of the technicals parked outside the building to the right.

He coaxed the van-shaped vehicle to pick up speed, even though the engine had maxed out at 167 kilometers per hour.

Akil lived for moments like this. He noticed something moving toward them in the night sky. Thought it was a reflection at first. Then saw the outline of a strange-looking attack helicopter swoop low until it was directly in front of them.

Seemed to be headed straight for the windshield.

"Hello, motherfucker!" Akil exclaimed. "What planet are you from?"

A second later the helo's twin cannons lit up. *Rat-t-t-t-t-*—Spitting out rounds so fast it was impossible to mark the space between them.

"Hold on to your nuts!!!"

Twenty-mm rounds tore a diagonal line across the hood. *Whap-whap-whap-whap!*

Saliha screamed, and Akil locked his eyes on the asphalt ahead, willing the ambulance forward, aware of the helicopter and big guns engaging one another in his periphery. Thought he saw another helo swoop in and he felt the ambulance losing power. Saw steam rise from the hood.

"Don't stop now!" he shouted, pounding the wheel. "Keep going!"

The firing above and to their right didn't let up, and the ambulance simultaneously created more space between them and lost speed, producing a big cloud of white steam and gray smoke.

Akil coaxed the vehicle forward, while Saliha lowered her head to her knees and dared not look.

Crocker, in the passenger seat of a yellow Jeep 4x4, heard the massive firing ahead, and was calculating whether the Nigerian helicopters would spot the big orange, blue, and white Gulf logo on the roof and let them pass.

"What should we do?" Alf, clenching the steering wheel, asked.

It was a risk Crocker was willing to take. "Don't stop! Keep going!"

One of the plant managers on the backseat pointed ahead and shouted, "What the hell is that?"

For the last twenty seconds Crocker had been wondering the same thing. Seconds earlier he had been focused on the attack helicopters and the firing from the technicals in front of the buildings to their left, but now he stared at the strange smoke-shrouded vehicle rolling toward them. Couldn't tell what it was or if the occupants were friendly.

"Stop!" he shouted, changing his mind. "Hit the brakes!"

Alf applied them forcefully and the 4x4 skidded to an abrupt stop, burning rubber and sending the contents of Crocker's stomach into his throat.

Then he heard one of the managers in back express exactly what he was thinking.

"You think it's a suicide bomber?"

If it was, they were goners.

All of them watched, sphincters clenched, as the strange vehicle rolled within ten meters of them and stopped in a swirling brume of steam and smoke.

When the cloud cleared for a moment, one of the plant managers noted, "It's an ambulance! I saw a cross on the hood!"

Alf responded, "So what?"

The question in Crocker's mind was what to do next. Turning to Alf, he said, "I'm getting out of here, then you quickly back up."

"Are you sure?"

Crocker wasted no time on explanation. Opened the passenger door, rolled out of the 4x4, and came up to his knees with the AK he was holding, aimed at the ambulance. In a crouch, he hurriedly circled right toward the fence, careful to maintain a distance of about ten meters between the vehicle and himself.

It didn't move.

Making out the silhouette of a driver, Crocker gestured forcefully and shouted, "Come out! Get out now! Hands over your head."

"Fuck you, Crocker!" came the retort through the driver's-side window.

What?

He tensed for a second, then his mind registered the identity of the voice. "Akil, you crazy bastard? Is that you?"

"Sure is, motherfucker. Nice way to greet a friend."

*　　*　　*

At the other end of the compound in Company Town, CT and Sally had moved from the VIP dorms to the headquarters building known as 50 Main. There they joined a French plant manager named Paul Pagon, who was trying to locate a satellite phone to use to communicate with Gulf headquarters in South Holland.

Terrorists had already searched the offices for hostages and money. Drawers were emptied and chairs overturned. They had just entered the Integrated Media Technologies (IMT) manager's office when Sally heard footsteps outside.

Turning to CT, she whispered, "Someone's coming."

"Inside," he said, steering Paul and Sally past a desk and toward a corner closet. When she started to resist, he held a finger to his lips and pushed her inside, followed by Pagon. Quickly covered them with a stack of boxes and shut the door.

He crouched under the desk along the wall with his AR-15 and pushed a chair in front of him.

All the time, saying to himself, *I'll be okay, baby. It's gonna be okay…*

Wasn't sure he was addressing God or his wife, Nasima, more than five thousand miles away in Virginia Beach. Last thing he wanted was to leave her with the burden of raising their three kids alone. Charles Jr. had just turned thirteen.

Nasima, I got this…

His heart skipped a beat when he heard the front door of the building crash in. His mouth turned bone dry, and he followed the sounds of the terrorists splintering wooden doors, starting with the first on the right side of the hallway. Heard every step and movement in detail thanks to the vent in the wall nearby.

The sounds formed a pattern—boots to door, doors breaking, and thirty seconds of lowered voices as the terrorists searched the room before the process started again.

Said goodbyes in his head to his loved ones.

Nasima, you warned me years ago that wherever I deployed, to never go to Africa. You had an intuition that night, and, baby, you were right…

CT heard the terrorists kick in the women's bathroom door. Now there was only one door left between it and the IMT manager's office at the end of the hallway, where he, Sally, and Paul were now.

Charles Jr., I know you're still a kid, and this isn't fair…But I need you to look after your brother and sister, and help your mom…

The footsteps approached the next office and stopped. Tears filled his eyes as he addressed his daughter. *Alyssa, my little angel…The moment I first saw you in the delivery room was one of the happiest in my life…*

He expected to hear boots against the door, and moved his finger to the trigger and prepared to start firing as soon as the terrorists entered the room. Instead, the footsteps turned right into the other hallway and continued out the back of the building to the exit.

It felt like a minor miracle.

Thank you, God…

CT counted the seconds of silence in his head. At twenty the trembling started in his hands and moved up his arms to his shoulders, and from his shoulders into his chest and torso, until his entire body was shaking and releasing tension.

Not only was he thankful to still be alive, he also had hope that now that the terrorists had searched the building a second time, they wouldn't return anytime soon.

Tiny Chavez sat propped against a wall in the Building A expat dorm lobby, his wrists chained behind him and a circle of C4 around his neck, trying to stop the stream of thoughts hurtling through his head, when he was jolted to attention by the sound of big guns firing, and men shouting. Glanced at the brown-haired woman named Zoe trembling and talking to herself.

He wanted to tell her not to worry, that thinking about the possible outcome would only make it worse. But last time he had spoken to her, the jihadist who he had dubbed *Pinche* ("dumb asshole" in Spanish)—round, nearly bald with dead eyes, had kicked him in the chest.

Through the cacophony outside he heard helicopters approaching and their cannons firing in a continuous stream. Wobbled between hope and dread.

Seconds later, the wiry, wild-eyed leader of the terrorists, who he'd dubbed *Chingado* ("crazy motherfucker"), burst in the front door, waving his arms and shouting. And Pinche and another guard pulled Tiny up from under his arms and dragged him through the lobby, and outside into the hellacious racket.

What now?

The sound hurt his ears. Cordite clogged his throat. The tops of his feet were raw from being scraped across the packed dirt and cement.

A woman beside him screamed, "Lord, have mercy!"

With difficulty, Tiny craned his neck up, and squinted into the early dawn light at a helicopter bearing down on them, smoke and sparks flying out of cannons below the cockpit. He wanted to wave at them or shout that he was an American, but his wrists were chained behind him and the noise was deafening.

Managed to take a deep breath, which he imagined would be his last. Then at the last second, the cannons stopped, and the helicopter passed overhead.

Mancini had spent the last fifteen minutes in the ceiling making a list of his favorite foods:

1. His wife's handmade manicotti.
2. Grilled rack of lamb with garlic and fennel.
3. Tom yum goong lemongrass Thai soup.
4. His grandmother's spaghetti and meatballs.
5. Fried calamari.
6. Lebanese fattoush salad.
7. Grilled New York–cut steak.
8. Chicken cacciatore.
9. Eggplant parmesan.
10. Broccoli rabe.

Imagined the taste of each in his mouth. When he finished that, he circled his feet and flexed his wrists to keep the blood moving. Felt like sausage meat stuffed in metal skin. Listened to make sure no one had entered the locker room below.

Whispered, "What are your names?" to the men above.

The Asian man answered, "Me? Haru."

"Haru, I'm Mancini. Call me Manny."

"Okay, Manny."

"You having fun?"

"Fun, not exactly. I'm thirsty."

"Me, too. In a few minutes I'm gonna climb down and get us some water."

"Too risky."

"We need water."

"We need food, too."

"We can go without food for more than a week. Water is more critical."

"Not for me."

"Haru, I've been thinking about food and decided it's a bad idea. I need to focus on something else."

"What?"

"I'm thinking...women."

"You like women?"

"Food and women together, even better. A delicious dinner, a good bottle of wine..."

"Woman? I thought you prefer *Jani*..."

"Johnny? Who's he?"

"*Jani* is Japanese term for slim, good-looking man."

Mancini chuckled. "You're making me laugh, Haru."

"I think you like my joke..."

"Yeah, and when we get out of here, I'm gonna kick your ass."

"You get us out of here, you can kick my ass all you want."

"You're funny, Haru. What do you do when you're not hiding in the ceiling?"

"I'm a metering engineer."

"How's your friend?"

"Jamisen isn't my friend. He's my boss. Very difficult man."

"All right, then fuck him."

"No, Jamisen is good friend. He's sleeping."

"Sleeping? That's not good..."

Mancini wasn't a corpsman, but like all SEALs he'd received trauma medical training. Now he squeezed his big head into the ventilation duct and past Jamisen's feet. Reached up, found his wrist, and took his pulse. It seemed normal. So did his body temp, as far as he could tell. The towel he'd wrapped around Jamisen's head had stopped the bleeding.

Running his hand along Jamison's chest as he squirmed down to where he had been before, Mancini discovered the phone in the chief engineer's pocket. Saw that it still had fifty percent charge.

Whispered to Haru above Jamisen, aware once again that the only thing he had on was another towel. "You know the password for Jamisen's phone?"

"Try his wife's name, Patricia."

Manny punched it in. "Doesn't work."

"Try his birthday, eleven twenty-four sixty-one."

"Nope."

"Try Barcelona FC. It's his favorite football team."

"No."

"Try Rambo. It's his favorite movie character. He named his dog after him."

"No shit?"

"His dog does shit. I hope so."

Mancini heard footsteps approaching in the hallway below. Whispered urgently, "Quiet, Haru! Someone's coming!"

CHAPTER NINETEEN

"He who will hold another in the mud must
stay in the mud to keep him down."
—Igbo saying

COLONEL NWOSU sat in the same Black Hawk helicopter he had flown to Yola two days earlier. Watched
as the sun spread its glow across the eastern horizon.
An hour ago, shortly after he had landed in Abuja and
was about to leave for home, he was informed of the
attack. Climbed in the same Black Hawk, and was
now on his way to a town near Utorogu.

It was 0748 on Friday the twentieth. In less than
five hours he was scheduled to be at National Christian Center in downtown Abuja to attend his grand-
daughter's christening. He clearly wasn't going to
make it back in time, not given the current national
crisis.

With the presidential election one year away, and
his cousin President Muhammadu Buhari planning to
run for reelection, he knew that the attack on the gas
plant was a potential disaster that could undermine his
and his cousin's future.

Hundreds of text messages and calls had already arrived at military HQs from people who escaped from

the Utorogu Gas Plant, relatives of workers trapped inside, and even those still hiding in the plant. As he traveled east, Colonel Nwosu read them on his laptop and tried to put together a coherent picture of the situation. He couldn't.

A SINCGARS Airborne radio beeped, and the aide seated next to him reported that the deputy commander of the Nigerian military outpost at Utorogu, Captain Tayo Contee, was on the line.

"We know anything about him?"

The aide shook his head. With his hand over the receiver, he said, "Speak loudly, Colonel, because the captain says he suffered some hearing loss in the assault."

"Okay. I will."

Colonel Nwosu took the receiver and covered his right ear to muffle the noise from the engine. "Captain," he asked. "Where's your commander?"

"Dead, sir."

"I'm sorry."

"Many dead. Very many, but it could be worse. Many men and women had gone home for the weekend."

"What's the situation now?" Colonel Nwosu asked.

"Which particular situation, Colonel?"

"The overall situation at the plant."

"Hard to know precisely, sir. We are about a hundred meters away. It's pretty clear that the terrorists have complete control. The men I have with me...I have roughly fifty soldiers, local policemen, guards, and volunteers. I have deployed them around the perimeter of the compound to help those who are able to escape."

"How many have there been?"

"People who have escaped? I would say more than a hundred. Mostly Nigerians."

"Any foreigners?"

"Very few."

The copilot, seated directly in front of Colonel Nwosu, indicated that someone wanted to speak to him over the helicopter's air-to-air communications system.

Colonel Nwosu, starting to feel overwhelmed, said into the SINCGARS receiver, "Hold on the line, captain. I've got to take this call."

Then he took the headset from the copilot and fitted it over his ears.

"Colonel Nwosu speaking. Who is this? Over."

"Colonel, Tiger-Delta-One, sir. NAF Makurdi. I'm the pilot of AH 7-2. We just completed our first series of passes over the Utorogu compound. Over."

"What were you able to observe, Tiger-Delta-One? Over."

"Colonel, the terrorists are everywhere. It's hard to tell how many. They engaged us with heavy machine guns that were stationed in front of two buildings at the north end of the compound. The map we have indicates that is where the expat dormitories are, sir. It seems that the terrorists are holding hostages there. Over."

This information jibed with other reports he had read.

"Tiger-Delta-One...Did you observe any hostages? Over."

"Yes, we did, sir. We saw several placed around the main building as human shields. Over."

Colonel Nwosu considered the bad press he and the government would get if his pilots gunned down foreign gas plant workers.

He said into the radio, "Tiger-Delta-One, suspend

any attacks until further notice. Do you read me? Over."

"I read you, sir, yes. Over."

"Tiger-Delta-One…Stay airborne and circle the perimeter looking for survivors. Are you in communication with Captain Tayo Contee? Over."

"Captain Tayo Contee…No, sir. I don't know who he is. Over."

"Tiger-Delta-One. Continue looking for those who manage to escape the compound and communicate their location to the TOC in Abuja. But do not fire at any targets in the compound until you hear directly from me. This is important. Do you read me? Over."

"This is Tiger-Delta-One. I read you, Colonel. Over."

"Good work, Tiger-Delta-One. Over and out."

Some light from the locker room leaked into the ventilation vent. Manny checked Jamisen's phone and saw that it was down to thirty-eight percent power. Cell reception had wavered from one bar to none. Now it held at two.

He tried punching in another code: Rambo.

This one worked.

Excellent!

He took a deep breath and calculated that eastern Virginia was five hours behind. So at 0750 where he was in eastern Nigeria, it was 0250 that morning there. Dialed the country code, number, and access code from memory.

A voice answered, "Emergency desk? Who's this?"

"O43-6-BCT."

"Mancini?"

"Correct."

"Mother's maiden name?"

"DiVincenzo."

"What can I do for you?"

"I need you to patch me in to Captain Sutter at ST-6 headquarters. It's an emergency."

"Hold on."

He heard footsteps resounding in the hallway below. Half a minute later, Sutter's Kentucky-accented voice came over the line.

"Mancini, where are you?"

"Sir, I'm currently hiding in a ceiling at a Gulf Oil plant in a place called Utorogu. I'm hiding, sir, because the plant is under siege by what I believe to be Boko Haram terrorists."

He heard Captain Sutter exhale hard on the other end.

"Did you say Boko Haram?"

"I did, sir."

"We just received a report about an attack on a Nigerian gas plant. But I didn't expect you would be there. You alone?"

"No, sir. Crocker, Akil, Chavez, CT...We're all here. We came to drop off some equipment from a group of Brits who helped us and spend the weekend. It's a long story. Suffice it to say that as I was getting ready for bed, the compound we're in was attacked."

"You said this plant is run by the Gulf Oil company?"

"That's correct, sir."

"Name?"

"Utorogu. Southeastern Nigeria. I'm hiding in a ventilation duct above the men's locker room in the expat dorm."

"Okay…Let me get this down. Vent…Men's locker room, expat dorm, Utorogu…Okay."

"Sir, I have no idea where my other teammates are located or if they're still alive."

"But you know they were in the plant with you?"

"Yes, we were all here when it was attacked."

"No cell or radio contact with any of them?"

"No, sir. It's a very big natural gas compound. They could be anywhere. They could be hiding, or they could have been taken hostage, or…"

"You said natural gas?"

"Yes."

"In Nigeria?"

"Correct."

"Is there still active combat?"

"I can't hear much where I am."

"Okay. Keep your cell turned on until you hear from me. I assume the desk has your number."

"They recorded it, yes. Please make it quick."

Festus Ratty heard Nigerian helicopters continuing to circle the compound, cementing in his mind the idea that they were trapped, and the Nigerians and their western partners were more inclined to fight than negotiate.

He made this observation soon after Umar Amine arrived in a technical with one of his aides Abu Abbas and three armed guards. They huddled in an office inside the main expat dorm. Festus finished with, "I don't like waiting. I want to act!"

Umar Amine—tall, serious, bearded, with a thick brow and high cheekbones—responded, "Let's remain calm and not make any assumptions." Then he pointed to a poster that featured the tennis player

Venus Williams in motion and the quotation: "I don't focus on what I'm up against. I focus on my goals."

On the floor was a plastic box filled with phones, wallets, watches, and other valuables taken from the expats and found in some of their rooms.

Ratty didn't care what some rich, spoiled tennis player said. He grabbed a framed photo of a young girl in a soccer uniform off the desk and threw it against the wall so that it shattered. Then he lifted the phone on the same desk out of its cradle and listened. Hearing no busy signal, he concluded that the compound electrical system was still down.

"No power, no phones, helicopters attacking us... What are we waiting for?"

Light-skinned Umar Amine remained the more sanguine of the two, stating, "There's nothing to worry about, my brother. We are in complete control."

Ratty didn't feel the same. "I just lost two men in the helicopter attack. This upsets me. My unit suffered one more casualty last night. You had one killed at the military outpost."

"I also have two badly injured," added Amine.

"So we're down to eighteen fighters, which is not good. Not good at all. This is a very large compound."

"Eighteen is all we need," Abbas said. "My men are setting barrels filled with explosives throughout the compound. The next helicopter that shoots at us, I'll order them to detonate one of them, and the crusaders will get the message."

"You came with three of your guards. Where are your other men now?"

Umar Amine, wearing a camouflage uniform and combat boots, walked over to the whiteboard on the opposite wall, erased the maintenance scheduled on it, and used a black marker to draw a crude diagram of the site. With left representing south and right north, it read from left to right—gas plant, company town, VIP bungalows, FN canteen and dorm, expat dorms A & B, central plaza with expat dining hall, and front gate.

"You're correct. I have three fighters with me. The other six are here," he said, pointing to the gas plant.

"None at Company Town?"

"No. We went through the area earlier and took three important hostages, all engineers. We captured another two foreigners in the VIP area. I brought them with me and left them in the lobby with the others. The engineers in the control room of the gas plant are cooperating. We have already mined the edge of the site and have missiles pointed at the main working facility. Now we're trying to get the gas turned on and flowing. It went off automatically when the alarm went off. What about you, my brother? What can you report?"

Ratty rose to his feet and pointed to the whiteboard. "Four men and one technical at the front gate. They also occupy the camera and security rooms there. The problem is that the cameras aren't working because the power is off."

"What about the other five men?"

"They're here with me at the main expat dorm guarding the hostages. I have two technicals outside."

"How many hostages?"

"We're finding more all the time. The last count was thirty-one."

"Good. Very good," Umar Amine responded. "The foreign hostages are important. They're our best bargaining chips."

Festus Ratty nodded. Now that Amine spoke about them that way, he felt proud of what he had accomplished. "I have them closely guarded, my brother. I'm using some as human shields to prevent more air attacks."

"Good, good, this is all very smart...It means we have achieved all our objectives of Phase One—control of both the plant and the base. Now we can begin to execute Phase Two."

"We only have two commanders and eighteen jihadists," Ratty reminded him.

"Brother, it only took nineteen of our brothers on 9/11 to destroy the World Trade Center and bring the infidel imperialists to their knees. Imagine what we can do with twenty men and millions of gallons of natural gas."

While Festus Ratty and Umar Amine were conferring, Amine's aide Abu Abbas sat in an adjoining office where he used a satellite phone to call Nigerian and Gulf officials. Abu Abbas's birth name was Abeo Cote, and he'd been born and raised in Toronto, the son of a Nigerian mother and French-Canadian father.

Abu Abbas's first call was to the Nigerian Federal Ministry of Interior, charged with administering all of the country's internal security, national police, prisons, and managing all national emergencies.

In perfect English, he read the group's demands to the assistant deputy minister on duty—a man named Bello Godwin Moro.

"One, the group that we call Written in Blood demands the release of all Boko Haram prisoners, Islamic State, and Al-Qaeda in the Islamic Maghreb prisoners held in Nigerian jails. They number 133 Boko Haram, twelve Islamic States, and twenty-four AQIM, according to our records. An associate of ours will email you a complete list of names.

"Two, any attempts to attack us from the land or air, or disable any part or function of the Utorogu facility will result in the immediate death of foreign hostages.

"Three, all hostages will be set free once your government meets the following demands: a) The release of all Boko Haram, Islamic State, and AQIM hostages. b) A promise by Gulf Oil company to immediately close down all operations in Africa. c) The publication of a three-page manifesto from our group Written in Blood on the front page of Nigerian newspapers *The Punch, This Day, Nigerian Tribune, Vanguard,* and *Daily Trust.* d) Payment of one hundred million US dollars into a secure, numbered account at Ras Al Khaimah in the UAE. e) The use of two Mi-17 helicopters and a guarantee of safe passage out of Nigeria.

"If these conditions are not met by 0001 on Sunday the twenty-second we will have no other option than to destroy the entire gas plant and kill the hostages. The responsibility for the lives of these people and the plant is now on you."

CHAPTER TWENTY

"Patience can cook a stone."
—African proverb

IT WAS 1426 Friday as Crocker crouched behind a second-story loft window in the steaming hot dining hall and watched as three terrorists approached from the expat dorms. Two of them carried AKs and grenades, and the third had an RPG slung over his shoulder.

As they approached and heat radiated off the pavement around them, Crocker wrestled with the question of how to respond. Part of his brain told him to mow down the savages who had cold-bloodedly killed at least a dozen unarmed foreigners. Another more reasonable aspect argued that by engaging the terrorists they would only invite more attention and violence.

Attention wasn't what Crocker, Akil, and the nineteen other men and women in the dining hall wanted, armed as they were with only four automatic weapons and a handful of pistols and mags. Another six critically wounded lay on counters in the kitchen, where nurses and medical workers like Saliha were trying to keep them alive.

The bodies of another eleven men and women had been wrapped in curtains and blankets and stacked inside the large walk-in refrigerator off the kitchen.

So far the water hadn't been shut off. And although the power was out, the pantry was stocked with ample food to keep them alive for days. A collective decision had been made not to run the generator because the sound would indicate to the terrorists that there were people inside.

Crocker used one of the walkie-talkie apps on a phone he'd borrowed from the facility staff to communicate with Akil, who was positioned near the front door.

"Romeo. Deadwood here. You read?"

"I read, Deadwood. Over."

"I've got three tangos in my sights. They're within ten meters of the front door."

"Shoot 'em, Deadwood, then send me a picture."

"The door bolted shut?"

"Check."

"Hold on, while I check in back…Kazumi and Eito, this is Deadwood here. You read me? Over."

Kazumi and Eito, two Japanese drivers who had previously served in their country's military, had volunteered to guard the rear door.

Of the two, Kazumi's English was better, so he responded. "Yes, Deadwood. We are here at the back door. Over."

"Instruct everyone in the kitchen to stay hidden, don't move, and be quiet."

"Done, Deadwood. They're still as mice."

"Hold tight."

Crocker wasn't one to get nervous, but he was

struggling so hard to hold back his impulse for revenge that sweat poured from his face and neck down the front of his black tee. The terrorists stopped eight meters away, and the one holding the RPG loaded a missile into the tube and went to his knees.

Crocker had him in his sights.

He whispered into the radio, "Romeo, take cover…"

Crocker ducked below the window when he saw the kid squeeze the trigger. A second later, a rocket exploded into the front of the building near the door. Shook the entire structure. Crocker half-expected the loft floor to give, but it held.

Smoke and dust curled up and filled the space, and when Crocker peeked through the little window again, the terrorists had moved out of sight.

He held down the button on the cell and whispered, "Deadwood, here…Romeo, you see where they went? Over."

"They moved out of my line of sight. I think they're near the front door."

Crocker couldn't see the front from his angle, either. Thought of the defenseless expats cowering in the kitchen. Seconds later, he heard boots kicking the door and hurried down the steps to help Akil defend it.

Found him on the right side of it against the wall. Went to his stomach. Whispered, "Ready."

Two seconds later, the rebels discharged their automatic weapons and bullets ricocheted off the metal door. Rifles ready and hearts in their throats, Crocker and Akil expected the terrorists to burst through any moment.

Heard one of the jihadists shout, and the firing stopped. When Akil reached up to unbolt the door,

Crocker grabbed his arm and stopped him. Heard the men outside talking urgently.

Akil mouthed, "What the fuck?"

The suspense caused Crocker to tighten his neck and shoulders. They were too close to risk even whispering into the radio.

Tense moments passed before Kazumi's voice came through. Crocker backed away and lowered the volume. "I see them from the side window. A ricocheted bullet hit one of them in the arm! They're helping him back to the expat dorm now...You copy, Deadwood?"

"I copy, Kazumi," Crocker answered. "Good for now."

Mancini's legs had started cramping and he was feeling dehydrated, so he tracked the silence below. After five minutes passed without a voice or footstep, he whispered to Haru above, "Wait here. I'm going to get some water."

"Good luck, friend. Be quick."

Remembering injured Jamison, sleeping above him, he checked to see that he still had a pulse. He did.

Then Mancini carefully moved one of the ceiling tiles aside, and climbed down.

The locker room was silent and dark. He reminded himself of the three things he needed—bottles, water, and clothes. Found a half-empty Rush plastic liter water bottle and a pair of old leather sandals in one of the lockers and flashed back to a discussion he had with his wife ten years ago when she had pointed out how uncool it was of him to wear socks with sandals. He had explained that he was following a very old tradition because a recent archaeological discovery had

shown that Romans had worn socks with sandals two
thousand years ago.

Carmen said then, as she had often done since,
"You have an answer for everything."

A month ago, days before they had deployed to
Nigeria, he'd shown her a photograph of Justin Bieber
entering a club in Los Angeles wearing sandals over
red socks.

His comment, "If he can rock 'em, I can rock 'em,
too."

He gathered four bottles, a half-eaten roll of Tums,
a year-old copy of *Time* with Hillary Clinton on the
cover, and his T-shirt and shorts. Pulled the shorts
over his naked bottom.

Decided that was a good enough haul for now. Was
headed to the bathroom to fill up the bottles and take
a leak when he heard footsteps in the hall and froze.

Someone stumbled and fell. Then he heard a
woman crying. Waited a few seconds before he went
to the door to peek out. The sound of more footsteps
and a man grunting stopped him.

Heard the woman plead in what sounded like a Scandinavian language, *"La meg være i fred…Jeg er ikke
amerikansk."* (Leave me alone…I'm not American.)

Couldn't resist opening the door a crack. Saw the
back of a jihadist leaning over a woman on the tile
floor. The desperate look on her face shifted to surprise when she saw Mancini.

The terrorist turned to look, too, and when he did,
Mancini sprung, smashing his forearm into the back
of the man's neck, which caused him to drop the automatic rifle.

Mancini lifted the terrorist off his feet with his left
arm, and used his right arm to hold the man's chin up

and twist his neck violently right. Heard his spine crack and saw the woman cover her mouth to muffle a scream.

"Shh…"

Dropped the jihadist's limp body, then quickly retrieved the AK and looked forward into the hallway to see if anyone was coming. Clear. Helped the blond-haired woman up and was about to help her into the locker room, when he heard something move behind him.

Turned and instinctively raised the AK. But wasn't fast enough to stop the rifle butt that smashed him in the nose and knocked him out.

Tiny sat propped against a wall looking around the room at the other thirty-one hostages, noting that he was one of the privileged few to wear a C4 necklace.

No hay pedo… (No problem…)

The room stunk so bad the terrorists had tied scarves sprayed with stolen perfume over their noses and mouths. Zoe, next to him, with her wrists and ankles chained together, was complaining to him about the lousy hygiene.

"They're pigs. They're worse than pigs. They're inhuman beasts…"

She was the same brunette who had been dragged out with him earlier to serve as a human shield. Now she whispered nonstop, even though the terrorists had ordered them not to talk.

"I'm not afraid to die…There are worse things than death…Like betraying yourself in a fundamental way…I'll never do that."

"Lady, you've got some stones…Now, be quiet."

Slightly delirious from his earlier brush with death, Tiny started to amuse himself by remembering some of the crazy shit he and his brother had done as kids, breaking into cars and hot-wiring them, painting graffiti, and playing pranks. Like the time they found a dead dog in an empty lot and tied its leash to the back bumper of the high school principal's car. They followed him on a motorbike as he drove through town until he was eventually pulled over by the cops.

We laughed our asses off…

"This whole thing is pointless," Zoe continued. "They kill us…We kill them…This world should be a paradise…That's the way it's supposed to be…"

Her whispering attracted the attention of the jihadist Tiny had dubbed Pinche—round, nearly bald with dead eyes. He wandered over, his AK slung over his belly.

"I tell you not to talk. You have fun?" the jihadist asked.

"Fun as shit, Pinche," Tiny answered, trying to divert his attention from Zoe. "If I ever get out of here, I'm going to look you up. Maybe we can hang. You got a wife? You got kids? You got a son you call Pinche Jr.?"

"You talk a lot of shit…"

A second terrorist, who Tiny referred to as *Coñazo* (big asshole)—short and lean with a perpetual sneer—passed in front of Zoe, slapped her head to stop her complaining, and then stopped in front of Tiny, and clocked him hard in the jaw.

Stars circled in Tiny's head and he half-expected the C4 necklace to go off and blow them all to smithereens. When it didn't, he gritted his teeth against the pain, looked up at the two terrorists and growled, *"Chinga tus madres."* (Fuck your mothers.)

"You…stupid, too?" Coñazo asked, poking Tiny with the barrel of his AK-47. "You Marine, yes?"

"No Marine...I'm Mexican," Tiny responded.

He'd been taught in SERE (Survival, Evasion, Resistance, and Escape) training in Southern California not to give up any information that could be of value to the enemy.

"Mexico, no...." the jihadist said. "Israeli."

It hurt to speak. "Palestinian."

Tiny had been inspired by the story of Lieutenant Colonel Nick Rowe, who had been one of thirty-four POWs to escape the Viet Cong. Separated from his fellow Green Berets, he was captured by Viet Cong in the Mekong Delta and held in a three-by-four-by-six-foot bamboo cage. He was interrogated for five years and frequently tortured. So obstinate that his captors referred to him as Mr. Trouble.

"No, Palestinian. Jewish."

"I can't be, motherfucker. I eat hot dogs."

An instructor at his SERE training course had said, "The enemy will force you to make decisions. It's up to you to decide what is right, and what is wrong."

Now the jihadists stood over him and taunted him together. "You Jewish. Jewish...piece of shit."

"You need to get your ears checked, boys. Your brains, too."

"You funny, Jew."

"You're funny, too."

"I laugh a lot when we kill you."

When the Viet Cong learned that LTC Rowe was a high-value target, they led him into the jungle to be executed. Rowe overpowered his captors, signaled a passing US helicopter, and escaped.

"You can laugh all you want, *hijos de puta* ..." — son of a bitch — "But one day you're going to face some-one like me, and it's not going to be pleasant...And when you meet your maker, whoever that is, he's gonna look you in the eye and say, 'fuck you!'"

The terrorists had left Mancini and the Scandinavian woman against a wall in the hallway with their wrists and ankles bound. And even though blood was streaming from Mancini's nose into his mouth and he had lost a couple of teeth, he had the presence of mind to try to comfort her, whose ankle had swollen to twice its original size.

"We'll get out of this. I've been through worse... Where are you from?" he asked, trying to get her mind off the pain.

She was short, middle-aged, and small-boned with almost white-blond hair.

"Are you Swedish?"

"Norwegian," the woman responded in a soft voice, craning her neck down the hallway to see if anyone was coming.

"Flink," he whispered back—"good"—using one of the dozen Norwegian words he knew. "You have a name?"

"Berit."

She was about to say more when the phone he had borrowed from Jamisen vibrated. He raised his chin to indicate for her to be quiet, then used his wrists to pull the phone out of the back pocket of his shorts, leaned as far right as he could, and used his thumbs to punch in the code as though it was no big deal.

"Captain?"

"Mancini, is that you? You sound funny."

"Dental issues...sir," he answered after swallowing the blood in his mouth.

"I'll make this quick before we're cut off. Do you

know the whereabouts of, or are you in contact with other members of the team?"

"No, sir."

"Crocker?"

"No."

"Do you know if he's alive?"

"Negative."

"Okay," said Sutter. "Here's the situation as I understand it. The terrorists are in complete control of the base. They're holding a large number of foreign terrorists. They've made a series of demands to the Nigerian government that the government has deemed unacceptable."

"Oh…" He heard the footsteps of multiple people approaching and figured that they weren't bringing good news.

"No point getting into that now. The terrorists have set a deadline of midnight tomorrow. They're threatening to blow up the plant and kill the hostages if their demands aren't met."

"Oh."

"Mancini, what are your chances of sneaking out of there and finding your way to safety?"

"Not good, sir."

Berit was making noises to indicate that the insurgents were approaching.

He kept leaning as close as he could to the phone. "We're talking to the Nigerians and exploring various options. Turn your phone on intermittently. I'll be in—"

A boot crashed into the side of his head near his ear, and he immediately lost consciousness.

CHAPTER TWENTY-ONE

"Knowledge without wisdom is like water in the sand."

— African proverb

CHICHIMA LOOKED down at her newly painted fingernails, then at the brightly colored Swaheelies sandals, and wondered if they belonged to her. A feeling came over her similar to the one she had experienced in the Sambisa—a partial shutdown of her mind and body like most of the lights in the house had been turned off, all the doors locked, and the part of her that vibrated lived hidden in the basement.

A woman behind the table, with an immaculate blouse and modern black-framed eyeglasses, smiled as she spoke. "We have designed this program specifically to help you catch up with your studies and reunite you with your former classmates."

Chichima nodded. She was sitting with three of her former classmates, who had also been kidnapped and later rescued. Today was their first day back in the Government Girls' School compound after almost two years.

Instead of being allowed to quietly slip back into

their classes and freely wander the campus to get reacquainted with friends, she and her classmates were in a room in the administrative office being counseled by Ms. Lawan and Mr. Obindu from the school, and another man who said he was a local government official.

Taped to the wall behind their heads were messages that read: Never give up. Believe in yourself. Shine like stars.

The government official warned the girls not to talk about their time with the militants and not to discuss their experience. He explained that they would all live together in a separate area of the girls' dormitory away from the other students.

"Why?" Chichima asked.

"It's for your own protection," he answered. "The other girls will be afraid of you. They might think that you have become attached to your captors."

"I think that's unlikely," said Chichima, looking to her friends for support.

The three of them wore shame on their faces and stared at their hands folded in their laps.

"Or they might worry that your captors will return to look for you, thereby putting them in jeopardy," continued the government official.

Chichima felt an impulse to leave the room, but her body didn't obey.

Ms. Lawan tried to soften the message, saying, "We know you've been traumatized. You were traumatized together; we want you to heal together."

"Forget the past and move forward," advised Mr. Obindu, the assistant director of the school.

"How?" Chichima asked.

"Maybe you're in what we call the red zone now.

Maybe you feel sad, and vulnerable, and even fearful. But that will pass with time."

Crocker checked his watch. 2214. Then slipped out the rear door of the dining hall dressed head-to-toe in black. Armed with a SOG knife and a Glock 9mm tucked into the waistband of his pants.

His heart pounding, he waited for his eyes to adjust to the darkness, then hurried along the back of the hall, past the swimming pool, and outdoor rec area, to the six-foot-high brick wall. A sliver of new moon hung in the sky, casting little light as the stars and spectacular Milky Way stretched east to west.

Catching his breath, he brought his head up and scanned the facility south. Saw artificial lights in the distance, indicating that terrorists were in possession of battery-operated torches or flashlights.

Otherwise his view of the two three-story expat dorm buildings sixty meters away was blocked by native scrubs and a series of port-a-cabins that Alf Knutsen said served as offices for the plant maintenance staff.

Saw that the one nearest him, at a thirty-degree angle, had been broken into. Its aluminum front door hung from a top hinge and the windows were shattered.

Climbed the wall, crouched along the opposite side, then ran to the closest port-a-cabin. Gave him a clear view of the plaza right and perimeter fence, all the way to the far east side of the front gate in the distance.

One thing stood out—a series of three barrels hidden behind the lip of the plaza wall and roughly ten meters from the dining hall. He had no doubt they contained explosives and were wired to a remote deto-nator of some sort.

From them he gleaned part of the terrorists' strat-egy and the reason why they hadn't probed the dining hall further. The jihadists were guarding the hostages, who were probably located in the expat dorms, and maybe in Company Town and the plant control room to the south. They would detonate the area he was in now in order to deter a possible Nigerian military at-tack or to press for concessions in any negotiation they were waging with the Nigerian and Gulf authorities.

Crocker confirmed this when he scurried close to the second port-a-cabin and made out three more bar-rels clustered and wired together between the second and third cabins. Decided not to try to disable them—one, because it was hard to see; two, because even if he succeeded it would call attention to the fact that there were survivors living near the expat plaza.

From the back of the third cabin, he had a clear vantage point to the expat dorms and technicals with big guns parked out front. It was alarming to see, be-cause he could only imagine the terror of the hostages inside, juxtaposed ironically with the complete silence and serenity outside. A peace interrupted occasionally by a very gentle hiss of a breeze and the call of some species of night bird.

Saw gas plumes from the burn-off stacks at the plant flickering in the distance. That indicated, ac-cording to Alf Knutsen, that the gas was flowing again—another plus for the terrorists. Meant that they could destroy the entire billion-dollar gas process-ing plant anytime they wanted.

Crocker considered turning back at this point. But the more cautious part of his brain lost, as it often did, and he proceeded south down the gentle embankment and up until he was only six or seven meters from the back of the first expat dorm—Building A. It was set back slightly from the second and had three technicals parked in front.

Lights glowed inside.

What now?

Before his reason could stop him, he was running as close to the ground as he could to the back of the building, dark with shadow. He crouched near the side of a stairway and caught his breath.

Froze when he heard a door open above him. Someone flung out a pail of liquid that splashed on his back and head. Smelled like urine.

Shook it off and crept around the north side. Stood on his tiptoes to try to peer into a window. Squinted into what appeared to be an office lit by light filtering from an inner room. Through a partially opened door, saw people sitting and lying on the floor with their wrists behind their backs.

The hostages!

Had to resist the impulse to hurl himself through the window. Trying to decide on his next move, he was interrupted by the sound of a vehicle approaching, no headlights. Couldn't tell what direction it was coming from, so he circled quickly to the back and almost ran straight into it. Dove behind the stairway wall where he'd hid before and waited.

Don't be stupid…

Miraculously, no flashlights shined on him or gunfire came his way. Instead, men's voices came so close they sounded like they were practically on his head. He heard them grunting as they climbed the stairs carrying something. When they disappeared inside, he popped his head up. Saw cases of five-liter water bottles in the open back of a Gulf truck. Also an RPG and several six-inch rockets, and an automatic rifle lying on its side.

Decided this time that it was too risky to try to enter the dorm. Chose instead to grab the RPG and two of the rockets and run.

It was a mischievous impulse, and one he hoped he didn't live to regret.

Colonel Nwosu was halfway through his third glass of Johnnie Walker Black. It was already midnight, and he was exhausted, and understood that he wasn't likely to sleep anytime soon. Because as much as he tried to anesthetize his brain with the scotch, the stream of ominous thoughts that ran through it wouldn't stop.

He was seated in the Eagle Mobile Military Command Post (EMMCP) parked on the outskirts of the town of Utorogu. It was a specially designed Toyota extended cab pickup with a tentlike extension in back that housed a communication center with the capacity to link all ground, air, and central command assets throughout the country.

On one of the many monitors, he watched a video feed from a Tsaigumi surveillance drone flying twelve thousand feet over the natural gas plant. Developed by Nigerian Air Force (NAF) engineers in collaboration with UAVision Portugal, the Tsaigumi was a car-sized air vehicle equipped with electro-optic infrared cameras, and to the colonel's mind an example of Nigerian national vanity. Instead of buying the relatively inexpensive and very effective Israeli-built Aerolight drone, his government had chosen to build its own.

The problem was that the Tsaigumi was so poorly designed and constructed that it was ineffective, as Colonel Nwosu saw now as the operator tried to zoom the electronic cameras in closer. All they saw on the monitor was an overhead view of the plant from three hundred meters.

"You can't zoom in closer?"

"No, Colonel. The mechanism isn't working."

"Useless," the colonel muttered under his breath.

He considered himself a tough, politically savvy man, but now felt alone on an island of responsibility and uncomfortably pressed from four sides—his government, Gulf Oil officials, his own sense of military obligation, and, though he would never admit it to anyone, the spirits of those who had died in the plant already.

His cousin, the president, had already announced to the world that his government would never negotiate with the group called Written in Blood—which most people believed was a splinter group of Boko Haram. By the military's count, at least thirty-seven people had died during the gas plant takeover. Many more would perish if the terrorists carried out their pledge to kill the hostages and blow up the plant if their demands weren't met.

Gulf Oil–Holland's Incident Management Team (GH-IMT), led by security operations VP Kenneth Whiteside, continued to communicate with the colonel directly. The company's decisions, he'd explained, were prioritized by the order of P-E-P—people, environment, and property.

Via satellite phone, the GH-IMT was in contact with some staff hiding within the complex and was aware that the terrorists had taken the control room and restored the flow of the very volatile natural gas. They were convinced that the terrorists would carry out their threat at the deadline, which was roughly twenty-four hours away.

Whiteside, on the phone again from South Holland, was asking for an update.

"I have no new news," Colonel Nwosu reported. "The situation remains stable."

"Stable?" Whiteside asked. "In what way?"

"There's no further terrorist activity at the plant. No killing of hostages, no additional destruction of property. We have the plant surrounded so the terrorists can't escape."

Whiteside said, "We have been in direct telephone communications with the terrorist spokesperson inside the plant. He says that their position hasn't changed, and we believe him. The terrorists will destroy the plant and the people if their demands aren't met."

"You know my government's position, Mr. Whiteside, and we hope you respect our national sovereignty."

"Of course, Colonel. We think there's maybe room for negotiation. Gulf Oil may be willing to pay some of the one hundred million the terrorists are asking for."

"My government won't accept that."

"Then is your government prepared to launch a rescue mission? Because if you are, we obviously know the plant better than anyone and would like to be consulted."

"We have no military operations planned at this time."

"No? Are you looking at one as a possible contingency?"

"No, Mr. Whiteside. We are not."

*   *   *

At 0105, Crocker was trying to keep from blowing up as he sat with Norwegian assistant plant manager Alf Knutsen, a second assistant plant manager, Jeremy Leiter from the UK, and Mark Greenway, the American general manager, in a circle on folding chairs in the expat dining hall. They'd been discussing the situation for almost an hour as Akil guarded the front, and Kazumi and Eito watched the rear door.

The mood in the room was tense, fueled by frayed nerves and lack of sleep.

All four men understood that they were basically sandwiched between the terrorists manning the main gate to the north, and what seemed to be the main body of terrorists stationed at the expat dorms around forty meters south.

Why the jihadists hadn't returned to the dining hall after their initial assault and recent foray was anyone's guess. But Crocker pointed out that there was nothing preventing them from doing so again, and all the expats had to mount a defense were two SEALs and two Japanese volunteers armed with automatic weapons and a handful of pistols and mags.

His assessment was blunt. "If the tangos decide to come at us, we're fucked. They've got explosives rigged outside, rockets, machine guns, and automatic weapons. We have four AKs and one RPG with two rockets. We'll be wiped out in a matter of minutes."

The other major problem was communication. Dining hall phone reception had been extremely weak since last night, and only a handful of those inside had their phones with them. The few they possessed had almost no charge left. Also, wi-fi throughout the camp had been disabled. So they no longer had a dependable way to communicate with anyone inside or outside of the camp.

In fact, the only secure method of communication with Gulf HQ in South Holland or the outside world was via the satellite phone in the 50 Main office in Company Town on the other end of the complex.

Company Town was key for another reason—it overlooked the central gas plant and control room. But as Crocker had seen during his recent surveillance, the outlet flames were on, which meant the gas was flowing again. That also indicated the terrorists had taken the critical control room.

"Look," Crocker said, "it's past one a.m. now. We've basically got another couple of hours to try to sneak out of here, or we remain sitting ducks."

"We try to leave, and we risk being shot," Mark Greenway remarked.

"Yes, but that's a risk we have to take, in my opinion."

"I'd rather put my faith in whatever negotiations are taking place," stated Jeremy Leiter.

"I think that would be a big mistake."

"Why?"

"I've been in hostage situations before," answered Crocker. "Terrorist aims are often what we might consider irrational. If they're jihadists, which these guys appear to be, they're willing to die for their cause."

"We don't know that for certain."

"I do."

"Don't you think you're falling into a kind of profiling to characterize jihadists as suicidal? Aren't they more strategic than that?"

"And what about the Nigerian government?"

Greenway interjected. "Isn't it possible that they're planning a rescue mission?"

"No, on both counts," Crocker answered, the tension building in his neck and arms.

"How can you state these things with such certainty?" asked Williams.

"I'm not an expert on the politics of Islamic radicals, but I know that most of them accept martyrdom as a central tenet of jihad," Crocker answered. "Secondly, I've been working closely with the Nigerian military for the last several weeks, and I've learned enough about their mindset and readiness that I wouldn't bet the farm on them in a situation like this."

"That's harsh."

Crocker stood. "Harsh or not, here's the deal…You gentlemen can sit and discuss this as long as you want. Me and my teammate are going to prepare to leave the plant at 0200. Anyone who wants to come with us is welcome."

CT was hunkered down in the IMT manager's office in 50 Main, showing Sally how to clean and reassemble an AK-47, when the Thuraya XT Pro satellite phone rang. The Thuraya was the primary choice of military operators, businessmen, and journalists in remote parts of the world for a reason. Not only did it have a very long battery life, it was also supported by a robust satellite network.

Paul Pagon answered and handed the walkie-talkie-sized receiver to CT. The three of them had been living on water, licorice, and Walkers shortbread biscuits found in the general manager's closet.

"It's your commander."

"Thanks."

"Crocker?"

"No, this is Captain Sutter. Is this Warrant Officer Charles Tanner Montgomery?"

"Yes, it is, sir. At your service."

"Were you sleeping?"

"Sleep is the last thing on my mind, sir."

"Warrant…We've had no contact with Crocker, Akil, or Chavez here at headquarters since the takeover. Do you have information on any of them?"

"No, Captain. The only one I've seen since the attack was Akil. And he left this location last night."

"What is that specifically?"

"My location? The IMT manager's office at 50 Main. I haven't heard anything from Crocker, Mancini, or Chavez. Have you?"

"Mancini, yes. He's hiding in the locker room ceiling of one of the expat dorms."

"That's excellent news, sir…He's okay?"

"What's your situation?"

"I'm in Company Town with one of the plant managers, and the emergency services administrator. Several terrorists entered the building earlier, but left before they reached our hiding place."

"There are three of you there?"

"That's correct."

"You're armed?"

"Two of us are, yes. Early this afternoon, the terrorists seemed to turn their attention to the gas plant control room, which is close by. We heard some combat from that location. The plant manager I'm with believes the terrorists occupy the gas plant control room now."

"We're aware of that. Yes. What are your chances of escaping the plant?" Sutter asked.

"Not good, sir. Not good at all. Since the terrorists are occupying the control room, they're practically looking down on us. Also the French manager who is with us now spotted snipers stationed at the top of the gas plant towers. Why do you ask?"

Akil remembered a pair of heavy-duty metal cutters in the back of the ambulance and was using them now to cut through the double-wired fence perimeter twenty meters behind the dining hall. He ignored the danger, and focused instead on getting the job done quickly and making sure the holes he cut were large enough to get the wounded through.

It was hard work, and there was no way to dampen the sharp "click" of every cut. He prided himself in being a man of action, and preferred to finally be doing something, instead of sitting around and waiting for the terrorists to act.

A thin sliver of moon hung in the sky. Owls hooted in the distance.

As he cut, he remembered the day he had told his Egyptian parents he was joining the US Marines. He saw horror on his mother's face and disappointment in his father's eyes. Two months later, when he returned home wearing his Marine dress uniform, his father had proudly taken him around their neighborhood in Detroit to show him off to relatives and friends.

It was an important turning point in his family's history, and the Marines had served as both a crucible for dealing with prejudice and a door to new opportunities.

Semper fi…Always do your best…Let the idiots and enemies eat your dust.

Sweat dripped from his chest and his arms and as he cut, he continued thinking about his family and the life they had made for themselves in the US. His father owned a jewelry shop, and his younger sister Dalilah was at the University of Michigan medical school studying to become an obstetrician.

Soon as he cut a five-foot-high, four-foot-wide half oval in the first fence, he pushed it back, and wired it to stay open. The part of this that bothered him was leaving behind their other teammates. It had been drilled into his brain to *never* leave a teammate behind, alive or dead. But Crocker was right. The more hostages who got out of the compound safely, the better.

Before Akil started cutting through the wire braids on the second fence a meter ahead, he looked over his shoulder to the outlines of the technicals parked in front of the expat dorms and said, "We'll deal with you fuckers later. One way or another, we'll be back."

Inside the dining hall, Crocker had just finished checking with Saliha to make sure that pieces of canvas tarps had been cut and tied to make stretchers for the wounded, and the six of them were ready to be moved. Then he reviewed procedures with Akil and Eito and Kazumi, who would be guarding the column.

"Remember, we walk single file, keep everyone in line. No panic, no confusion. If we're discovered, me and Eito in back will engage the enemy and try to draw fire, while you and Akil continue ushering the expats out."

Kazumi nodded.

"Get as many of them out as you can. Keep moving. Don't worry about us."

Now he was rechecking the things he was planning to carry on his person, when managers Whiteside and Leiter approached.

"Crocker?"

He didn't look up. "What?"

"We think it's better if we leave at sunrise," Whiteside said.

"Why?"

"If we go now...in total darkness...we'll have to use flashlights to see where we're going, which will make us targets."

Crocker finished taping the one extra mag to his belt. "We're not using flashlights until we're at least twenty meters beyond the fence. Everyone needs to know that. Me and my guys will carry the flashlights, no one else. Like I said before, no shiny objects, belt buckles, metal glasses frames...Phones and watches... conceal them in pockets. Hide anything that can reflect light...Wear dark colors. Make sure everyone understands that."

"What about the Nigerian soldiers?" Leiter asked.

"What about 'em?"

"They're out there beyond the fence, correct? They're surrounding the plant...How do we alert them? I mean, if they hear us approaching, aren't they going to shoot?"

"Akil and I will walk in front once we get through the fence. We'll take care of that."

"How?"

"Leave that to us."

CHAPTER TWENTY-TWO

"However long the night, the dawn will break."
—African proverb

AKIL WAS the first person through. Paused to look back at the line of expats. The wounded came first in improvised stretchers carried by men with arms strained to the limit. All of them silent, heads down.

He held the second fence back, ears focused on any sound from the expat dorms or beyond the fence, counting each person as they passed, then pointing to the thicket of trees, ten meters from the fence and whispering, "Wait there. Don't run."

A few of the expats still inside the compound couldn't control their legs, either because of fear or physical trauma. One man stumbled and fell. Crocker ran to help him up, terror on the man's face.

"Sorry…"

"*Ssh…*"

A wounded man on a pair of crutches called out, "Angie, I'm coming! Angie, don't go."

Saliha hurried over, held him up, and cupped a hand over his mouth. Tense moments passed as Crocker looked over his shoulder at the expat dorm, waiting for a light to come on or an engine to start up.

He was the last person through. Raised his thumb to Akil.

Reaching the trees beyond the compound, the men and women huddled around him. Some of the expats wept with relief.

"We're almost there," Crocker whispered. "Keep silent. I'm going ahead to alert any Nigerian authorities. You follow with Akil twenty meters behind."

"Why?" someone asked.

"For your safety...No questions."

Saliha handed him a white towel, which he attached to the end of the RPG. She'd been poised and helpful throughout. He remembered she told him that in her spare time she taught Brazilian dance.

Now he picked his way through the trees and up an embankment, the white towel held over his head. Saw the Nigerian soldiers before they saw him. Two of them up ahead near a large tree. One of them was taking a leak.

Crocker called out, "Americans! We're Americans! Over here..."

A panicked soldier fired a shot over his head that tore through the improvised white flag. He froze. Calmly dropped the RPG and raised his arms.

"We're hostages from the plant...Expats, Americans..."

The Nigerian soldiers approached, fear in their eyes, waving their rifles, shouting, *"Ala! Ala! Onye o bula ala! Onye a bula n'ime ala!"* (Down! Down! Everyone down to the ground!)

As Crocker went to his knees, he pointed behind him and said, "We're expats from the gas plant... There are more behind me. Peace!"

*   *   *

Tiny sat with his back against the wall of the lobby of expat dorm Building A, counting the minutes and hours in his head, and trying to hold back thoughts of torture and death. Many of the roughly twenty hostages in the space with him were asleep. Some moaned, some wept, some occasionally called out for water or use of the metal pail that served as a toilet.

Tiny was determined to stay alert to every sound, smell, movement, or shift in the mood of the terrorists. They seemed to have grown weary, too. He saw the strain on their faces. The doubt in their eyes.

What are they thinking? What have their leaders planned?

The pace of new hostages being dragged in had lessened to a trickle.

The last had been a tiny blond woman with a badly swollen ankle. She sat at a right angle to him with her back against a planter. Her head was cast down so that her hair covered her face. Couldn't tell whether she was conscious.

A metal door slammed behind him. Turning, he saw two terrorists dressed as soldiers dragging a very large man. The only thing he had on was a pair of blood-covered shorts.

Poor guy got the shit kicked out of him…

The man's body was covered with bruises and his chin hung to his chest. The terrorists dragged him to a wall on the left side of the room, and let him go. And when they did, the prisoner's head snapped up, and Tiny saw that the swollen face belonged to Mancini. He was immediately filled with rage.

Motherfuckers! Savage…fucks!

He had to grit his teeth to keep from shouting. The anger brought such a surge of energy that he imagined he could burst free of the chains. Reason quickly reminded him he couldn't.

So many emotions clashed inside him—anger, frustration, hopelessness, indignation.

Saw that his teammate's eyes had rolled back into his head, but his ribs were moving, indicating he was still alive.

Somehow…some way, he said to Mancini in his head, imagining he could communicate with him telepathically. *I'm gonna get us out of here. And you and I are gonna liberate everyone and defeat these motherfuckers. So help me God!*

It took approximately two hours for the expats who had escaped to be processed and bused to nearby hotels, and the wounded to be treated at clinics and hospitals. Crocker and Akil had turned down the offer of showers, beds, and hot meals. Their minds were still focused on the hostages at Utorogu.

Wearing the same clothes as before and sipping chicken soup out of cardboard cups, they were driven to the Eagle Mobile Military Command Post where they were greeted by an exhausted-looking Colonel Nwosu.

"Welcome back, gentlemen," he said. "Your escape is a victory for all people across the world who value justice and freedom. It's a ray of hope in what has been a long, dark, difficult night."

First thing Crocker wanted to do was touch base with his command. Now he stood outside under an arbor of plants with white and yellow blossoms as the sun started to rise, talking on a sat phone borrowed from the colonel.

After checking in with the duty officer, Captain

Sutter came on the line. "Dammit, Crocker. You really had me worried."

"Akil and I are safe, sir."

"Good to hear your voice. How many hostages did you get out?" Sutter asked.

"Twenty-five in all. Most of them expat workers and supervisors. Six are being treated at local hospitals."

"How bad are the injuries?"

"Mostly gunshot wounds, Captain. None are critical. We lost a number of people in the initial attack. We had to leave their bodies behind."

"You and Akil okay?"

"No worse for wear, sir. Running on fumes, but we're good."

"What about the others... You see Chavez, or know his location?"

"No, sir. I haven't seen him since the raid last night, nor am I aware of his location. I have some clues, but no confirmed sighting."

"What clues?"

"I did some surveillance before we left, and saw a number of hostages being held in a ground floor room of the main expat dorm. There's a strong terrorist presence around the two buildings, particularly the one closest to the main gate."

"That's north, correct?"

"Yes, sir. It's called Building A."

"I don't know if you're aware, but we've been in contact with Mancini and CT."

Crocker took a moment to compose himself. "That's a huge relief, sir. They're okay?"

"Mancini is hiding in a ceiling of one of the expat dorms, and CT is holed up in an office in the Company Town."

He didn't know his information about Mancini was outdated and incorrect.

"I'm very glad to hear that, sir," Crocker responded. "Text me the numbers they're calling from and I'll check in with them as soon as I can."

"Consider it done."

Crocker had a lot on his mind. "Sir…I just learned the terrorists have established a deadline of midnight tonight. What's going on in terms of negotiations?"

"There's been no further contact between the terrorists and the Nigerian government. As far as we know the two sides aren't talking."

"That's bad news, sir. Very bad…"

"We haven't been briefed by Gulf Oil in terms of talks they're engaged in…Overall it's extremely frustrating, and it doesn't seem as though our government has much influence. The White House and State Department are lobbying Nigerian officials. I know that they've sent the deputy director of the NSC to Abuja. He should be there now. Other countries are applying pressure. Japan, France, the UK, Norway…But none of them seem to have made headway, as far as I know."

"I'm disappointed. Extremely disappointed. Many lives are still at stake."

"I know that, Crocker. Not to mention a several-hundred-million-dollar natural gas operation. But the terrorists have made their demands, and the Nigerian government has their reasons for not conceding. We'd probably do the same under similar conditions."

Crocker glanced at his watch. "According to what I just heard we're looking at a deadline that's about twelve hours away."

"That's correct. Midnight."

"Something has to be done to save the people inside."

"That's not up to us, Crocker. I hope you understand that. The Nigerians are sensitive to any kind of foreign intervention. They're also one of the top oil and gas producers in the world."

"You think I give a fuck about that?"

"Crocker!"

He gathered himself. "Sir, I'm with Colonel Nwosu now. I'm gonna debrief him and offer our services. Then I'll get back to you."

"I hope we understand each other, Crocker. Let's be absolutely clear on this… You're not to take any action on your own. Do you hear?"

"I hear you, sir."

"You're not to launch any kind of rescue operation into the plant without Nigerian government and White House approval."

"Colonel Nwosu is waiting."

"I can't tell you how happy I am to hear that you and Akil are safe and sound."

"Safe, yes, but not sound until we get our teammates out."

"Dammit, Crocker…"

"I'll be in touch."

Colonel Nwosu was feeling sorry for himself as he paced the narrow trailer. "They've put me in an impossible position, Chief. Absolutely impossible… If I could resign right now, I would. As soon as this nightmare is over, I'm going to retire and return to my farm. No more military or politics…"

Crocker finished the soup and set down the empty cup. "Colonel, I understand your distress. I feel it, too.

It's our job to focus on the challenges we face now. Maybe you're right, and the situation is near impossible. But you and I are going to change that."

The colonel grimaced and took another sip of scotch. "How? Are you a magician with a magic wand?"

"Colonel, I believe in myself, and my teammates, and the power of good over evil."

"Nice words...Very nice..."

Crocker got to his feet and stood in the colonel's path. "Let's agree to no more regrets about our situation. Let's accept the reality for what it is, sir, and figure out what we can do."

"You're an interesting man."

"Tell me what you've learned from surveillance, and from people who know the plant."

Colonel Nwosu shook his head. "It's not a good picture. It's confusing and incomplete."

"Let's see what you've got."

The colonel snapped his long fingers at a military aide and pointed to a stack of still pictures on a counter along a row of monitors. The uniformed aide brought them and set them on a little round table. Colonel Nwosu pointed to a chair and nodded to Crocker, who sat. The colonel examined the photos first.

"They're no good," he said with disgust. "It's the same poorly engineered drone that for two whole years couldn't locate the girls in the Sambisa Forest. Here..."

Crocker examined the surveillance photos using a magnifying glass provided by the aide. Indeed, many of them were out of focus, or partially cut off by a thick black bar, and all of them had been taken at high altitude. Still, with the use of the magnifier, he was able to identify some important features of the plant.

He gestured to Akil to join him. The colonel stood, gazing out a small rectangular window.

"You can tell their personnel concentrations by the placement of the technicals. Here, at the front gate…Here, around the expat dorms…And at the south end near the plant control room…"

"They're pretty spread out."

"I count six technicals…So we're probably looking at something like forty fighters."

"Yeah." Akil scratched the thick growth of beard on his chin. "Like I said before…they're very spread out."

"Only one technical at the front gate."

"The entire plant is probably rigged with explosives…"

"I saw some barrels before, but they're hard to make out," Crocker said, pointing to one of the clear photos of the expat dorms and plaza. "See.…"

Akil nodded. "Boss, I'm starting to get a picture…The tangos are smart. They've got no illusions that the government will concede to their demands, and are ready to blow up the entire plant."

"It appears that way, right?"

"And I don't think they're expecting a raid…Not the way they're spread out."

"Maybe not…"

Crocker looked up at the colonel, who was holding a tumbler of scotch. He asked, "Colonel, when were these taken?"

"Yesterday afternoon. Approximately 1600 hours."

"Where's the drone now?"

"It's at a base near here, being repaired. The navigation system isn't working."

"What kind of drone is it?" asked Akil.

"A Tsaigumi," the colonel answered.

Akil looked at Crocker and shrugged. Neither of them had ever heard of it.

"What's the likelihood you can deploy another, or get that one patched up and airborne?"

Colonel Nwosu groaned and shook his head.

At 1221 Saturday Festus Ratty Kumar twitched with excitement as he sat across from Umar Amine in the office of Building A. The two jihadists were discussing what action to take at midnight if and when the Nigerian government refused to meet their demands.

Umar Amine, a devout man, was prepared to blow up the plant and sacrifice himself and his men to the cause of jihad should the Nigerians not concede.

Festus had other ideas, which he expressed with almost delirious energy. "My brother…My good brother…This is the moment of opportunity. The sword of the Messenger is in our hands. The whole world is watching!"

Umar Amine frowned. Not only had his molars been bothering him all day, but Festus Ratty's reference to the Messenger Mohammad concerned him. He'd taken two Motrin for the tooth pain, and now he swallowed another with a swig of water mixed with vinegar, which he kept in a bottle tied to his belt.

Festus Ratty pointed to his head. "I receive messages, too. And the message I have received says there is a way to destroy the plant and punish the infidels, and outwit them at the same time."

"What are you talking about, brother?" Umar Amine asked.

"I'm talking about surviving this situation so we

can continue to fight the crusaders in the future. Allah wants that…Our alliance pleases him and our mission isn't over."

"Does he tell you how to achieve this?"

"He does…" Festus Ratty opened Google Maps on his laptop and zoomed in on southeastern Nigeria. "As you can see, Brother Umar, we're only forty kilometers from the Cameroon border. Forty kilometers is nothing!"

"Forty kilometers is forty kilometers."

"I know a path through the brush that will get us to the border quickly. They call me the Leopard, and I know this terrain like the back of my hand."

"Have you forgotten about the Nigerian soldiers who are probably surrounding us now? If you know the path, my brother, they'll know it, too."

"No, I haven't forgotten them. It's important, as we've discussed before, to know our enemies. And I know them."

"Of course."

Umar Amine remained skeptical of any of Festus Ratty's plans. It was hard to accept him as someone chosen by Allah. Instead, he clung to the belief that angels and beautiful virgins would be waiting for him near a fountain beyond the gates of heaven.

Mischief danced in Festus's eyes, his face and body animated as though possessed by a spirit. "Brother Amine…Oh, my brother…Here is the truth: when the plant explodes the Nigerian soldiers will be in shock. They'll be unprepared for what comes next."

"Maybe, maybe not."

Festus Ratty pointed to his forehead. "I can see these things unfolding…I've been granted this power. Once we set off the first explosions, the military will rush into the compound and try to rescue the hostages. They already have orders in place to do that…"

"How can you be sure?"

"I know…So we will deliberately spare the expat dorms so they think there is an opportunity to save the hostages there."

"And then what happens?"

Ratty's enthusiasm grew. "This is the most clever part, brother Amine. Listen carefully…" He pulled his chair to within inches of Amine for dramatic effect.

"We leave the compound a few minutes before the explosion, and we set it off remotely by phone…Our trucks are already painted to resemble Nigerian vehicles, and we're wearing army uniforms, so it will be confusing, yes? We leave through the gate behind the gas plant."

Umar Amine rubbed his jaw as he half-listened. The pain clouded his brain.

"The Nigerians will be confused. They won't be expecting that. We leave, they rush into the north side of the compound, and the explosions go off. Ka-boom! Everything is panic and chaos. Meanwhile, we're riding in our trucks toward the Cameroon border. I will even call some of my local fighters and get them to clear a path for us. It's brilliant, yes?"

"It's interesting…" Umar Amine said. He was a careful man who didn't like to jump into things unprepared. "What about the hostages? Will they all die in the explosion?"

Festus Ratty jumped to his feet. "No! We will take some of the hostages to use as bargaining chips, and eliminate the others before we leave!"

"Eliminate them?"

"Shoot them. Yes."

"And what happens when the Nigerians launch their airplanes and helicopters?"

"Brother, I am clever. Their closest base is Makurdi, which is at least fifteen to twenty minutes away by air. By the time they get here, we'll be across the border in Cameroon. And, if for some reason their planes arrive quicker, the land we'll be passing through is covered with trees."

"If their planes are in the air already, they will find us."

"And we have missiles that can shoot them down!"

CHAPTER TWENTY-THREE

"A wise person will always find a way."
—Tanzanian proverb

AT 1640, Crocker sat with Utorogu plant managers Alf Knutsen and Mark Greenway in a little schoolroom across from where the Eagle Mobile Military Command Post was parked. An energy bar in one hand, a can of Coke in the other, he listened as Greenway related the latest report from Gulf Oil headquarters, which was basically advising everyone to stand down.

They don't get it, he thought. *Standing down isn't an option. It cedes complete control to the terrorists, and that's not smart.*

Crocker saw Akil trying to get past the two soldiers guarding the door.

He shouted, "He's with us. Let him in." Then turning to Greenway, "Excuse me for interrupting."

His head hurt from all the confusing talk, his own exhaustion, and the many actors and moving parts. What he really wanted to do was get a consensus on a plan and start putting it into motion. But crisis moments like this were never easy. Fear, preconceived ideas, nerves, and limited options and resources always figured into the outcome. He knew that his goals had to be clear, and whatever action he chose to take to achieve them, he shouldn't expect support.

Akil whispered, "Spoke to CT. He says hoo-yah."

"He okay?"

Akil raised a thumb. "He's hanging in there."

"Tiny and Mancini?"

Akil shook his head.

Greenway repeated the message from Gulf, and Crocker frowned, thinking that he'd try Mancini again as soon as this was over. In a part of his brain, he'd been concerned about him the whole time. Knew that his longtime teammate hadn't been right since the action near the border.

Rubbing blood into his face, Crocker said, "I don't know what that means," when Greenway finished.

The red-haired American looked annoyed. "It means they're talking."

"Who's talking?"

"Gulf Oil company officials and the jihadists."

"The Gulf Oil official you spoke to said that?"

"Not in those exact words. But he implied it."

"Come on, Mark…People's lives are at stake. Things have to get more specific."

"It means Gulf is advising us to stand down and not interfere with whatever they've got under way. Why is that so hard to understand?"

Crocker sat on the impulse to go for Greenway's throat. Took a deep breath. "First thing…Don't ever speak to me like that again. Second, while you're speculating on what your bosses are or aren't doing, the terrorists are holding twenty hostages and there are another twenty or more very frightened people hiding inside the compound. Two of them are my teammates. Nobody's going to tell me not to interfere when I don't know what they're doing."

Greenway swallowed hard. "Like I said before… they're talking, they're negotiating. I assume that means that they're close to some kind of resolution."

"You assume?"

"Yes."

"I'll tell you the truth…I don't really give a fuck what Gulf Oil wants me to assume. My goal is to get every single one of the hostages out of there alive."

Greenway, his face red, rose to his feet and started to leave. Akil stopped him and pointed to a metal chair.

"Sit down."

Greenway obeyed.

Crocker continued, "I'm going to start making plans, and I'm going to press hard to get it done. You can cooperate if you want, or you can decide not to. That's up to you. But if you, or Gulf, or anyone else tries to get in my way, you'll have hell to pay. Make no mistake about that."

A kind of resigned monotony had set in. Tiny could see it on the faces of the terrorists and hostages alike. He'd seen it in the two leaders who occupied the office to his right, and strode out every twenty minutes or so, to go outside, or bark orders into their radios.

The energetic smaller man with the crazy eyes— who he'd named *Chingazo*—struck him as violent and unpredictable. The other taller, lighter-skinned man worried him more. He had the vacant look of either a psychopath, or someone who was resigned to some kind of violent, apocalyptic ending, or both.

Then suddenly a pale, spectacled terrorist hurried into the office as though he was carrying important news. He left an electric current of expectation that hung in the air.

Something's up.

Through the open front door, he saw the sky starting to darken. Tiny was exhausted, his mouth and throat were parched, and his empty stomach throbbed, but he still didn't think of his situation as hopeless.

I gotta keep looking for opportunities, he thought, aware that it might seem ridiculous given the fact that he wore a C4 necklace around his neck and had his wrists chained behind his back.

I've gotta be prepared for whatever comes.

It came as no surprise to Crocker that after the meeting Greenway stormed off and his fellow assistant plant manager Alf Knutsen offered to cooperate.

"He's not a bad person, really," the tall Norwegian explained. "None of us are used to handling this kind of pressure."

Akil removed the pretzel from his mouth and said, "I don't trust him."

Crocker was more diplomatic. "I get it. I've been in hostage situations before. I know that parties box themselves into corners, and things get weird as the clock ticks down. The important thing is not to lose sight of the human suffering of those caught in the middle."

"I respect that," opined Knutsen.

"Akil and I are going to need help."

Knutsen said, "I have some positive news in that regard. There are about a half dozen security officers from other Gulf facilities south who have volunteered to lend their services. Most of them know Moxie and Rufus and some served with them in the Royal Marines."

"Where are they now?"

"They're waiting in a town nearby. You want me to call them?"

"Please. Contact them now and ask them to meet us here a-sap. I'm going to set up shop in this room and start looking at contingencies."

"Does Colonel Nwosu know about this?"

"He knows we're exploring other options."

Knutsen swallowed so hard his teeth clicked together. "You're actually thinking of raiding the plant?"

"Yes."

"You think the Nigerians will help you?"

"Probably not."

"So how is your plan going to work?"

Crocker shook his head. "I don't know yet."

Akil saw the concerned look on the Norwegian's face. "Nothing's impossible."

"I'm not sure why I'm saying this, but I believe you...What can I do to help?"

Crocker started to compose a list. "We're gonna need weapons, ammo, radios, grenades, smoke bombs, explosives, armored vests, flares, cell phone and radio jamming equipment, and a very detailed schematic of the plant. I'm sure there's more...We're also going to need your ideas and guidance on how to gain entrance to the control room, and how to turn off the gas."

"I'll do my best."

Akil said, "Part of the plan is to get out alive."

The Norwegian grinned. "Of course."

"There's a beautiful woman staying in an inn nearby and I plan to make love to her later tonight," added Akil.

"I understand."

CT was on the phone with Crocker. Saw Sally standing at the window, peering through the closed blinds toward the front of the building.

Whispered, "You see something?"

She turned and shook her head. "Just darkness."

"Where's Pagon?" CT asked, referring to the French manager who had been hiding with them.

Sally answered, "He's across the hall watching the back of the building."

"Good." Then CT turned his attention to Crocker on the phone. "Sorry, boss."

"Everything stable?"

"Yes."

Crocker asked about CT's specific location in terms of access to the plant control room, how he was armed, and his physical condition.

After CT answered his questions, he asked, "What's the plan?"

Crocker hesitated, then remembered the satellite phone was encrypted so the terrorists couldn't be listening. "We're gonna strike around midnight, and we're gonna need your help. I'll call with specifics later. Let me know immediately if anything changes in or around the plant."

"Roger that."

Chichima's dorm room was dark except for the little pool of light from her reading lamp. One of her three roommates snored gently in the bunk below. The book that had been assigned for her literature class—*Beloved* by Toni Morrison—lay open in front of her. Even though the story of Sethe held many parallels to her own, Chichima had a hard time relating.

Her memories weren't filled with longing and regret like Sethe's were in the book. Hers burned with intensity to the point that her brain felt like it was about to explode and her entire forehead was on fire. The experience in the Sambisa had become part of her and would never go away. Nor did she feel any need to deny it, or feel sorry for herself, or turn herself into an object of pity.

Why? What do I care what journalists or anyone else thinks of me? Where were they when my friends and I were being held in captivity?

So little of what she had experienced fit into other people's narratives. It was hers and she embraced it and wanted to learn from her experience. If other people expected her to think of herself as a victim, and act like one, she wouldn't. She didn't feel that way.

Her parents had taught her that the real world is what it is. Sometimes it was violent and unpredictable. The role of an honest person was to try to understand it. And maybe out of that understanding could come positive change.

Chichima burned with energy as she lay in the dark. She felt the souls of her ancestors stir around her.

She didn't want to be imprisoned, coddled, or protected the way she was now.

Longing to connect with someone, she closed the book and opened her laptop and started searching. Gossip and beauty tips didn't interest her. When she reached the Vanguard news site, she read for the first time about the crisis in Utorogu, and connected immediately with the terror and hopelessness the hostages were experiencing there.

Once again, it sounded as though the government was making excuses and being passive. Journalists and citizens were standing apart and watching like viewers of a motorcar race or circus.

Compelled to at the very least express her frustration, Chichima logged in to the popular Nigerian social media website Nairaland.com and wrote the following:

My fellow Nigerians...My name is Chichima and I'm one of what are popularly known as the Sambisa girls. Yes, I was one of the many schoolgirls who were held as slaves and hostages of Boko Haram.

As I read now about the crisis at the Utorogu gas plant, all my feelings of anger, frustration, and hopelessness return again. Once again our government and our military claim that they are unable to take action to free the hostages! They said the same when me and my fellow schoolmates were being raped and brainwashed in the Sambisa Forest.

My fellow citizens...When are we going to say that this is unacceptable? When are we going to make our voices heard and remind our government and our military that their primary responsibility is to protect the people who live and work in Nigeria?

When are we going to make them realize that
people—living, breathing people, whether poor
and disenfranchised or rich and politically
powerful—are more important than principles or
ideas?

When ideas become more valued than people, all
of us become irrelevant. Petition the government
to free the hostages at Utorogu! Make your voices
heard!

"It's like trying to raid an army base with a can
opener," cracked one of the British Gulf security
officers.

"That's why we have to be creative and as precise
as we possibly can." Crocker glanced at the clock over
the blackboard at the front of the room, which was
covered with a map of the plant. It read 1943 local
time—a little more than four hours from the terrorists' deadline.

"And willing to take bloody insane risks," another
of the Brits offered.

They sat in a tight cluster snacking on sunflower
seeds and water. All six were heavily tattooed and
had bulging muscles, which qualified them as work-
out warriors. Crocker didn't know what they had to
offer in terms of operational prowess. His brain was so
shredded with exhaustion that he was having trouble
remembering their names.

"Risk is good," Akil said, challenging them with his
eyes.

"Whatever, mate…"

"I'm serious."

Crocker cleared his throat. His voice had turned hoarse. "Any of you guys familiar with the plant?"

Two of them pointed to a colleague slumped in his chair, arms crossed over his chest and a black Maserati hat pulled over his eyes.

"Reg spent six months in Utu...Yo, Reg, wake up!"

He snorted awake and his colleagues chuckled.

Crocker thought as time pressed him, *This is like herding cats.*

The compact guy in the Maserati hat sat up. Had the build of a wrestler—thick torso, short arms and legs. "Sorry, mate. Got zero sleep last night. What'd you ask?"

"I hear you know the plant."

"Yeah, yeah, Chief...I worked with Moxie, Rufus, and the mates...A year and a half. That's the reason I'm here. You think there's a chance any of them are still alive?"

Crocker shook his head. "Sadly...no."

Reg kicked the empty chair in front of him so that it slid across the floor and hit the wall. "Bloody fucking bollocks!" Then quickly composed himself. "What's the question?"

"We're trying to figure out where the hostages are being held...and working on the assumption that the majority of them are gathered in the same location."

"Yeah...Yeah. Sounds about right."

"Our informed guess at this point is that they're located in the expat dorms."

"Yeah, mate. Makes sense."

"What can you tell us about the two towers?"

Reg sat up, removed the hat, and scratched his

head, which was covered with short sandy-colored hair.

"Towers? Hardly...Both three stories...Kind of a bland grayish aluminum siding."

The biggest of the six Brits cut in. Tall good-looking guy with tribal tats running up both arms. "Don't be daft, Reg. Like anyone gives two shits about the décor."

"Up yours, Potter..." he said, then, turning back to Crocker, "Entrances fore and aft. Zero fortification if that's what you're asking. In other words, common as dirt...Made by a company called Alibaba...Prefab...I was there when they went up. About twelve rooms each floor with two bathrooms and showers."

"Good. Continue..."

"Building A, the one closest to the gate, has an office and large lobby-slash-reception room on the first floor. Very basic. Several steps down from a Marriott....Sucks about Scott and the mates."

"And the other building?"

Potter said softly, "Focus, Reg."

"I'm trying...Building B. A little entrance on the first floor, and a steam room, and rec area with lockers on the second."

It matched Captain Sutter's description of the area where Mancini was hiding.

"So the only place that could accommodate twenty-some hostages would be the lobby of Building A?"

"Yeah, Chief. That's correct."

"Okay, Reg. That's good...Very good. We're making progress."

When Crocker looked up from the notes he was taking, he saw Alf Knutsen standing in the door holding a satellite phone.

"Who is it?" Crocker asked.

"Your commander."

"Find out what he wants."

"He says it's an emergency. He needs to talk to you now."

CHAPTER TWENTY-FOUR

"War has no eyes."
—Swahili proverb

TINY SAW three of the terrorists—Pinche, Coñazo, and the dark-skinned leader he'd nicknamed Chingado—standing over Mancini slumped against the wall to his left. They fed him water from a plastic bottle, then emptied the rest over his head.

Chingado stepped back and laughed. Tiny wanted to carve him a new one, but was more concerned about Manny and his condition. Prayed he'd hold on. When the terrorists backed away, he saw his big teammate breathing and sitting up.

Filled him with hope. He'd always admired Manny, how he conducted himself in the teams, constantly fed his brain, appreciated his family, and enjoyed life. Now if he could only get some sign of recognition from him, he wouldn't feel so alone. But the skin around his teammate's eyes was so badly swollen, Tiny wasn't sure he could see.

Noticed the other jihadist leader, who he'd dubbed Aaron because of his resemblance to the former NFL player and convicted murderer Aaron Hernandez, waving from the office door.

Chingado joined him, and the slight terrorist with the round glasses popped his head out. Then Aaron whispered something to Chingado and the three men entered the office and closed the door behind them.

What the fuck is going on?

Tiny focused on the watch on Pinche's wrist, halfway across the room. Made out the space between the hands at the top. Seeing the narrow strip of white between them, decided that it was almost 2300.

Said to himself: *Something's up.*

Crocker was trying his best to temper his anger. People removed from the field almost never understood the full emotional dimension of things on the ground.

They tended to see crises through the lenses of policy and strategic goals. The policy that distorted their vision now was the US and Nigerian governments' refusal to negotiate with terrorists.

Crocker understood the reasoning behind it. But public policy and behind-the-scenes negotiations were separate in his mind.

Captain Sutter had just informed him that Gulf Oil officials were talking to the terrorists and close to reaching a deal.

"They're in direct communication?" Crocker asked through the satellite phone.

"Yes, and have been for some time."

"Why are the terrorists talking to them, and not us?"

"Because it's their plant, and their employees," responded Sutter. "I don't see why it matters."

"Because Gulf has their interests, and we've got ours."

"They're the same, Crocker!"

"How do we know if we're not even part of the conversation?"

"It's not your business… This is positive news. I expected you to take it that way."

Crocker was trying hard not to let his emotions get in the way. "Have you heard the specific terms?"

"No. Not yet."

"We've got less than an hour."

"I'm well aware of that."

"Akil and I are standing by. We've recruited a half-dozen volunteers, and we're ready to take the plant if needed."

"With eight men? Are you insane?"

"No."

Sutter exhaled deeply on the other end. "Crocker, I've always admired your courage and determination. But now we're dealing with a very fluid, volatile situation. Things could change at the last minute. The important thing to understand is that you're not to do anything without Nigerian military approval."

"We can't anyway, so no need to worry."

"Are we clear about that, Crocker?"

"Yes, sir."

"Better yet, why don't you and Akil get some rest and let the Nigerians handle this?"

"That's impossible."

"Why?"

"Neither one of us will be able to sleep until our teammates and the rest of the hostages are safe."

Inside the office of Building A, Abu Abbas, Umar Amine, and Festus Ratty sat around the desk, waiting for a call from Victor Balt. Forty minutes ago, Abu Abbas had conveyed the news that Gulf Oil–Holland had agreed to wire $40 million into Balt's numbered UAE bank account if the Written in Blood terrorists abandoned the plant and left all the national gas pumping and processing equipment undamaged.

The terrorists had also been promised safe passage to Cameroon.

Now the three jihadists were waiting for confirmation from Victor Balt that the money had arrived in the escrow account.

Festus Ratty was the only one of the three who didn't seem pleased. He said, "I don't trust the Westerners. Never will."

Umar Amine nodded as he rubbed his jaw. "Me neither."

Now Abu Abbas spoke. "Balt said that once the money is released from the UAE escrow account, he will quickly move it to other secure accounts that can't be touched. He knows his business."

"When will it be released?" Festus Ratty asked.

"Midnight. Balt will let us know."

Festus Ratty shook his head. He still had doubts. "What prevents the Nigerians from attacking us as we leave?"

Umar Amine winced from the pain in his mouth. "They double-cross us, we can always destroy the plant remotely using a cell signal."

Abbas said, "Part of the deal with Gulf is that we turn off the flow of gas before we leave. They will be able to confirm that from the burn-off stacks."

"We can always detonate the other explosives."

"And," Festus Ratty suggested, "we can take as many hostages as we can hold in our trucks to serve as human shields."

"I like that idea. But what do we do with them

when we reach the Cameroon border?" Umar Amine asked.

"Whatever we want."

"We can use them for propaganda purposes," Abu Abbas suggested. "Then we either release them or sell them back to the Westerners."

Umar Amine started to smile, but the pain from his teeth stopped him.

Festus Ratty waved his arms vigorously. "No, no, brother...I have a better idea. We shoot them. We kill all the hostages as a final 'fuck you' to the infidels!"

Umar Amine frowned as though he objected. But before he could express anything, the phone rang.

Abu Abbas answered in English, "Yes."

The other jihadists' eyes locked on him as he listened.

Half a minute later, Abu Abbas said politely, "Thank you," and hung up the phone.

"That was Victor. He says the deal is done. The money is ours!"

"All $40 million?" asked Umar Amine.

"Yes."

Festus Ratty shouted in triumph and the three men embraced and danced around the room like schoolkids, shouting "Allahu Akbar!" over and over.

At 2311 hours, Colonel Nwosu remained in the Mobile Command Center twelve kilometers outside the plant. He'd recently showered and changed from his uniform into a blue Puma warm-up suit he'd received for his birthday. Now he was sipping broth out of a coffee mug and cursing Gulf Oil officials under his breath. Crocker sat, hands grasped in front of him on an upholstered bench.

"Colonial attitudes never change, my friend... They're so deeply entrenched in the European mindset they aren't even aware..."

"I believe you, Colonel," Crocker said. "But I'm worried about the hostages. Based on what you've told me about the agreement, the disposition of the hostages isn't clear."

"No, Chief. It's not clear. Nothing is clear except the orders I have from my government to cooperate with the agreement, and to guarantee the terrorists safe passage to Cameroon once they leave the plant."

"Then what happens?" Crocker asked.

"It's out of our hands. The Cameroons will not cooperate with us, so there's nothing to discuss."

"Are you sure there's nothing in the agreement that is more specific about the hostages?"

Colonel Nwosu picked up a printout from in front of the monitors and handed it to Crocker. "Here... Read it yourself."

Crocker read:

Written in Blood agrees to relinquish control of the Utorogu Gas Plant and leave the entire gas pumping and processing plant and its assets intact, and abandon it by 0001 Sunday. In return, Gulf Oil–Holland agrees to transfer $xx,xxx,xxx to a secure numbered account provided by the representative of Written in Blood, and the Nigerian government promises the safe passage of Written in Blood commandos across the Cameroon border. At that point all hostages still under Written in Blood's control will be released.

Crocker let the document fall to the floor and shook his head. "This assumes the terrorists are taking some of the hostages with them."

"Yes."

"What's to prevent them from killing them once they reach Cameroon?"

"I wasn't consulted. I don't know."

"The money has already been transferred?"

"That's my understanding. Yes."

Crocker squeezed his head between his hands. "This is a disaster."

"I'm ashamed to say that some officials in my government have probably accepted money for their compliance. And, then, there's this…"

Colonel Nwosu removed another document from the counter and handed it to Crocker. It was a printout of the blog Chichima had posted on Nairaland.com.

"What about it?"

"Look at the number of likes. More than two million in less than three hours. My government won't be pleased about this, either. They're going to be looking for someone to blame."

Crocker got a little satisfaction when he recognized the name as one of the rescued schoolgirls he had recently seen at Yola.

He said, "Colonel, the agreement seems to assume that at least some of the hostages are going to die, one way or another. You realize that, don't you?"

The two men's eyes met, and Colonel Nwosu slowly nodded, *yes*.

"Will you allow me and my men to pass through your lines and raid the plant and free the hostages before the terrorists leave?"

"I'm sorry, Chief, but that's impossible. The

terrorists will blow the plant sky high and everyone will die."

"What if we promise to disarm the terrorists' explosives before we attack the plant?"

"How the hell will you do that?"

Crocker ran from the Mobile Command Post to the schoolhouse across the street where Akil and the six Brits were checking their gear, and Alf Knutsen, Eito, and Kazumi waited to lend their assistance.

"What's up?" Akil answered.

Crocker crossed straight over to the corner where Knutsen was standing, talking on a cell, and grabbed him by the shoulders.

"I need you to get your hands on a cell and radio jammer immediately!"

Knutsen terminated the call and slipped the phone into his pocket.

"Where?"

"I have no idea. But I need one! It's critical."

Knutsen consulted with Eito and Kazumi and the three men tore off.

It was 2347 and CT had moved to another office down the hall, which afforded him a view of the gas burn-off towers. He carried the satellite phone and was followed by Sally. Both were armed with AR-15s.

Crocker spoke calmly over the phone. "What do you see?"

"I see the burn-off flames are still burning. And I can see two armed terrorists standing guard on a concrete wall outside the control room."

"Only two? Are you sure?"

"Yes, that's all I can see. Two."

"Any technicals or other terrorists nearby?"

"The technicals moved north about ten minutes ago."

"Perfect. Hurry back to your hiding place and call me as soon as you get back."

Three minutes later, CT called from the office in 50 Main.

Crocker got right to it. "CT, this is a review of what is about to happen…In a few minutes the burn-off flames will go out when the central gas-fed pipeline is turned off. Seconds later, one or more terrorists will leave the control room and two British snipers are going to take them out as well as any guards in the vicinity. Then you and the two Brits will make a mad dash for the control room."

Crocker didn't explain that the gas was being turned off by the jihadists according to the terms of the agreement they had reached with Gulf Oil. He was adhering to need-to-know.

CT said, "Got it, boss. The two Brits will know I'm coming?"

"They've been briefly about you, yes."

"I will have a volunteer with me. An Irish woman named Sally. The third person with us has elected to stay here."

"Sally know what she's getting herself involved in?"

"I believe so."

"She know how to handle a gun?"

"She does."

"Then thank her for me. And make sure you carry the sat phone. The second you reach the control room, call me. Cell phones won't be working."

"Will do."

"Hold the control room and don't move until we

get there. We're hitting the other end of the plant first, so it might take time."

"Godspeed, boss."

"Godspeed."

Tiny was trying to stay focused in spite of the nervous exhaustion and thirst that were messing with his head. The amalgam of signs the last fifteen minutes had raised set off all kinds of alarms. First the shouts of *Alluhu Akbar,* and the terrorists high-fiving one another in celebration, then the nauseating smile of triumph on Pinche's face.

He had wanted to see them as a positive development that would lead to their release. But whatever hope he had was quickly dashed by more kicks, punches, and slaps from the terrorists, who were now dragging the American and European hostages— Zoe, Berit, Mancini, and others—to the front of the room. Some of them appeared barely alive.

He was next.

"Where are you taking us?" he asked Pinche, who stood over him.

"Disneyland…" the terrorist answered, pulling him by the ear.

Outside on the driveway, Pinche held him, while Coñazo removed the C4 collar from around Tiny's neck.

"You treat your wife this way, too?"

Another punch to the face and more stars circling in his head. And when he saw clearly again, he realized he was being dragged toward one of the trucks where more armed men were waiting. Beyond his right shoulder other terrorists were using hand trucks to move barrels of what he assumed were gasoline or explosives into the building. There were more than a dozen hostages still inside.

Are they going to blow it up and kill the rest of the people inside?

It didn't make sense.

What about us? Where are they taking us?

Things were happening so fast it was hard for Tiny's brain to keep up. Saw Mancini, still bare-chested and swollen, being dragged to the back of one of the technicals. Zoe and the little blond woman with the swollen ankle followed. Both looked to be in varying states of shock.

They don't deserve this…

He so badly wanted to stop one of the terrorists and ask for an explanation. Two jihadists he'd never seen before picked him up from under his arms and carried him past the driveway to a grassy patch in front of the building and before the road that ran along the fence. Another woman and a man with longish blond hair joined him.

The night air caressed his face. Birds cawed in the distance.

Tiny turned to the man on his left, and whispered, "You have any idea why they put us here?"

The man's eyes never stopped staring at the ground. Tiny got the impression that he was afraid to answer.

CHAPTER TWENTY-FIVE

*"You must act as though it is impossible
to fail."*

—African proverb

AT **2352,** CT watched through the 50 Main windows as the twin burn-off flames shut off. He stood and, squinting through the shadows around Sally's face, said, "Wait here with Paul."

"Hell with that... I'm coming with you."

Outside, everything had turned dark, which caused him concern at first, because he couldn't locate the Brit snipers. A heartbeat later he heard suppressed sniper shots, and figured the guns were equipped with night-vision scopes. Gave him hope.

We can pull this off... I know we can... Crocker thinks of everything.

He was halfway down the grassy embankment to the fence that separated the gas processing facility from the rest of the compound, when he realized that he hadn't been on his feet for almost twenty-four hours. A second later, his legs gave out and he fell and tumbled three or four meters until he crashed into the fence. Knocked the air out of him.

Sally helped him up.

Before he could whisper "thanks," he saw sparks flying out of the barrel of a gun close by and pulled her down with him onto the ground. Prayed the shooters were friendly.

Took a deep breath, and somehow managed his way over the fence and up a set of concrete steps. Stepped around a body, then realized he'd dropped the sat phone near the fence. Six feet from the entrance, he was about to turn back, when he saw a flash directly in front of him, and heard Sally grunt in pain.

Still only partially conscious and with no time to raise his rifle, he flung himself at the dark shape that was shooting. Caught him just below the waist the way his high school coach had taught him. His body moving automatically, he spun, locked his massive right forearm around his neck, and squeezed hard.

Heard the crack of the jihadist's thorax, pushed the limp body away, and looked for Sally. Saw shapes against an instrument panel in the dark room ahead, and Sally, on her knees, leaning against the right side of the door.

Whispered, "What happened?"

Sally whispered back, "Duck," and lifted the AR-15 and fired past his ear to someone in the darkest part of the room.

He heard a man groan. Then flashlight beams crisscrossed the floor and lit up the faces of two frightened-looking engineers, their faces covered with several days' growth of beard.

"Don't shoot…Please," he said with a Scandinavian accent.

Heard someone with an East London accent ask, "We okay here?"

"I think so…Yeah."

Hands helped him up. Saw Sally behind him still leaning against the door. A big man with a sniper rifle was holding her up.

As he caught his breath, CT asked, "You okay?"

"Got hit near the elbow," answered Sally. "I'll live."

"Let me see."

Saw that it was a pass-through just below the joint. Removed his belt and used it as a tourniquet.

Then he remembered and said, "Wait here. I've got to get the phone."

Soon as Akil received the radio call from Crocker, he gunned the yellow school bus the Nigerians had provided down the road to the gate. Stopped inches away, high beams on, motor running. Two surprised terrorists in Nigerian military uniforms hurried to the driver's-side window, poking their AKs in his face and chest, shouted:

"Puo!" (Get out!) "Kedu ihe i choro?" (What do you want?) "Aka elu!" (Hands up!)

He did as they said, and spoke back in Arabic. Threw in some *Allahu Akbar*s every so often.

The jihadists seemed confused not only by his speech, but also by the fact that he looked Middle Eastern and was dressed in black and wore a black bandana around his head.

One of them pressed an AK into Akil's chest, while the other reached for his handheld radio. Neither of them saw the two Brits who had snuck out of the back emergency door of the bus and now took them down with suppressed fire from their MP5s.

Nor did they know that concealed under one of the bus seats was a very high-powered cell and radio jammer with a range of three hundred meters, which was capable of isolating and jamming signals from all countries.

"Well done," Akil whispered to the Brits, his face and chest spattered with blood and more blood streaming from his nose.

They pumped more rounds in the terrorists to make sure they were dead. Then one of them pointed at the blood and asked, "That yours or theirs?"

"Both."

Akil used the bottom of his tee to wipe it away, and retrieved an MP5 with suppressor and RPG from the side storage compartment of the bus.

"I've got a date later. Let's do this quick!"

They scanned the area for more terrorists, then took up positions behind a concrete guard pylon. Saw some technicals speeding toward them.

"Here they come, mate!"

"Hoo-yah!"

Crocker was seventy meters away on the other side of the security fence in back of Building A when he saw the headlights at the gate and gave the order.

"Go!"

Reg and Potter held the wire fences open for Kazumi and Eito. Crocker followed them through the same holes they had exited through the night before.

Sensed then that he'd return, and here he was, flying on adrenaline, hurrying up the loose dirt incline, MP5N in his right hand, RPG slung over his shoulder, grenades, rockets, mags, a Glock, and a sheathed SOP knife tucked into his belt and vest.

He led the way to the back of Building A. In his periphery saw three technicals speeding toward the gate. Stopped and went to his knees, waved the other guys past him. Quickly loaded a rocket into the RPG and aimed for the explosives he had previously seen clustered under the ramp to the dining hall, aided now by the headlights of the first technical speeding toward it.

Hands shaking, the first rocket missed.

Focus, fuckhead...

Took a deep breath and steadied himself. *Whoosh!*

The second rocket hit inches in front of the barrels, and the resulting explosion ignited the gasoline inside and sent a column of fire rocketing thirty meters into the sky. Spectacular and eerie. Lit the entire north side of the compound and tossed two of the technicals against the far fence, their headlights still on. Seconds later one of them erupted in flames.

Akil, you can thank me later...

Before Crocker realized what he was doing, he was already back on his feet and halfway up the steps at the back of Building A. Ran right past Kazumi and Eito, positioned where they were supposed to be on either side of the door, and almost smacked into two terrorists hurrying out of the building.

One of them pulled his trigger, sprayed a volley of bullets in the floor and walls. The flash burned the right side of Crocker's face and a ricochet grazed his left triceps. He managed to hold on to his MP5 and knock the terrorist back and off his feet with a suppressed blast directly into his chest. Eito nailed the second one in the neck, blood spurting everywhere. Finished the terrorists off with a Mozambique—two center mass, then one to the head.

"You hit?" Eito whispered.

Both of them panting on either side of him.

"Let's go..."

He signaled forward, leading the way down the hall toward the ground floor lobby.

The blood kept flowing from Akil's nose, which he figured was broken. Spit the mess out of his mouth and kept firing at the one technical that continued toward them. His face throbbing, thinking he wouldn't be doing any kissing later, all he saw was dust and headlights. The 12.7x108mm rounds from the heavy DShK machine gun were tearing up the concrete pylon, making it hard to aim or even raise his head.

Reg had already been blinded by concrete dust to the eyes. Was growling, "Can't see fuck-all!"

"Stop whining…"

"Bugger off."

The truck kept bearing down on them. Was so close it was running out of room to maneuver with a guardhouse and other structures to the right. It was either going to crash into the barrier they were hiding behind or veer sharply left.

When it was within five meters, the driver did the latter so abruptly that the gunner in the back bed manning the DShK flew out like a projectile and crashed against the fence. The truck itself spun out of control and flipped over.

Akil growled, "Last man to the dorm pays for drinks!"

Tiny didn't care that he had shit his pants. What he had witnessed so far had to be the greatest spectacle of his life. First, headlights at the gate, then the three technicals that had been parked in the driveway in front of Building A speeding off. Then the bluish-white trail of rockets launched from behind the dorm, followed by a huge explosion. Now two of the technicals disabled, and one of them burning like a torch by the fence.

It was like watching the coolest action movie imaginable and wanting to jump out of your seat and cheer. But in Tiny's situation he had his ankles wired together and his wrists chained behind his back.

Scooted to his right to get a better vantage. Now facing Building A at three o'clock. Saw another technical speeding south. Manny and the other dozen hostages looking scared and vulnerable huddled together on the concrete driveway where the terrorists had just left them. More jihadists clambered aboard the two remaining technicals parked between Buildings A and B.

Tiny hoped that whatever force had hit the front gate was big and well-armed, because more enemy firepower was coming at them. He had no idea the attackers consisted of Akil and two Brits.

Then Tiny spotted two figures moving in the dark shadows between Buildings A and B. Couldn't tell who they were at first, even when the reflection of the fire lit up their faces. Saw them drop to their knees, lift RPGs onto their shoulders, and line up the technicals in their sights.

He nearly passed out with excitement. Then realized he was almost directly behind the line of fire. Lowered his head and fell right as rockets hit the trucks and exploded in front of him. Was so hyped up on adrenaline that he was hardly bothered when shards of hot shrapnel burned into his shoulders, neck, and chest.

From the ground, Tiny saw the column of flames and heard terrorists' screams.

Fucking awesome!

Pushed himself up in a sitting position and beheld what to him was a thing of beauty: the two men with camouflage paint on their faces finishing off panicked jihadists. Then bullets ripping into the grass around him. Farther left, he spotted a crazed terrorist with a burning uniform running toward him, AK blazing.

Fuck this…

Eyes shut tight, every part of his body clenched, he expected a bullet to enter him next. Heard a gun discharge nearby, and bid goodbye to Eleena.

Until we meet again…

Nothing happened. When he found the courage to open his eyes again, spotted an Asian man at the door holding an MP5, and a terrorist face-planted three meters away.

Nix that, sweetheart, I'm coming home!

Crocker burst into the big ground floor room like a bolt of lightning. All the pent-up anger and frustration of the last several days poured forth as he picked out targets. A terrorist kneeling in a corner. A terrorist hiding behind a planter. Another holding a hostage by the hair. Down, down, down!

A jihadist aiming an RPG at one of the barrels near the front of the room. Fired and nearly took his head off. He was pissed, and filled with more ferocious energy than his body could contain.

Needed to let it out. And didn't need more than a split-second glance and a sniff to measure the degradation the hostages had suffered. One big one with a gray face looked at him wide-eyed and grinned sideways.

Nodded back. Saw that Kazumi and Eito had already exited out the front.

Brave men.

He heard peals of automatic fire. Then spotted someone leaning out of the office and aiming at Kazumi and Eito's backs. Before his brain warned him not to, Crocker raised the RPG, and fired across the room still half-filled with stunned hostages. The resulting explosion obliterated the office doorway, the terrorist standing in it, and bit out a section of the wall. Also sent flying a little piece of concrete that landed in his mouth.

Temporarily deaf and half blinded by the dust and smoke, he spit out the concrete and crossed to the office. Entered firing his compact MP5N at moving targets.

CT heard the distant battle from the inside of the control room as he searched the drawers for painkillers. The two Brits—Chase and Pete—kept guard out front while he was served as de facto medic to Sally and the two engineers. She had sustained a minor gunshot wound to her forearm and a sprained knee, and both engineers were suffering from blinding headaches.

No ibuprofen, but he did locate bottles of water in a closet near where the terrorists' bodies were bleeding out.

He was wondering when he would hear from Crocker when Chase leaned in the entrance, and said, "CT, we need your help."

"Coming…"

Quickly handed out the water, grabbed his AR-15 and hurried outside. Found Chase and Pete standing behind the concrete wall at the top of the steps watching a pair of headlights approach.

"Friendly?"

"No. Looks like we've got unwanted company, mate."

CT saw the outlines of the big gun in back. Whether it was a DShK or a 50mm, he knew they had no way to stop it. No grenades or RPGs. All they had arms-wise were a couple AR-15 automatics, two M2010 sniper rifles, and pistols.

Chase said, "We need you and the lady to hold the fort, while we scurry up the right."

"You cool with that?"

CT saw that the right embankment would give them a better vantage. "Go for it, bros."

The Brits tore off, running down the steps. Once the big gun was in range it started firing. Tore up the fixtures and wall behind him, showering dust and glass over his head and shoulders. Sally came hobbling out with her rifle.

"Down! Get down, all the way to your belly."

CT knew that if terrorists regained the control room, the entire mission and compound were in jeopardy. And if they hit the plant with a missile, they'd all be blown to hell.

Through a drainage slit at the base of the wall he made out the silhouettes of the Brits climbing up the embankment on their hands and knees, M2010 sniper rifles slung over their backs.

In his mind, he urged them to move faster. Understanding that they needed cover, he squirmed on his stomach to the first step, lined up the technical between the three dots of his Trijicon night sight, and squeezed the trigger.

Managed to knock out one of the headlights at forty meters. The truck skidded to a thirty-degree angle and stopped. Then the big gun started up again.

Sally shouted, "What do you want me to do?"

"Stay down. Take out anyone approaching the fence."

He was already halfway through the thirty-round mag, and had one more in his back pocket.

Bam-bam-bam…

The 12.7x108mm rounds were so powerful they were ripping through the wall. CT scurried to the bottom of the steps, saw the Brits prone to his right, then the *pft, pft, pft* of their sniper guns, followed by shattering of glass. The DShK went silent.

Brilliant!

A small moment of triumph, then a strong light from the technical lit up the incline and the half-dozen terrorists opened up on the Brits.

Run!

The Brits were exposed and dashing for cover. He saw a bullet rip into the back of Pete's leg. He stopped. Chase turned back to help him. Then the DShK started up again.

CT raised his head above the wall and fired, aiming at the side of the Toyota Hilux, praying one of his bullets would find the gas tank. Ran through the mag in his rifle. Ducked down, removed the spent mag, and slammed in his last. Moved right and came up shooting again.

Didn't see the two terrorists who had entered the fence to his left. A bullet tore into the skin behind his left hip, and he kept focus, aiming and firing. Hit the jihadist behind the big gun, then saw the first flicker of flame.

"Sally! Left!"

Another round glanced off his AR, and tore a ribbon into his right forearm. The weapon jammed.

Sally was unloading at the terrorists less than ten meters away.

They screamed "Allahu Akbar!" and returned fire. It was hell with terrorists closing in, and CT reaching for his pistol, only to find that his right arm had lost strength because the bullet had torn into his extensor muscles.

Heard Chase shout, "Bloody bastards!"

Then a flash from the truck and a split-second later, the deafening boom of the vehicle's gas tank exploding.

Rounds from Crocker's MP5N raked the tallest of the terrorists across the chest. Saw a weird look of satisfaction as he folded to the floor. Was processing dozens of impressions when a second man screamed from the cloud of smoke and dust to his right, and came at him shrouded in white powder, firing a pistol. Two rounds embedded in Crocker's armored vest and knocked him back.

He stumbled, and held himself up against the wall to keep from falling. His finger had never felt the trigger of the MP5N, and now he squeezed off a salvo at eight hundred rounds a minute, cutting the terrorist's legs out from under him. Completely shredded his knees so that he collapsed in a heap and writhed in agony.

The room spun off-kilter. Crocker needed a few seconds to steady himself. Heard movement and shattering glass, and saw a third man crash through the window.

Where the fuck did he come from?

Screaming, blood dripping down his arm and chest, Crocker climbed out after him.

Festus Ratty was already halfway up the embankment and a third of the way to the port-o-cabins. Half conscious, his brain in a muddle, he wasn't thinking about how the infidels had betrayed them or whether Umar Amine and Abu Abbas were dead.

As he ran, he imagined the shock he was about to bring to the world, and remembered the lyrics from his boy Vector: "I'm gonna spray to the end of the game…Kill everything in my way."

He imagined he was starring in his own music video, gun in hand and every inch the gangster, creating space between himself and the big man behind him.

"Turn a body to a spirit…I'm sick dope enough to go against the world…"

Crocker aimed at the dark shape near Cabin 3 and squeezed the trigger only to realize that he was out of ammo. Threw the MP5 aside and reached for the Glock in his waistband.

Where the fuck did he go?

Acrid smoke from the smoldering technical thirty meters away burned his eyes. Heard the diminutive terrorist laughing like a hyena and hit the ground. Bullets sailed over his head and tore into the side of Building A behind him.

It wasn't hard to intuit what the jihadist was planning to do next—set off the barrels of explosives Crocker had spotted previously between Cabins 3 and 2. He knew they contained more than enough firepower to obliterate them both and probably level Building A, as well.

No time to call for help, or wait to catch his breath even though he felt his body running out of energy, probably from the loss of blood.

Saw a dark shape move around the back of Cabin 3. Maneuvered with such fluidity that he thought it was a large animal at first. Willed himself up to his feet. Legs wobbling, he moved as fast as his body would take him across the gap between the two prefab structures, pistol in his right, his chest heaving and burning. Couldn't find the terrorist in the golden glow of the burning technical.

Where is he now?

Rubbed his eyes, blinked, and spotted a figure in a half crouch near the barrels at the side of Cabin 2.

No…

He raised the Glock and squeezed off a volley of shots, but his hand was shaking so hard they sailed over the terrorist's head. The click of the empty chamber made him realize he was out of rounds again.

Festus Ratty took a moment to look up at the sky and locate the brightest star he could find—Sirius, aka Canis Majoris.

He called out loud, "Allah knows best!" and removed the grenade from his belt.

Crocker saw a strange blue light issue from the jihadist's hand. Alarmed and fascinated, he watched the jihadist hold up the grenade for him to see, his face and the grenade bathed in blue light as a final, eerie "fuck you."

Winced when the jihadist, grinning ear to ear,

pulled the pin. Knew he could never cross the four-and-a-half-meter gap in time. Not at the rate he was dragging his body, the SOP knife in his right.

He was within three meters when someone fired and hit Festus Ratty from behind. Crocker saw the terrorist drop the grenade and stumble forward. And the *oh shit* look on his face as he fell on top of it.

Akil shouted, "Boss, hug the ground!"

He used the split second before it exploded to throw himself belly to grass and cover his head with his hands. The blast lifted Crocker three inches off the ground, but the sound wasn't as sharp and painful as he expected.

Holding his breath, he waited for a bigger explosion from the barrels. Instead, clumps of Festus Ratty's body spattered his back and pieces of shrapnel punctured his arms.

He sighed "thanks" to the heavens.

And passed out.

CHAPTER TWENTY-SIX

"What you give you get ten times over."
—Yoruba proverb

CROCKER CAME to propped against the front wall of expat dorm Building A, a bandage around his left shoulder, an IV drip in his right forearm, his face wiped clear, but blood and tissue still clinging to his T-shirt and pants. He peeled off the former and tossed it aside.

It appeared as though he'd missed the mop-up operation, the arrival of Nigerian army troops and ambulances, and the landing of medical helicopters. Made him wonder for a moment if the last several hours had been a nightmare.

He was still coming down from the high of the excitement, questioning what it all meant, how many hostages had been rescued, if any of the jihadists had escaped, and what he had to do now.

Akil's deep voice nearby was easy to hear. "Wait, Saliha…The thing is…I still want to see you later."

"After everything that's happened?"

"Yes."

"Seriously? You need to get your nose and the rest of your head looked at."

Crocker located the couple near an ambulance a few meters away. Remembered Saliha leaving the compound with them the night before, and realized that the remarkable woman must have returned with the medical trauma team. Saw her hand him an instant cold pack, and watched Akil squeeze it, popping the water pouch so that it mixed with aluminum nitrate inside.

Holding the cold pack to his swollen nose, Akil asked, "You still dig me, right?"

She shook her head. "You're impossible."

"So you'll see me later?"

"I've got work to do. I'll text you."

"Cool, babe. I'll wait."

Their conversation brought a smile to Crocker's face. Some things never changed.

He experienced everything from inside the bubble of his own sense of mission success. They had rescued the hostages, and saved the plant. Didn't care that the Nigerians were taking all the credit, or that reporters had gotten it wrong, or his left triceps burned, or his chest hurt, or every muscle in his body ached.

Did care that some of his men were hurt, Mancini most notably. Mancini and Tiny had already been medevaced to Ramstein.

He had just called Germany from Yola. Word from the medical staff was that both men were being treated and were out of critical danger.

Now he watched as CT pulled on a clean T-shirt and examined himself in the mirror.

"I thought you got shot in the ass," Crocker said.

"Technically known as the gluteus medius and gluteus maximus. Yes."

"How's that going?"

CT gently patted the bandage over the gunshot wound. "Sore, but functional. I'm probably gonna be spending a lot of time on my feet."

The room they were in was filled with bouquets and stuffed animals from well-wishers. A big pink bear sat in the corner next to Akil's bunk.

CT said, "I'm going into town to meet up with some of the folks. You coming?"

"Which folks?"

"Some of the locals and expats we met inside."

"Sally gonna be there?"

"Sally, Saliha, Greenway, Knutsen, Reg, et cetera."

"Akil?"

"You know it."

He wondered if Zoe would be there, too. "Where?"

"The Babz Lounge. It's on Ahmadu Bello Road. We've reserved the entire patio for the afternoon and evening."

"Sweet."

Life-and-death situations drew the humanity out of people and brought them together.

"You gonna join us?"

"Later, yes. I've got a couple things to take care of first."

He sat alone staring at his laptop, staving away the emotional void that followed difficult missions, and thinking of who to call via Skype when the secure Iridium Extreme 9575 sat phone rang.

"Crocker, it's Les at ST-6 HQ. The captain wants to speak to you."

"I'm secure. Go ahead."

It was the first time the two men had talked since the raid.

"Crocker?"

"Captain."

"You in one piece?"

"I'm alive, sir."

"And mentally?"

"About sixty percent. What's up?"

"I've been hearing all kinds of remarkable reports out of Nigeria. Sounds like someone took some serious risks and saved the hostages and the gas plant."

"I'm hearing the same, Captain."

"I'm not even going to ask you what your specific role was. I'm assuming you were supporting Nigerian Special Forces per your rules of engagement."

"That's my understanding, sir."

Sutter guffawed. He still had a sense of humor. "I'm assuming you were inside the wire, and that's where your men were injured."

"If you're referring to Mancini and Chavez, that's correct. As hostages they were badly abused by the terrorists. They've already been medevaced to Ramstein, and the doctors say they're out of danger."

"I'm very glad to hear that. So overall would you call the training mission a success?"

"I would, sir. A number of very positive things have come out of it, including increased operational awareness and confidence, and force-to-force cooperation."

"In other words, Colonel Nwosu is covering your ass?"

"I'm not sure what you're referring to, Captain."

"Whatever role you played, congrats. The command and the White House are pleased, which lets you off the hook."

"That's exactly where I prefer to be, sir."

"I'm assuming you, CT, and Akil are at the Yola base now."

"That's an affirmative, sir."

"Then I'm ordering the three of you to return to home as soon as you get your gear together. Corporal Timmons will arrange your travel."

"Copy, captain. Mission accomplished."

"Mission accomplished, and report to my office upon your return."

First he had the 72 AFSF driver take him to the market where he purchased colorful glass bead necklaces and bracelets, and *geles* for Jenny, Cyndi, Cyndi's daughter, Amy, and Manuela, and carved-wood bead-and-ivory bracelets for Jenny's boyfriend, Bogart, and Manuela's son, Nash.

Then he directed the driver to the Government Girls' School in Yola. His left arm in a sling and carrying a large bouquet of lilies, he told the guard that he wanted to see a student named Chichima Okore.

"That's not possible," the guard answered, "unless you have the director's permission."

Now he stood opposite the school's assistant director, Mr. Obindu, as the afternoon sun bore down hard on his head and shoulders. Mr. Obindu explained that the Sambisa girls weren't allowed visitors and were being guarded from the public.

"Maybe you can return in two weeks, when they've had time to adjust to their new circumstances."

"I'm leaving tomorrow."

"Then I'm sorry, sir."

Crocker didn't want to be rude, but he wasn't going to be deterred, either.

"Can you make an exception? All I want to do is say goodbye before I leave for the States."

"My apologies. It's not permitted at this time."

Crocker took a deep breath. "Do I have to put Colonel Nwosu on the phone, and get him involved in this?"

"The colonel is an acquaintance of yours, sir?"

"We're colleagues. We work together."

Mr. Obindu nodded to the guard, who unlocked the gate and let him in.

He sat waiting in the lobby of the modern-looking building studying photographs of Nigerian farmworkers. The faces were amazing, he thought, filled with strength, beauty, and light.

He'd decided he wanted to return to Nigeria someday as a civilian, maybe in the company of Cyndi or Manuela, and explore the rest of the country.

He was imagining what sights he'd like to see, when a woman entered and led him to a small classroom. Chichima sat waiting, wearing a blue and white school uniform. Her face lit up when she recognized him.

They embraced and he handed her the bouquet of orange and white lilies.

"Thank you, Mr. Crocker. They're so beautiful, and it's good to see you again."

"I wanted to stop by before I leave Nigeria and see how you're doing."

"Better," she nodded. "Every day…gets easier. But they treat me like some kind of delicate object. And I'm not that, you know."

"No, you're not." Crocker compared the bright-eyed teenager to the mud-covered girl he had first encountered. The change was remarkable. "Be patient.

Experience is everything. People think they know, but they don't understand. You're a strong young woman with a whole life in front of you."

"Thank you," she gushed, emotion building up inside her. "I owe you so much."

"You've already repaid me, Chichima. What you did the other night was instrumental in saving those people at the Utorogu gas plant."

"Me? You mean my blog post and the millions of likes it got?"

He leaned closer under the watchful eye of the teacher at the door.

"What you did on social media convinced the Nigerian authorities to allow us to raid the plant, which led to the freeing of the hostages."

She gasped. "Really? You did that? You saved those people like you saved me and my friends?"

"I'm not here to talk about myself...It was you, Chichima, and the power of your words that gave us the opportunity in the first place."

"No."

"Yes. You spoke and millions of people responded. You did that, Chichima. Your conviction and your voice moved your fellow Nigerians. The reaction to your post had a profound effect."

Tears gathered in her eyes, and her voice quivered. "Are you sure it convinced the authorities?"

He took her hands in his. "It did. Yes."

"Mr. Crocker, thank you. Thank you so much. You have restored my faith...in humanity."

"Chichima, I know you suffered. But you're strong...and you made it through. Believe in yourself and the lessons you learned. Your strength and wisdom can change the world."

ACKNOWLEDGMENTS

We would like to thank our families and friends for their love and support, especially Don's daughter, Dawn, and Ralph's wife, Jessica, and his children, John, Michael, Francesca, and Alessandra. This book wouldn't have been possible without the help of our agents, Eric Lupfer and Mel Berger, and the expert guidance and work of a number of skilled professionals at Mulholland/Little, Brown, including Emily Giglierano, Pamela Brown, Elora Weil, Ben Allen, and others. In terms of inspiration, we get that from the men and women who do the kind of work described in this book. Thank you for your service!

ABOUT THE AUTHORS

Don Mann (CWO3, USN) has for the past thirty years been associated with the US Navy SEALs as a platoon member, assault team member, boat crew leader, and advanced training officer, and more recently as program director preparing civilians to go to BUD/S (SEAL Training). Until 1998 he was on active duty with SEAL Team Six. Since then, he has deployed to the Middle East on numerous occasions in support of the war against terrorism. Many of today's active-duty SEALs on Team Six are the same men he taught how to shoot, conduct ship and aircraft takedowns, and operate in urban, arctic, desert, river, and jungle warfare, as well as close-quarters battle and military operations in urban terrain. He has suffered two cases of high-altitude pulmonary edema, frostbite, a broken back, and multiple other broken bones in training or service. He has been captured twice during operations and lived to tell about it. He lives in Virginia.

Ralph Pezzullo is a *New York Times*–bestselling author and award-winning playwright, screenwriter, and journalist. His books include *Zero Footprint: The*

True Story of a Private Military Contractor's Covert Assignments in Syria, Libya, and the World's Most Dangerous Places (with former British Special Forces commando Simon Chase), *Jawbreaker* and *The Walk-In* (with former CIA operative Gary Berntsen), *At the Fall of Somoza, Plunging into Haiti* (winner of the Douglas Dillon Award for Distinguished Writing on American Diplomacy), *Most Evil* (with Steve Hodel), *Eve Missing, Blood of My Blood, Full Battle Rattle, Left of Boom,* and *Ghost*.

MULHOLLAND BOOKS

You won't be able to put down these Mulholland books.